secrets that kill

A SHELBY NICHOLS ADVENTURE

Colleen Helme

www.colleenhelme.com

Publisher's Note: This is a work of fiction. Names, characters, places, and incidents are a product of the author's imagination. Locales and public names are sometimes used for atmospheric purposes. Any resemblance to actual people, living or dead, or to businesses, companies, events, institutions, or locales is completely coincidental.

Book Cover Art by Damonza.com Copyright ©2013 by Colleen Helme
Book Layout ©2013 BookDesignTemplates.com

Secrets That Kill/ Colleen Helme. -- 1st ed.
ISBN: 1482628708
ISBN-13: 978-1482628708

Dedication

To Tom, as always, with love

ACKNOWLEDGMENTS

I would like to thank my wonderful family for all of the support and enthusiasm you give me. I couldn't do it without you! A big thanks to my great editor Kristin Monson. You're the best! A huge shout out to Gary Widdison for teaching me how to play poker as if I could read minds, and for making the poker scenes so fun to write. Thanks so much! To Holly Murphy, for help with all of my Florida questions. To Damon for the fabulous cover art. And last but not least, to everyone who loves the Shelby Nichols series. You keep me writing. Hope you enjoy this next adventure!

Shelby Nichols Adventures

Carrots
Fast Money
Lie or Die
Secrets that Kill
Trapped by Revenge
Deep in Death
Crossing Danger
Devious Minds
Hidden Deception
Laced in Lies
Deadly Escape
Marked for Murder
Ghostly Serenade

Devil in a Black Suit ~ A Ramos Story
A Midsummer Night's Murder ~ A Shelby Nichols Novella

Contents

Chapter 1

When I was a kid, the best part of my trip to Disneyland wasn't the park, the rides, or the entertainment. It was the swimming pool at my cousin's house where we stayed. I loved going to their house after a long hot day and gazing into the pool's clear blue water. With the pool light turned on, there was just something about that water that made me want to jump in. With the dark starry night overhead, it was soothing and magical.

That's why, on the last day of our vacation to Orlando, I found myself sitting beside the pool. It was late, and most everyone had gone to bed, so I was there by myself. If I could have gone swimming, I would have, but the pool had just closed for the night. So I sat back in a chair and gazed into the water, smelling the slight odor of chlorine and feeling the tension ease out of my body.

It felt so good to have my thoughts to myself that I almost cried. Hearing people's thoughts in all the crowds these last two weeks had been murder on my poor brain. I had put up my shields as much as I could, but it left a constant tension between my eyes; and worse, I was sure I had new wrinkles to show for it.

I had no idea there were so many different theme parks and attractions in Orlando. We had visited at least five parks, with several other attractions thrown in. Although we'd taken a couple of days off in-between to recover, mostly for my benefit, the constant barrage of thoughts had gotten on my nerves, making me irritable and short-tempered. I'd done my best, but I knew that Chris and the kids were happy to leave me at the pool and go inside for bed. Chris tried to understand, but I knew it bothered him.

It bothered me too, but for different reasons. Sure, I had the 'super-power' of reading people's minds, but this vacation had proven that even I had my limits. I might have handled one week, but two was over-kill. Today had proven that. I cringed to remember how I'd yelled at the father who was only 'thinking' his cute daughter was a pain in the butt, and today was one of those days he wished she'd never been born. I'd told him to quit being so selfish and enjoy this time with her. That she'd grow up before he knew it, and he'd be sorry and full of regret for his poor attitude.

The problem was, she was just a baby and had thrown up all over him. So I had probably over-reacted. His first thought in reaction was guilt that I was right. But his second impulse quickly over-rode the first, and hot anger turned his face red. How dare I chastise him in front of all these people when he hadn't done anything wrong?

Acting fast, Chris wisely pulled me away and apologized over his shoulder, telling the guy I had forgotten to take my medication. My outrage at Chris quickly changed to embarrassment and then self-loathing. Chris couldn't believe I could be so callous and mean. What was wrong with me? Where were my shields? My behavior was totally unacceptable. Not only that, he was so embarrassed he could hardly stand it.

But he only 'thought' all of those things, so I couldn't be too angry. Especially when he also thought being privy to everyone's thoughts had to be rough on me, so he needed to cut me some slack. Still...

Shame and regret flowed over me, so I shoved the memory away and glanced up at the stars. Our flight tomorrow didn't leave until three o'clock in the afternoon, so we still had some time in the morning to relax. Or at least Chris and the kids did. I had an errand to run for Uncle Joey. He was the mob-boss I had to work for since he knew my secret.

Although he compensated me for my time, we had a tenuous relationship. It had evolved over the last few months, and I liked to think it was now based on mutual respect rather than fear that he would kill me. Still, it was a balancing act to work for him on my terms rather than his.

When he found out I was coming to Orlando, he'd asked me to deliver a letter for him. Not a big deal, right? So I'd saved his errand until the last moment, hoping it wouldn't ruin my vacation. That was a big mistake, since thinking about delivering the letter every day had done exactly that. I should have just delivered it the first day we'd gotten here instead of dragging out the torment. That was just plain stupid.

First thing in the morning, I'd take care of it. Then we could go home. Our vacation was over. With the exception of that embarrassing incident today, we'd had a fun time here, and I was grateful we'd come, but now I was eager to go home and get back to normal. Plus the extra space from all the people wouldn't hurt.

Ha! Who was I kidding? I could hardly wait to be alone in my own house. Just thinking about it brought such a profound sense of relief that I was a bit giddy. Did that mean I was losing it? Had the stress finally gotten to me? Maybe I did need some kind of medication. What I'd done today was... I shook my head and sighed. A cool breeze brushed my skin, making me shiver. It was time to put a stop to these gloomy thoughts and go to bed.

Chris checked the address one more time. "Are you sure you'll be all right delivering this by yourself?" He was thinking how worried he was about me, and wishing I hadn't waited until the last moment to do this. He could have come with me if I'd gone earlier. What was I thinking?

"Yeah. It's no big deal. I'll be fine." I gave Chris a reassuring hug and kiss, wanting to ease his worry and escape his criticism. "See you at the airport. Bye kids." Engrossed in their packing, they absently waved.

I took the elevator to the lobby and hurried out the door. A cab was waiting for me, and I got in, giving the driver the address. "How long will it take to get there?" I asked.

"About twenty-five minutes," he replied.

"Okay good," I answered. It was a little before ten a.m. and I didn't have to be to the airport until one, so I had plenty of time. I would probably get to the airport long before Chris and the kids, but I wanted to play it safe and not miss my flight.

"How far is it from this address to the airport?" I asked the driver. I probably should have checked a map since I was basically clueless as to where I was going.

"Um... probably about twenty minutes," he said.

"So do you think I'll make it by one?" I asked mostly for his benefit so he'd know I was on a schedule.

"Of course," he said. "Unless you plan on staying for more than a few minutes, you should be to the airport by... eleven-thirty or so."

"Oh, okay. Thanks." Maybe I shouldn't have left so early, but with my luck it was probably better to plan for extra time.

I spent the drive making sure I had everything in my carry-on bag that I needed for the flight. Chris was in charge of my luggage, so I didn't have to drag it around with me, but I still felt loaded down with both my carry-on and my purse. Luckily, my carry-on was just a big bag so I could carry it over my shoulder. In fact, if I moved things around, there was probably enough room to stuff my purse inside as well.

That accomplished, I heaved a sigh of relief, grateful I wouldn't have to worry about keeping track of both bags. Before zipping it all up, I found the letter from Uncle Joey that I'd put in a special compartment, and pulled it out.

It was addressed to Warren Peace, which I knew had to be a fake name, or maybe even a code of some sort, and I held it gingerly. Getting rid of this couldn't come fast enough for me. I'd tried to tell Uncle Joey to mail it, but he wouldn't, saying he needed my 'special touch' so I could tell him what Warren was thinking. That worked fine as long as Warren didn't take it out on me. Especially since I had a feeling that the message it contained couldn't be good.

The cab pulled next to the curb and came to a stop. I glanced up at an apartment complex and realized I was in trouble if he wasn't home. What was I going to do then? I didn't even have a phone number.

"I'll only be a minute, if you don't mind waiting," I told the cab driver.

"No problem, as long as you know the meter's still running." He sent me a friendly smile and settled back in his seat to wait. He hoped I'd take my time and pulled out a book to read.

I got out, taking my bag with me, and scanned the apartment numbers. I found the one I was looking for on the lower level, which had about five steps leading down to the door. The outside light was on, and for some reason that made me nervous. Did that mean he wasn't home? What would I do then?

Taking a deep breath and letting it out, I started down the stairs and rang the bell. I heard some rustling inside before the curtain parted and someone glanced out at me. I caught sight of a bearded face and glasses, before the door opened a crack.

"I'm not interested," he said, and began to close the door.

"Wait," I said, pushing against the door. "Are you Warren Peace? I have a letter for you. Then I'll go. Here..." I held it out, "Just take it."

His eyes widened because of the name I'd called him. Joey "The Knife" Manetto was the only one who called him that. He glanced behind me, then stuck his head out the door to look up the stairs. "Are you alone?" he asked, frowning.

"Yes. I'm only here to deliver this letter and take your response back to Uncle Joey."

He hesitated, then his thoughts filled with about every swear word imaginable. I would have held my hands to my ears if it had done any good. "All right," he finally said, still not taking the letter. "You'd better come in."

I hurried inside and he closed and bolted the door behind me. "Did anyone see you come here?" he asked.

"Well, no... just the cab driver. He's waiting outside for me."

This time he cursed out loud. "You've got to get rid of him! A yellow cab like that will draw attention. Quick, before someone notices."

"I can't," I said, alarmed that he was freaking out. "He's taking me to the airport. Just read the damn letter and tell me your answer!" I tried to shove the letter into his hands, but he held them up.

"I don't have to read it. I know what he wants, and I just can't do it." He sent a searching glance at me, desperation filling his eyes. "You'll have to do it for me, or I'm a dead man. Please... I just need you to take what Manetto wants back with you. You can give it to him for me. If you don't, I swear I'll be dead by morning." He grabbed a wad of bills from his pocket. "Pay off the cabbie and I'll take you to the airport. It's not safe for you or me with him sitting out there like a yellow beacon. Manetto has no idea what he's gotten you into here... Hurry! Go!"

Waves of anxiety poured off him, infecting me with his fear. I took the cash and hurried out the door. He wasn't lying about my safety, or anything else he'd said, and that scared me. I paid the cabbie, giving him an extra twenty for a tip, and hustled back to the apartment. Warren waited at the top of the stairs, watching up and down the street until I came back. He ushered me into the apartment, locking and bolting the door behind us.

"Hopefully, we have a little time," he said. "At least I've prepared for this moment. I just didn't know Manetto would make his move so soon." He was thinking about everything he needed to get before we left. He had stashed all his cash along with his passport and ID in the freezer.

"Wait," I interrupted. "Read the letter first, and then tell me what's going on." I shoved the letter into his hands, and planted my feet in front of the doorway to the kitchen.

With great reluctance, he tore open the envelope and pulled out the letter. As he read, I heard the words in his mind.

Warren...I need the information you've obtained for me. I know it might put you in danger, but I've discovered through my sources that it's time you moved on anyway. Bring it to me without delay, and I'll help you disappear. The lovely woman delivering this letter is Shelby Nichols. Tell her you'll bring the item to me, and then send her on her way. If anything happens to her because of you, you're A Dead Man. Don't keep me waiting. Yours...etc...Joe E. Manetto.

Warren glanced at me and licked his lips. Maybe he'd been too hasty in sending the cab driver off and enlisting my help. Manetto didn't make threats he wasn't ready to keep. "What time does your flight leave?" he asked.

"Three o'clock," I answered.

"Oh good," he said, checking his watch. "We've got plenty of time. Should be a piece of cake." He was thinking it would be close, but it could still work. As long as I hadn't been spotted by Carson's goons. "I'll get my stuff, and we can leave in a few minutes."

"For the airport?" I asked.

"Yeah," he nodded.

He was lying. Folding my arms, I lifted one of my eyebrows and tilted my head. It was a look I had practiced on my kids and had down to perfection. "We're going straight to the airport?" I asked again.

He pursed his lips, knowing he'd been caught in a lie. How could I tell? "Not straight. I just have to make a quick stop on the way." He was thinking of the thumb-drive that Manetto wanted. He had to get it out of hiding. The thumb-drive had given him a certain amount of leverage, but he'd known it wouldn't last. Sending it with me to Manetto would buy him the time he needed to disappear. It was perfect. He could end his association with Manetto and

Carson at the same time. It might just keep him alive long enough to make a clean break.

"I'll get my things and we can go," he said.

He passed me and entered the kitchen. I leaned against the doorframe and watched him take three large bags of chicken breasts out of the freezer. He opened up the first and dumped out several wads of cash. The second held more cash, and the third had a combination of cash and two passports, along with various ID's and credit cards.

He stuffed them all in a backpack, then disappeared into a bedroom. A few minutes later, I heard water running in the bathroom. Was he taking a shower? I thought we were in a hurry here.

While waiting, I took out my phone and contemplated calling Chris to tell him what had happened. I pursed my lips and put the phone away, knowing that calling him would just make him more worried about me, especially when there was nothing he could do about it. I'd call if I really needed him to know what was happening and not a moment before. Besides, everything could still work out, right? I had plenty of time to get to the airport, and Warren was afraid of Uncle Joey, so he'd make sure nothing happened to me.

Even with those reassuring thoughts, my stomach clenched, and a sense of impending disaster came over me. Suddenly weak-kneed, I plopped down on the couch and tried to get a handle on my nerves. Uncle Joey's letter to Warren was lying on the coffee table in front of me, so I snatched it up. With my name in it, my instincts to protect myself kicked in, and I quickly stuffed it back into my bag.

I started guiltily as Warren came out, but he didn't glance in my direction and missed it. He looked so different, I hardly recognized him. He had shaved off his beard and clipped his hair short. His glasses were gone too, and he was dressed in tan slacks and a white polo shirt. He carried a nice leather bag that I figured contained his clothes and personal items along with the backpack.

"Okay, I'm ready," he said. "Let's go."

Relieved, I stood and followed him to the door. He unlocked it, but hesitated, and turned back to me. "Stay here while I take a quick look around." At my nod, he pulled the door open and moved to the stairs, cautiously peeking over the concrete wall to the street. "Shit!" He rushed back inside and locked the doors. "They're here. We'll have to go out the back way."

My heart started to race. This was bad. What had I gotten myself into? I followed Warren to the bathroom where he immediately pried open the window and pushed out the screen. He threw his bags out onto the concrete, then beckoned to me for my bag. After it disappeared, he helped me climb onto the toilet seat and outside. It was a short drop from the window, but somehow, I managed to fall on my butt. I quickly got up, dusting off my hands and moved out of the way, grateful I'd worn my jeans and running shoes. At least I had that much going for me. I reached for my bag and quickly slung it across my shoulder.

Warren dropped down just as a loud banging sounded from the front door, and I heard someone yelling a command to go around to the back. Warren grabbed my wrist, and we ran across the parking spaces to an alley where a black Mustang was parked out of sight. Warren popped the trunk open, and we threw in our stuff and jumped into the car.

I had barely closed the door when Warren put the car in first gear and peeled out. The alleyway turned into another parking lot, and Warren made a hard right, the back tires skidding on the pavement. I cringed, hoping no one was coming our way, and grabbed the seatbelt. I clicked it in place and glanced up to find the lane coming to an end.

Warren pushed on the brakes and deftly pulled between two parked cars, continuing to the turnout leading onto the street. He glanced both ways before taking a left and pulling into traffic.

He let out a breath, thinking that was close, but we'd made it out. Good thing he'd been ready to leave in a hurry. He glanced at me, noticing my hands braced against the dashboard. "Are you okay?"

"Sure," I answered, tucking my hands into my lap. I didn't want him to see how shaky they were. "Where are we going?"

"I've got to pick up the... item Manetto wants. Then I'll take you to the airport." He was thinking he would probably just drop me off somewhere and let me catch a cab. He'd paid for my cab fare to his house, so I should be good for it. Besides, Carson would probably be watching for his car at the airport, and taking a cab would be better for both of us.

If he hadn't thought that last part, I would have been mad at him. But his reasoning made sense, and I was more than happy to leave him behind. "So who's this Carson person?" As soon as it was out of my mouth I realized he'd never said the guy's name out loud. Damn! Why did I do that?

Warren looked at me, his eyes round with horror. "How did you know? Did Manetto tell you? Does he know anything else?"

"Manetto doesn't know anything," I assured him. "Earlier, you said something about Carson's goons, and hoped they hadn't spotted me or the yellow cab. I'm assuming that's who was after us, and I was curious, but hey, you don't have to tell me anything. I was just trying to start a conversation. That's all."

He remembered thinking exactly that, but he could swear he'd never said it out loud. But he must have if I'd heard it. He'd better come up with something, as long as it wasn't the truth. "He's just some guy who thinks I owe him some money. No big deal."

"Okay," I said.

When I didn't pursue it, Warren relaxed. He was thinking that Manetto never needed to know he had used the information he'd gathered for him to blackmail Carson himself. Although Carson had no idea how much information Warren really had on the thumb-drive, his threats were enough to put him on Carson's hit list. With them watching, and me showing up, it had to have been the incentive they needed to take him out. Probably not the smartest thing he'd ever done, but he needed the cash to disappear. Too bad Carson had decided he wouldn't take it anymore. With both Carson and Manetto on his tail, he couldn't get out of town fast enough.

I could hardly believe it. This guy was nuts. Trying to pull something over on Uncle Joey was bad enough, but using his information to blackmail someone else was even worse. Plus, from Warren's thoughts, I knew this Carson person was all kinds of bad. I needed to get away from Warren as fast as I could. I didn't care about the thumb-drive. It wasn't worth my life.

"I've changed my mind," I blurted. "Why don't you just let me out, and I'll take a cab to the airport. You can figure out how to get the... um... whatever it is Uncle Joey wants without me."

Warren's brows drew together in confusion. Why was I changing my mind? "Wait. No, you have to help me."

"I'd really rather not," I said. Warren wasn't buying it, so I played my trump card. "Besides, I don't think that's what

Uncle Joey had in mind when he had me deliver the letter. You don't want to upset my Uncle now, do you?"

"Um... of course not." His face paled as he realized that I'd called Manetto my Uncle several times and he'd missed it. "But, please... don't bail on me now. I promise... I won't let anything happen to you."

I sighed. He wasn't making this any easier, and his desperation was heartfelt. He really needed me to do this. Argh! I hated being in this situation.

"We're almost there," he continued, sensing that his pleas were getting to me. "All I need to do is get the thumb-drive and give it to you. It won't take more than a minute. Then you can jump in a cab, and that will be the last you'll see of me."

"Where is it? Where are we going?"

"To a restaurant where I used to work. I hid the thumb-drive there. It's about five minutes away. You can even wait in the car if you want."

"No," I said forcefully. "I don't want to wait in the car."

"That's okay. You can come in. I'll even buy you a drink and give you some money for the cab fare if that will help."

I let out a breath. "All right," I said, exasperated. "I'll do it, but you don't have to buy me a drink, and I still have some money left over from the first cab fare, so I'm good."

He sighed, relieved that I'd agreed. "You'll be safe, I promise." He was thinking he'd do whatever it took to get me back to Manetto in one piece, mostly because he didn't want Manetto to send Ramos after him. He knew how that would end. A picture of Ramos holding a gun to his head and slowly pulling the trigger came to his mind. He blinked, shaking his head to clear the vision, scared to even think about it.

It scared me too, given how Warren had visualized Ramos. In his mind, Ramos stood at least seven feet tall, was big and bulky, and had a sneer on his face like a crazy person. I sure wouldn't want to run into that vision of Ramos either. Strangely, something inside me settled down, and I didn't feel so nervous anymore. It was like Ramos was here protecting me, even though he wasn't. How crazy was that? Still, maybe this could work out after all.

We pulled into the parking lot of a restaurant with the name "The Blue Heron" posted above the entrance. It was a few minutes before noon. Although the place wasn't crowded, there were still several cars in the parking lot. Warren parked in a far corner, backing in for a quick get-away. I glanced up and down the street, but there wasn't a taxi in sight, and I had no idea where I was.

Warren started toward the restaurant, and I panicked. "Wait! I need my bag out of the trunk."

"Oh, yeah." With his mind focused on the thumb-drive, he had forgotten about everything else. He popped open the trunk and glanced around, thinking this was dangerous because Carson's people knew he still worked a few shifts here. Since they hadn't caught him at his apartment, they might send someone here, so we had to hurry.

Oh great! So he lied about that, and still worked here? This was worse than ever. Warren hurried inside, but I followed more slowly, wanting to keep some distance between us, especially if there was someone watching for him.

I entered the restaurant and blinked into the dark interior until my eyes adjusted. Warren walked toward the back of the restaurant like he owned the place, so I waited at the hostess desk wishing I could disappear. The hostess approached with a smile, asking if I'd like to be seated and how many were in my party.

"Just me," I blurted, in self-preservation. "Could I sit at that table?" I pointed to a booth in the furthest, darkest corner there was. From there, I could also watch the door, and it was only a few feet from where Warren was talking in hushed tones with a waitress.

"Um... sure." She grabbed a menu and thought that I was probably meeting up with someone I shouldn't, like I was cheating on my husband, mostly because I looked so nervous. I should have dressed nicer though, since a theme park t-shirt and jeans made me look like a tourist. Hmm... maybe that was the idea. She bet I wouldn't order anything but a soda.

What? I liked my t-shirt. It was white with cap sleeves, and had brightly colored blue and green sequins on it in the shape of waves with dolphins jumping out. I didn't think it was that touristy. Annoyed, I pursed my lips and slid into the corner of my booth, stuffing my big bag down by my feet.

I took a moment to scan the thoughts of the few people here and relaxed. At least no one seemed to be paying any attention to Warren or me. As I focused on Warren's thoughts, he noticed me sitting at the booth.

With relief, he pointed the waitress in my direction, hoping to use me as a diversion while he got the thumb-drive out of the... cleaning supply closet? The waitress was not so easily deterred, and from her mind, I realized she was an old girlfriend who was seriously ticked off. Pointing me out only escalated her anger. How dare he bring another woman here?

Good grief! I needed to get out of here and call a taxi. This was getting out of hand. Before I could slide out of the booth, a man with a stone-cold face stalked into the restaurant, and my stomach clenched with fear. This guy was pure muscle and sported snake tattoos on his biceps. He spotted Warren and frowned in confusion before putting together who he was without his beard and glasses.

Warren noticed him and stiffened with alarm. Then he glanced my way before making the decision to leave me behind and run. He took off through the back, and the snake guy took off after him, passing me as he went. I picked up that he wasn't alone, and I was afraid it might be the end of the line for Warren.

If they caught him, would he tell them where the thumb-drive was? Should I try to get to it first? Before I could even think about it, another man entered the restaurant, scanning the people, and looking for a woman with long blond hair and a touristy white t-shirt. Yikes! That was me!

I ducked under the table and held my breath. Listening intently, I realized he hadn't seen me, and I sighed, clenching my eyes shut with relief. A few seconds later, I sensed him turning around and leaving to find the back exit. I peeked over the table, making sure the coast was clear, then slowly sat up on the seat.

Had Warren gotten away? Were the men still outside? Should I make my escape while they were busy with Warren? I tried to get my legs under me and stand, but I couldn't move; my muscles felt frozen to the seat.

A sudden shriek sounded from the back of the restaurant, shocking me into action, and I ducked back under the table again.

"Call nine-one-one!" a feminine voice yelled. "He's been stabbed!"

From her thoughts, I knew it was the waitress Warren had been talking to, and she was thinking that Warren was bleeding so bad he was going to die. I jumped up and pushed through the crowd to the kitchen. Warren was lying on his side in a pool of blood with a meat cleaver in his back.

He glanced at me, moving his lips in a silent message. Even though I couldn't hear him, I knew what he was trying to say. He was sorry for getting me into this mess, but that wasn't the message he was intent on telling me. Before his eyes rolled back into his head, his blood-chilling message came through loud and clear. *They think you have the thumb-drive.*

Chapter 2

Stunned with shock, I hardly noticed the paramedics who pushed me aside to get to Warren. I watched them take his pulse before all that blood got to me, and I started to feel light-headed. I lurched out of the kitchen and back to my corner booth, sliding into the bench. I lowered my head onto the table and took a few deep breaths.

The ringing in my ears slowly abated, and I began to hear the commotion around me. One voice stood out, and I realized it was Warren's ex-girlfriend, explaining to someone that he'd come into the restaurant with me.

That caught my attention, and I sat up. Glancing around the restaurant, I was chagrined to find it flooded with police. Crap! I should have left before they came. Now I had to talk to them, and I would have to make up something fast, because I certainly couldn't tell them the truth.

That stupid ex-girlfriend was ruining everything. A cop came over to my booth and took a seat across from me. He was thinking that I looked as white as a sheet, something he'd never imagined seeing in sunny Florida. He figured I was from out-of-town, and that made him a little suspicious.

"Are you all right?" he asked.

"I think so," I answered. Just then, the paramedics walked down the aisle carrying their equipment back to their vehicle. One of them was feeling bad that the guy had died, but there wasn't much any of them could do about it. A meat cleaver that big, and hacking right into the liver... they'd done everything they could, but he didn't stand a chance.

A sudden wave of nausea passed over me and I closed my eyes. "Maybe not so much after all. Could I get a glass of water?" The cop nodded, hoping I wasn't going to be sick all over the table, and left me alone.

Grateful for the space, I concentrated on pulling myself together, but it was hard. Poor Warren was dead. I pretty much knew that already, but it was still a shock. Tears flooded my eyes, but I wiped them away. I needed to keep an emotional distance if I was ever going to figure out how to answer the questions from the police without arousing their suspicions about me and what I knew.

That meant I needed to focus on the policeman's thoughts so I could figure out what to say. In other words, I had to lie. I hated lying, especially to the police. It didn't sit right, but if I wanted to go home, did I even have a choice?

He came back before I was quite ready with a glass of ice water. I took several swallows and felt my nerves settle down a bit. The cop was going to ask about my relationship with Warren so I spoke before he could.

"This guy came into the restaurant," I explained. "He had tattoos of snakes on his biceps and his head was shaved. He walked right past me. He looked like he was after the guy who got hurt. Is he going to be all right?" I turned to look back toward the kitchen, catching a glimpse of Warren's shoes behind the propped-open door.

The cop frowned. If I didn't know the victim, then what was the waitress talking about? "Um... I'm afraid he's dead."

"Oh no! That's awful!" I said. "I heard the commotion and ran back to see what was going on, but I get queasy at the sight of blood, so I came back here to sit down. So he's really dead?"

"Yeah," the cop said. He was thinking that I obviously didn't know the guy, and the waitress must have made a mistake. But why would she lie to him? Something was off. My description of the man with the snake tattoos fit what the others had seen, and if I could identify him it would be helpful. He'd make sure the detectives talked to me when they got there. Maybe they could figure out what was going on.

"I need to ask you to wait and talk to the detectives who are coming to investigate. They'll have a few questions for you, and then you can go home. Just don't leave until you've talked to them. Okay?" he asked.

"Sure," I said. "Anything I can do to help." I was pretty sure if I seemed anxious to leave, he'd pick up on that. I also needed to let him believe that home wasn't so far away, or I might not ever get out of here. I checked the time and cringed, twelve-forty and counting. I still had some leeway to make my flight, especially since I didn't have to check a bag. I could still make it.

The minutes ticked slowly by with no sign of the detectives and, try as I might, I couldn't help thinking about Warren's last words to me. His sudden death was a shock, but now I had to worry about the guys who'd killed him and the fact that they were after me. How had this happened? When had they seen me? Warren hadn't even had a chance to retrieve the stupid thumb-drive, and now Carson, whoever he was, thought I had it? Could things get any worse?

I considered looking for the cleaning closet to see if I could get the thumb-drive but decided that was a bad idea. It was safer in the closet than if I had it. Not only that, it was safer for me to leave it alone. Plus, someone might be watching me and wonder what I was doing. No, I just had to sit tight and try not to freak out.

Ten long minutes later, two men in suits and ties walked into the restaurant. They talked to the policemen and examined the body, which was still lying on the floor of the kitchen. Just thinking about Warren lying dead a few feet away was giving me the willies, and I tried not to listen to the Detective's thoughts about how he died. They made his death sound so clinical, like he wasn't even a person. I sniffed, feeling bad all over again, and wished I could just go home.

More cops entered the restaurant, taking pictures and documenting the crime scene. I was grateful to be out of the way in my booth. The detectives came out of the kitchen and started making the rounds of talking to all of the witnesses. I hoped they'd talk to me before the ex-girlfriend, but she butted in like she was the most important person there. Great. I kept my face averted and tried to ignore her as she pointed them in my direction. I glanced up as they came to my table.

"I'm Detective Fitch, and this is Detective Castro. We'd like to ask you a few questions." Fitch was clearly in charge and had the gray-streaked hair and fine lines in his face to show he'd been on the force for a long time. Castro was younger and was thinking this was his first case with Fitch. He was excited to learn from the best.

"Sure," I agreed, hoping I didn't sound as nervous as I felt. If Fitch was that good, I might be in trouble.

They slid into the booth across from me, each studying me in their own way. Fitch immediately concluded that I was involved, mostly because I looked spooked and panicked, a sure sign that I knew what was going on.

My heart rate doubled. This was bad.

"How long have you known the victim?" he asked.

"Known him?" I drew my brows together in confusion, knowing I had to play this just right. "I don't know him."

Fitch narrowed his eyes. What was I trying to pull? "His girlfriend said he was with you."

"I don't know what you're talking about," I answered, keeping the confusion on my face. It wasn't too hard since she had changed from being an ex to a full-fledged girlfriend. "What girlfriend?"

Fitch glanced toward the back to find her, but she wasn't in sight. He'd have to get her over here and get to the bottom of this. He glanced at Castro and slid out of the booth. "Go find her while I ask... sorry, I never got your name."

"Shelby Nichols," I said.

"Shelby. Okay. Apparently there's been some misunderstanding, but I'm sure we can clear it up. Detective Castro will get the waitress."

"What waitress?" I asked.

"The waitress who is the girlfriend who says you came with the victim," he explained. He was beginning to think I really didn't know what was going on.

"Oh... okay," I said. Fitch slid back into the booth and tried to figure me out. To distract him I asked, "So what was his name? You keep calling him the victim, but he was a real person. Who was he? Why was he killed? Was he in a gang or something? That guy I saw had snake tattoos on his arms, and his head was shaved. Is he the person who killed him?"

"The victim's name was Warren Pearce. Tell me what you saw," Fitch said.

I explained how I came in and the hostess seated me in this corner booth. "I wasn't too far from the victim... Warren, and noticed him talking quite loudly with a waitress. Must be the girlfriend?" Fitch nodded and I continued. "Now that I think about it, she did give me a dirty look, although I had no idea why."

Fitch was thinking Warren must have told her I was his new girlfriend to get her off his back maybe, but why? "Go on," he said.

"Next thing I know this guy came rushing down the aisle toward the back like he was after somebody. Right after that I heard a scream, and a woman yelling to call nine-one-one, and shouting that someone had been hurt. I went back to see what was going on and saw the guy... Warren, lying there and... it didn't look good." I grimaced and swallowed. "All that blood. It gave me quite a shock."

"Did you get a good look at the guy's face? The one with the tattoos?" he asked.

"Yeah. He was big and looked really mean." I gave him a more detailed description, finishing up just as Detective Castro brought the waitress to our table.

With her hands on her hips, and mascara running down her face from her tears, she still managed to sneer at me. "Warren said he was with you. He wouldn't have told me that if it wasn't true. He knows how mad I get."

Everyone focused on me and I shrugged. "I didn't come in with him. Just ask the hostess. She saw me come in alone and seated me here."

"But why would he tell me that?" the waitress asked, anger drying her tears. "You're making this up. I'll get Molly and prove it." She stalked off to find the hostess.

I tried not to sigh with relief and shook my head. "I don't get it either. But there's clearly something going on. I hope you can figure it out."

"We'll get to the bottom of it," Detective Castro assured me. He followed after the waitress, leaving me alone with Fitch again, who was thinking that once this matter was cleared up, he could send me on my way. My description matched those of the other witnesses, although I was the only one who got a good look at his face, so he really didn't think he needed me to stay.

Only... he had a feeling there was something he was missing. It was on the tip of his tongue to ask me what I was doing in the restaurant in the first place, but before he could, Castro returned.

"The hostess said she came in alone," Castro said. "So the victim must have lied to the girlfriend for some reason." He glanced at me. "The hostess also said it looked like you were meeting someone."

Did he really expect me to answer that? They both glanced at me, wondering what I would say. Fitch thought if I told them to mind their own business, it meant I had something to hide. Put that together with what the victim said to his girlfriend, and it could mean something.

"I wasn't meeting with anyone," I said. "I'm just here as part of my job. I have my own consulting agency, and I'm doing some work for a client."

Fitch's eyes glinted. There was a definite ring of truth to that. This must be what he was missing. It made more sense to him now, unless it had something to do with Warren. If I didn't tell him exactly what it was, and said some stupid thing about client privilege and all that, he'd know I was keeping something from him that was important to the investigation. "Did it have anything to do with Warren?"

Damn! Now I had to make up something really good. “No. It’s not about that.” Thinking fast, I lowered my voice and leaned toward them. “It’s about a secret recipe. My client wants to know if this restaurant stole hers. I was going to do some snooping around... ask a few questions. But... after this, I’ll have to come back some other time.”

I sat back in my seat. “You won’t tell anyone, will you? It’s supposed to be confidential, and I don’t want anyone here to know.”

“No,” Fitch said. “Of course not.” He was caught off guard, and had a hard time wrapping his head around my explanation. A secret recipe? Here, in this dive? Of course, he’d never eaten here before. Maybe the food was really good. He’d have to give it a try. He wondered what dish it was and glanced at the table, just in case there was a menu handy.

“If that’s all, I might as well go,” I said, catching his attention. “There’s nothing more I can do for you is there?”

“No, I think that’s everything,” he answered. “Could you give me your card in case we need to get in touch?” He was thinking if I were lying I wouldn’t have a business card to give him.

Good grief! Was he always this suspicious of every little thing? “Sure.” I rummaged through my bag and found my purse, then pulled a business card out of the pocket where I kept them. “Here you go.”

“Thanks.” He eagerly studied it, thinking that it looked authentic. The number had a different area code than Florida, but that wasn’t too unusual. “This looks like a business number. Do you have a personal cell phone number you could give me?”

“Yeah, sure. Let me write it down on the back of the card.” Dang, he was good. After getting my name and consulting agency in the paper for finding all that stolen bank money, I'd had to get a business line for all the phone calls. Now I couldn't ditch Fitch so easily.

"Thanks. I'll call if I need anything."

"Okay." I took my time stuffing my purse back into my bag, waiting for him to be the first to leave the booth. I didn't want to look too eager to get out of there. I checked the time. It was one-thirty-five. Could I still make it to the airport? I had to try.

A group of people came into the restaurant wheeling a gurney to pick up the body. The grim sight reminded me that I wasn't out of danger yet. Not with Warren's warning rattling around in my head. Were Carson and his goons watching for me? My stomach tightened. I needed to get out of here.

I walked to the front of the restaurant and glanced out the window. Lots of police cars and yellow tape surrounded the entrance and filled the parking lot. There was no way I would find a taxi without calling a cab company. I turned back to search for the hostess and ask for a phone book.

She was sitting in a booth with another worker, and stood as I approached. "I need to call a cab," I said. "Do you have a phone book or a number handy?"

"Yeah, we keep the number at the hostess desk for emergencies," she said. She was thinking that the police and yellow tape had probably scared my lover off, so now I had to pay for my own ride home.

I could hardly believe how judgmental she was and decided that she'd been watching too much TV. From my experience listening to people's thoughts, I knew most regular people didn't do half the things other people assumed they did. "Here it is," she said, handing me a laminated piece of paper with the phone number on it. "Do you need a phone?"

"No, but thanks." I took a seat in the waiting area, needing some space to get my purse back out of my bag where it was stuffed. I pulled out my phone, only to realize I'd missed several calls and text messages...all from Chris. Oops. I sent a quick text telling him I was fine and I'd call soon. After that I called the cab company. Lucky for me the paper had the name and address of the restaurant at the top, so I could tell the cab people where to pick me up.

"We'll have someone there shortly," the cab operator said.

"How long will that take?" I asked, feeling the time ticking away.

"Um...about ten minutes or so," she answered.

I thanked her and ended the call, worried about the "or so" part of her answer. Usually when people added things like that, it meant at least five to ten minutes more than what they said, but since I couldn't hear her thoughts over the phone, I was just guessing. Maybe this time I'd be wrong, and the cab would be here a few minutes early. Now I was just kidding myself. With the way things had gone so far today, I didn't stand a chance.

I should probably call Chris now and let him know, but I didn't want to do it where someone might overhear my conversation. I pushed open the door and stepped outside, glancing up and down the street. A few policemen stood inside the yellow tape beside me, and the coroner's truck with Warren's body was just pulling out. A small crowd had gathered to gawk, and I noticed a news reporter talking into a camera. She spotted me and hurried over to get an eyewitness account.

Yikes! I ducked back into the restaurant. No way was I going to get my face plastered all over the news. I'd just have to wait until I got into the cab to call Chris. I stood by the window where I could see when the cab arrived, and settled in to wait. It wasn't long before the other people in the restaurant began to leave, and I watched the reporter pounce on them. It kept me entertained for a little while until the reporter and cameraman packed up their stuff and left.

After that, the seconds passed slowly, stretching my nerves to the limit. I wanted to get out of there so bad I couldn't stand still, tapping my foot and changing position every few minutes like a crazy person. I stared out the window, chewing on my fingernails, worried that the cab could find a place to park that wasn't a block away. Then I worried that he'd wait for me to walk that far once he got there. Where was he? Fifteen long minutes had come and gone and still no sign of him.

As the cab finally pulled up across the street, the detectives finished up, and were just walking toward me to leave. I wanted to get out of there before them, but Detective Fitch beat me to the door and held it open for me. I told him thanks and rushed out before he could question me about why I was still there.

I quickly crossed the street to the cab with Fitch's thoughts coming through loud and clear. The fact that I was still at the restaurant after so long had aroused his suspicions, and now he was wondering why I was taking a cab. He wished he had gotten my home address. Maybe he should ask me to wait before it was too....

I closed the door, blocking out the rest of his thoughts, and told the cab driver to take me to the airport as fast as he could. As we pulled away, I glanced out the window. Detective Fitch had opened his car door, but paused to watch me leave. He was still standing there when the cab took me around a corner and I lost sight of him.

That was close. I buckled my seat belt and pulled out my phone. Chris answered on the first ring. "Hi honey," I said, keeping my voice cheerful so he wouldn't know how much trouble I was in.

"Where are you?" he practically shouted. "You should have been here an hour ago. Why haven't you called before now? What's going on?"

"I'm in a cab on my way there," I explained. "Hang on a minute, and I'll ask the driver how long it will take to get to the airport."

The driver had been listening, but waited for me to ask before he told me. He was thinking it would take about thirty to thirty-five minutes if we were lucky. "I can get you there in about forty-five minutes if traffic isn't too bad," he said. "This time of day, you never know. Could be more, could be less. We'll just have to wait and see." He was thinking I would give him a better tip if he got me there before he'd said he would.

I thanked him and turned back to Chris, going with the shortest time. "About half an hour. Will that work? Do you think I can make it?" I heard him sigh before he replied.

"Maybe," he said. "But if you're any longer, you probably won't. Maybe we should wait and take a later flight."

"No, I don't want to do that. I want to get home." I had to take the chance that I'd get there because I didn't want to stay in Orlando another minute longer than necessary. "Listen, if I don't make it, I'll take a later flight and you guys can go ahead. It's not what I want to do, but I still think I can make this flight, so let's not change anything."

"Are you sure?" he asked. "I mean... I'd hate to leave you behind."

"If it happens, it happens... I'll deal with it," I said. "I'm sure there's another flight later today that I can get on. Since you've already gone through security and the bags are checked onto the plane, you might as well go. Besides, I think I can still make it. So what Terminal and Gate should I go to?"

"Have the cab take you to the A side of the Main Terminal. You'll need to check in, but just do it curbside through a skycap. I think that will be faster. From there you'll need to go to Airside Terminal One, and Gate Two. Got that?" he asked.

"A side, Airside Terminal One and Gate Two," I repeated. "Got it."

"Good. There wasn't a long line at security when we got there, so you might be all right."

"Sure," I said. "I'll make it."

"I sure hope so." He sighed. "So what happened? Why are you so late?"

"It's kind of a long story," I hedged. "I had to take a detour and some things happened to delay me, but I'm okay now."

"Now?" His voice sounded anxious. "What does that mean? When weren't you okay?"

I tried to figure out how to respond with the cab driver listening to every word I said. He was pretty interested to know what had happened to me, especially since he'd seen the yellow crime-scene tape and heard on the radio that someone had been killed at the restaurant where he'd picked me up. Was I involved in that? Was that why I was so anxious to leave the city? The cops might be interested to know he'd taken me to the airport. Let's see... A side, Terminal One, and Gate Two... he'd be sure to remember that.

"Sounds good," I said cheerfully. "I'll see you soon and tell you all about it. Love you too! Bye!" I disconnected. Shame and remorse coursed through me. I had just hung up on my husband. Not good. That made me a bad wife. He was going to be so mad. But I didn't have a choice! Not with the stupid cab driver listening to every word I said. Damn! I sent a quick text telling Chris I'd explain everything later and slipped the phone into my jeans pocket.

"How close are we to the airport now?" I asked the cabbie.

"Um... about half an hour. When does your flight leave?" He was thinking it would be good to know my destination as well.

"If we're there in half an hour, I've got plenty of time," I answered. I wasn't about to tell him anything, not after I had to hang up on Chris because of him. He was too nosey for his own good. What happened to people who didn't want to get involved? Why couldn't I have gotten a taxi driver like that?

I silently fumed, feeling helpless as the seconds ticked by. I checked my phone, hoping Chris had replied to my text, but there were no new messages. I sent another one telling him I was almost there, hoping it was true. I perked up when signs for the airport came into sight. It couldn't be too far away now. Five minutes later, my cab pulled into the exit for the airport. My phone chirped with a message from Chris. He said to hurry because they were now boarding the plane.

All ready? My heart sank. I checked the time. It was two-forty. I couldn't give up now. I might still make it. Only a few more minutes and I'd be there. I took out my ticket, texted Chris back saying that I would hurry, and got ready to jump out of the taxi.

The cab driver checked his rear-view mirror several times, and as we got closer to the drop-off point, he was thinking about the car behind us. It had been following for a long time, maybe even since he'd picked me up. He glanced at me, concerned that I was hiding something from the police after all. This might get ugly. I might get shot or taken into custody without paying him. He wasn't going to let me out until he saw green.

My heart raced, but I resisted the urge to look out the back window. Who could be following me? It was either Detective Fitch or Carson's goons. At this point, I hoped it was the detective. "I've got to hurry," I said. "How much do I owe you?" I'd kept the cash from my earlier ride in my jeans pocket, and pulled it out to show him.

"Fifty should do it," he said, then added, "Since I got you here in good time." He named a higher price because he didn't think I'd leave a tip. He was right about that.

I undid my seatbelt and counted out the cash, then reached between the seats and placed it on the passenger seat. "There you go... it's all there," I said, answering his unspoken question.

"Good," he nodded, and pulled to the curb.

I threw my bag over my shoulder and jumped out as soon as the car stopped. Rushing to the skycap with my ticket, I glanced back and caught a glimpse of the car behind the taxi. It kept going, then quickly pulled over, and the passenger door flew open. A man stepped out, glancing toward me. I gasped. It was the same guy who'd been looking for me at the restaurant.

"Is that your ticket?" The skycap asked.

"Oh, yes." I handed it over, keeping my attention on the man following me. My mouth went dry, and my pulse raced. He started to get in line behind me, but another person beat him to it, so he got behind that person.

"Um... I don't think you're going to make it," the skycap said. "The plane has already boarded."

"I've got to try," I said. "My family is on that plane."

"Then you'd better run." He shook his head, thinking it would be close. "Here's your boarding pass. It's Airside One, Gate Two. I'll let them know you're coming."

"Thanks." I grabbed the pass and ran toward the sliding doors, hoping the guy was too far away to hear where I was headed.

I pushed into the crowd of people, looking up at the overhead arrows to make sure I was headed toward Airside One. I followed the arrows and ran toward the security gates. It was hard to keep going since my legs were shaking so badly. If the guy was following, I hoped I could get through security before he caught up with me.

My shoulder blades itched, as if someone were aiming a gun at my back, but I couldn't turn around and look, so I did the next best thing. I focused my mind on the thoughts of those behind me.

I caught a few random thoughts before I zeroed in on his mind. He was there, but keeping a small distance between us. He was trying to figure out how to stop me without anyone noticing. If I made it to security, he'd lose me for sure.

Yikes! I had to make it now. In the distance, the black security screening monitors and metal detectors came into view. I was almost there! Hope swelled in my heart, and I heard the guy cursing in his mind that he couldn't catch me.

I jogged the last few steps toward the checkpoint and lurched into line in front of a couple of people, who gasped in displeasure. "Sorry!" I said. "But I'm late, and I can't miss my flight."

The guy following me was thinking this was his chance to grab my arm and tell me to move to the back of the line. I dodged to the side and he missed. Before either of us could make another move, a Passenger Service Agent jumped into the fray. "What's the problem?" he asked.

I spoke almost before he finished, cutting off my assailant's complaints. "My flight is boarding with my husband and kids. I've got to get on. Can you please help me?"

"Do you have your boarding pass?" he asked.

"Yes." I handed it to him. "The skycap said he'd radio ahead."

He took the pass and shook his head. "I don't think you're going to make it."

"Yes I can. Please. I've got to try."

"Okay. We'll see what we can do. Come with me."

I followed him to the frequent flyer line where he ushered me to the front, showing my ticket to the agent stationed there. "They'll need to see your driver's license too," he said.

I got it out and started placing my bags and phone onto the conveyer belt. Glancing back as I did, I noticed the goon talking into his phone. He was thinking that he'd failed to catch me, but from the looks of things I was probably going to miss my flight, and maybe he should stick around to see if I'd come back out. Or the boss might want him to buy a ticket and follow me to Terminal One, Gate Two. If the boss thought it was worth it, that's what he'd do next.

The agent handed back my boarding pass and my driver's license, telling me I needed to take the AGT train to Airside One, Gate Two as fast as I could. "I'll let them know you're coming, but I'm not sure how long they can wait."

"Thanks so much," I said. He was thinking I wasn't going to make it, but he'd seen some pretty crazy things happen before. As long as they didn't close the cabin door to the cockpit, I had a small chance.

While he spoke into a radio, hope poured over me. He thought I had a chance. I started to walk through the metal detector, but the security guard stopped me. "Your shoes," the guard said. "You need to take them off."

"Right, okay." Flustered, I slipped them off and put them on the conveyer belt, waiting for the security guard's nod before passing through the metal detector. No warning bells rang, and I heaved a sigh of relief. Now all I had to do was get everything put back together and run to the train. I slipped on my shoes, grabbed my things, and managed to jump on the train right before the doors closed.

According to the voice over the intercom, I now had sixty-eight seconds until the train pulled into Terminal One. That was fast, right? I checked the time. Two minutes after three. Would they wait? The train slowed to a stop and I rushed out, frantic to follow the signs to Gate Two. My lungs were heaving by the time I got there.

The PSA worker at the desk was watching for me and took my boarding pass. Hurry," she said, ushering me toward the door. I started inside, but an agent coming down the aisle stopped me. He shook his head. "Sorry, the door is closed. We can't let you on."

"Really? Are you sure?" I asked, panting for breath.

"Yes," he said, his face creased with sympathy. "We waited an extra five minutes. But when the captain says it's time to go, there's nothing we can do about it." He was thinking one minute faster, and I would have made it. "Let's see if we can get you on the next flight out."

As he ushered me back to the desk, I swore under my breath and clenched my fists. I'd missed it by one lousy minute? How could I be so close and not get on? The plane was right there! Why couldn't they just open the damn door and let me in? I took a deep breath and tried to calm down. Freaking out wasn't going to get me anywhere. But after everything I'd been through, this was almost too much.

The PSA lady who'd waited for me was busy at her computer, trying to find an empty seat on the next flight that left at five-twenty. She pursed her lips, thinking the best she could do was put me on standby. The flight after that wasn't until eight-ten, but it was full too.

She checked all the upcoming flights heading to my destination, and the only one that had an empty seat wasn't until the next day in the afternoon. If it were up to her, she wouldn't sit around the airport all day, hoping to get on standby. She'd take the sure thing of the empty seat the next day, since that was the one I'd probably end up on anyway.

She glanced at me, thinking she hated this part of her job when she had to deal with people who were going to be disappointed and upset. They always acted like it was her fault. Was I going to be like one of them? She'd just have to remind me that it was my fault for being late in the first place.

As I listened to her thoughts, I watched the plane slowly back away from the gate. I followed the plane's progress toward the tarmac and a feeling of sadness came over me. Tears gathered in my eyes. I hated being left behind. What if something happened to me and I never saw my family again?

I reached for my phone and quickly called Chris, but it went straight to voicemail. They'd probably been told to turn off all their electronic devices. I left a message. "Hey Chris," I said, wiping my eyes. "I'm standing here watching the plane leave the gate. It's awful to be this close and not be on it with you. I hate being left behind. Anyway, they're going to try and get me on the next flight, so call me as soon as you can, and I'll give you an update. I love you. Bye."

Chapter 3

I didn't feel safe leaving the terminal, so I told the worker to put me on standby for the next few flights. She'd heard my message to Chris and was feeling sorry for me. She also booked the open seat on the flight the next afternoon, but didn't have the heart to tell me that was the one I'd probably end up on.

After getting the boarding information from her, I found a seat in the boarding area and sat down for a minute, trying to decide what to do next. The worker left a few minutes later, leaving me abandoned and alone. The place was practically deserted, and I glanced nervously at anyone new, wondering if the bad guy had bought a ticket and was going to show up any moment now.

My hands shaking with nervous tension, I knew it was time to call Uncle Joey.

He answered cheerily. "Hi Shelby. You must be back. How was your vacation?"

"Which part?" I asked. "The part where I had a good time with my family, or the part where I'm stuck alone at the airport because of a letter I had to deliver?"

"I take it, it didn't go so well?" he said.

"No, and now they're after me."

"They're after you?" he asked. "Who's after you?"

"Carson's goons," I said, slightly satisfied to make him nervous.

"What?" he shouted. "What the hell's going on?"

I explained that Warren had begged me to deliver the package to Uncle Joey for him. "He said he'd die if I didn't do it, so I..."

"Wait a minute," he interrupted. "All I told you to do was deliver the letter. That's it! Why would you go along with Warren? He's a... a... oh, never mind." I heard him take a deep breath. "Just tell me what happened."

I told him the whole story and ended with missing my flight. "That guy is either going to wait until I come back out, or he's going to buy a ticket and show up here. He knows where I am. What should I do?"

"And the thumb-drive is still in the cleaning closet?" he asked.

"I guess."

"Okay, go hide in the restroom until I call you back." The line went dead and I put my phone back into my pocket. Hide in the restroom? Was he serious? I thought about it, but couldn't think of anything better, so I found the restroom and took a seat on the lounge chair just inside the door.

I pulled the book I was reading out of my bag, hoping reading would distract me while I waited for Uncle Joey or Chris to call me back. After reading the same paragraph over and over again, I couldn't even remember what I'd read, so I put the book away, too nervous and distracted to concentrate. If it was this bad now, how was I going to last until tomorrow afternoon?

A few people came in and out, and each time the door opened I held my breath, worried the goon had found me.

Soon, my nerves were shot. Maybe I should just leave. But where would I go? My phone vibrated, interrupting my paranoid thoughts, and I eagerly grabbed it from my pocket.

"This is what we're going to do," Uncle Joey said. "I'm sending Ramos in my private jet. He just left for the airport. He'll be there in about two and a half hours."

"He will?" I asked. I didn't know Uncle Joey had a private jet. "What should I do until he gets here?"

"I want you to go back to the shops and buy a hat or something to disguise yourself with, and find a place to eat. Try to sit at a corner table and order some food. Maybe read the paper or a magazine to cover your face. Stay there until Ramos comes. He'll text you when he lands and you can meet up with him. Whatever you do, don't leave the secure part of the airport. Can you do that?"

"Sure," I said. Why hadn't I thought of a disguise? He made it sound so simple.

"Great. Call me at once if you get into trouble."

"Okay, I will."

"Don't worry, you'll be fine. I'll talk to you soon." Uncle Joey disconnected, and an odd feeling of warmth spread through me. He was sending Ramos in his private jet, just for me. That was so nice.

Wait a minute. There had to be more to it. Uncle Joey never did anything without an ulterior motive. The only thing I could think of was the thumb-drive. Ramos probably had orders to get it while he was here... still, I could hardly begrudge him that.

I slipped out of the restroom, walking purposefully toward the shops and restaurants, ducking into the first shop I came to. Since Orlando was the theme-park capitol of the world, most of the t-shirts had Disneyland or Harry Potter stuff on them. I finally found a pink t-shirt with

Orlando printed in flowers across the front, and got the large so I could wear it over my clothes.

There were lots of hats, and I thought a floppy one would cover my hair and face better than a baseball cap. I found a cute white one with a pink flower on the side and tried it on. It did a good job of covering my head, but I looked kind of silly. The store worker was thinking the same thing, so I put it back.

Then I found it. The perfect hat. It was called a hair-hat, and had what looked like a visor with short hair poking out the top. Excited, I found a pink one with whitish-blond hair sticking up and hurried over to a mirror to try it on.

I twisted my hair and tucked it into the top of the cap, pulling the hat in place. It looked kind of real. This was great, plus I'd always wondered what I'd look like with short hair. With it standing up like that, I looked like a punk kid, or a pixie. If I could find some pointy ears to put over mine, it would make a great Halloween costume. I liked it.

The lady at the counter smiled, thinking if I were trying to surprise someone, they wouldn't recognize me at first with that hat on. She rang up my purchases and even cut the tags off so I could wear them. After slipping on the shirt, I went back to the mirror and got the hat on right. This time it looked even better. Satisfied, I waved at the clerk and left the store, feeling relieved and a little hopeful that I could get through this.

I was even ready to eat something. Knowing I had over two and a half hours to kill, I wanted to find a table and chair that was soft as well as out of the way. Since I didn't think the goon would recognize me now, even if he did manage to get a ticket, I took my time to wander around like a real tourist.

My phone vibrated in my pocket, and I quickly pulled it out. It was Chris calling me back. I felt a moment of panic, but decided to tell him the truth that Uncle Joey was sending Ramos for me. Of course, that meant explaining what had happened to Warren. Did I really want to do that now?

"Hi honey," I answered. "How's the flight?"

"Not good," he said. "Mostly because you're not here. What happened?"

"I missed it by one lousy minute," I exclaimed. "I was right there, and they wouldn't let me get on. It was awful."

"So what's the plan now? Are you coming on the next flight?"

"The next flight with an open seat isn't until tomorrow afternoon, so I'm booked on that one."

"You're kidding! What about stand-by?" he asked.

"They put me on stand-by for the other two flights that are leaving later today, but the PSA worker didn't think I'd get on either of them."

"So what are you going to do?" he asked.

"I've got another plan in place," I said. "But I can't really talk about it right now. Can I call you back? I'm going to find someplace to sit down and eat. I'll call you back in just a few minutes."

He sighed before agreeing. "Okay. I'll give you ten minutes." We said goodbye and disconnected.

With my attention on the phone call, I hadn't been watching for Carson's goon, and quickly glanced around me to see if I'd missed anything. Luckily, nothing stood out and I continued toward the food court.

On my way there, I bought a magazine that I never would have read at home, and at last, came upon a restaurant with waitresses and everything. Relieved to get this far, I asked for a corner table, and the hostess led me to the perfect spot. From here I could see people coming and going as well as those wandering in the corridors. Plus it was private enough to talk on my phone without worrying about someone listening in.

I waited until the waitress had taken my order and brought me my Diet Coke before I called Chris back.

"You're late," he growled.

"I know, sorry. I had to get situated and...

"Just tell me what's going on," Chris interrupted. "The whole story. Start after you left this morning."

"Okay." I sighed and took a deep breath, explaining as simply and quietly as I could what had happened to Warren, and his last thought about me, and how Carson thought I had the thumb-drive. "The police needed to talk to me before I could leave for the airport, and once I got here, one of Carson's goons was following me. I lost him at the security gate, but he was thinking about getting a ticket and coming to this terminal, so he might still be here looking for me. That's why I was late."

"Uhng," Chris mumbled.

"So I called Uncle Joey," I quickly continued, worried how Chris was taking it. "He told me to buy a hat and a magazine to hide behind, while I ate some food and waited for Ramos."

"Ra..Ramos? What the...? How...?"

"Oh... he's sending Ramos in his private jet to come get me." I waited for a response from Chris, but the line was silent. Had we been cut off? "Are you there?" I asked. "Chris?"

"I... I'm here," he answered. "Just give me a minute..." I waited, visualizing how Chris was probably rubbing his forehead right now and trying really hard not to get angry. Or yell and ask me what I was thinking. "Okay," he said. "Anything else?"

"Not really. I'll be fine," I said, wanting to reassure him that he didn't need to worry about me. "Ramos should get here about the same time you get home. I don't know what the plans are after that, but I should be home later tonight, or maybe tomorrow. It all depends... I mean, if I know Uncle Joey, we'll probably have to get the thumb-drive before we head back. So it might be tomorrow. But at least I won't have to worry about that guy chasing me with Ramos here. Right?"

"Yeah... right." I got the definite impression that Chris wasn't happy about this arrangement. "Just... do me a favor."

"Sure," I agreed.

"When he gets there, call me."

"Oh... of course," I said.

"And then I want to talk to him. Got that?" His voice was hard and unyielding.

"Uh... sure. What about?" I asked, suddenly nervous.

"You don't need to worry about that," he said with a placating tone. "It's just between him and me. Something I need to tell him."

Now was one of those times I wished I could read minds over the phone. I had an idea of what Chris might say, and upon reflection, decided it was probably better to stay out of it. "Okay. I'll make sure you get to talk to him."

"Good," he sighed. "I guess... I mean with..."

"Go ahead," I said. "Just say it. I'm pretty sure you're mad at me. I would be too if I were you. It's okay if you want to yell at me."

"It's not that exactly... well, I guess it is. If I'm going to be honest, then yes... I'm upset. But yelling at you won't change anything. It's just... this is a mess! Why does this always happen? You need to stop getting into these kinds of situations. It's too much."

"If it makes you feel any better, Uncle Joey was pretty mad at me too. I should have just delivered the letter and left. It's all my fault."

"No it's not!" Chris' voice was low, but his anger came through loud and clear. "This is Manetto's doing. You can't work for him anymore. Not when things like this happen. I think I might just have to talk with him and settle things once and for all."

"Wait!" I cried. "Don't do that. He's sending his private jet with Ramos to get me. He doesn't have to do that, and I'm sure it's going to cost him a lot of money. Just wait until I get home and we'll figure it out. Besides, you need some time to cool off, and I need to get out of trouble. Then we'll figure it out. Okay? You can wait, right?"

I was repeating myself, but this was serious. I couldn't have Chris yelling at Uncle Joey now. I heard him exhale through the phone and waited for him to get under control.

"You're right," he finally said. "I'll wait. Just be careful. And call me as soon as Ramos shows up."

"I will," I promised. "Oh, here comes my food... I'd better go." We said our goodbyes and disconnected.

The waitress set my food down in front of me, but I wasn't really hungry anymore. I thanked her and she quickly left. I checked the time and cringed. Now I had two hours to wait before Ramos got here. Two hours to feel sorry for myself.

The waitress returned with a refill of Diet Coke and I felt better. Nibbling on a hot French fry, I caught a glimpse of my magazine and learned that one of the hottest celebrities was in deep doo-doo with his fiancé. Probably even worse than I was with Chris, and it made me feel better.

Engrossed in the article, I was startled to hear my name over the intercom system. What? Had I heard that right? Then it came again: "Shelby Nichols, please report to the service desk."

I didn't know what to do. Was it a trick by Carson to find me? If that was the case, how did he know my name? Maybe it was the airline trying to tell me they had a seat for me on the next flight home. Since I had no intention of taking it, maybe I should just ignore it. On the other hand, since no one from the airport knew what I looked like, it might not hurt to take a peek and see who wanted me. Plus, if it was someone who knew me, I could probably get away with looking, since I was wearing this hat and a different shirt.

My curiosity got the best of me, so I told the waitress that I had to use the restroom and would be right back. I hurried out into the corridor and glanced up at the signs to find which direction to go for the service desk. Following the signs, I eventually came to the center of the terminal and found the service desk by the trains.

Two men stood beside the desk, observing all the people coming and going from the trains, clearly looking for me. As I got closer I recognized the detectives from this morning, and my step faltered. Some chairs and cushioned benches lined the corridor with plants arranged between them, and I quickly sat down, turning my back toward the men. I opened my magazine, holding it up to block my face.

Detective Castro noticed me, but his thoughts were focused on looking for a woman with a white touristy t-shirt and long blond hair, so his gaze slid right past me to the next woman in the area.

I breathed a sigh of relief and kept my back toward them, realizing that if Detective Fitch saw my face, he would be more observant and probably figure out who I was. Taking a deep breath, I tuned into their thoughts, focusing mostly on Detective Fitch.

He was thinking that I was in trouble, and hoped I would show up soon. He couldn't quit thinking about the car that pulled out behind me after I left the restaurant in my taxi. He hadn't been able to shake off the feeling that he'd missed something, so he'd called the taxi company to find out where they'd taken me. The airport had been a surprise, and the driver had even given him the terminal and gate he needed to check.

It hadn't taken long to track down my scheduled flight, and then to figure out if I had actually made it onto the plane. When it turned out I hadn't, he was even more concerned and suspicious. Where was I now? Who was after me and why? I had to know who killed Warren.

Explosive swearing drew my attention to a man coming down the corridor toward me. Of course it was only in his mind, but it certainly caught my interest. I peeked over my magazine, noticing his Hawaiian alligator print shirt before focusing on his face. My breath caught. It was the guy who was after me!

He was thinking it was his dumb luck to run into the detectives like this, but hoped they wouldn't recognize him. It had been a while since he'd had a chat with Fitch. Maybe Fitch wouldn't remember him.

He kept his face down as he approached the train, and another thought popped into his head. If the detectives were at the service desk, they were waiting for someone. What was the name he'd heard over the intercom? Shelby... Shelby something. Were they looking for the same person he was? This might be helpful after all. If only he could get by without being recognized.

I held my breath as he walked past me, then cringed as the lady at the service desk said my name again asking me to come to the desk. Damn! Now the guy knew my name. He passed the detectives, his mind full of smugness. Since he hadn't been able to find me anywhere in the terminal, at least he could tell Carson what my name was. It wasn't a total...

The train doors closed and I lost his thoughts. I focused back on Detective Fitch who was thinking that the guy looked familiar. Didn't he know him from somewhere? He asked Castro if he'd seen the guy in the alligator shirt. Castro was looking for me and didn't notice. This disgusted Fitch who was thinking Castro was practically worthless if he couldn't be more observant than that.

Since I wasn't there yet, he didn't think I was going to show up, so he pulled out his cell phone and found my card, hoping I'd answer my phone and explain what was going on. My phone was set to vibrate, but I still got up and hurried back the way I had come. Should I answer and tell him I was fine so he'd leave me alone and go after the real bad guy? When my phone began to vibrate, I couldn't bring myself to answer. It was probably better not to get involved with the detectives if I could help it.

With that thought, I hurried back to the restaurant, hoping I'd done the right thing. At least I didn't have to worry about that guy finding me now. Though that didn't mean he had given up. He could still be watching the main terminal for my exit, but since I had two hours to kill, I didn't think he'd wait around that long. My food was still waiting for me, and I eagerly sat down to eat. All this snooping around had given me an appetite.

Two hours and several Cokes later, my phone chirped with a text message, and relief poured over me. Woohoo! Ramos was finally here! I texted him back, and he told me to meet him in the main terminal just past the security checkpoint by the baggage carousel. I couldn't wait to get out of the airport and quickly gathered my things.

After a quick visit to the restroom, I rushed through the corridors and got on the train. It reached the main terminal and I got off, staying close behind some people to keep out of sight. Almost to the security checkpoint, I slowed and glanced at my phone as a pretense to watch for any sign of the alligator shirt.

When I couldn't see or 'hear' him, I put my phone away and, keeping my head down, walked past security and into the main terminal. I arrived at the carousel but couldn't see Ramos, so I ended up pacing back and forth in front of it. I knew it would take him a few minutes to meet up with me, but I couldn't stand still any longer. I was just about to turn around when I heard his voice behind me.

"Babe," he said. "What's with the hat hair?" His chuckle rumbled deep in his chest.

"Ha, ha," I said turning toward him. He was dressed casually, wearing jeans and a dark blazer over a tight-fitting shirt, with a duffel bag slung over his shoulder. It was hard not to throw my arms around him, so I went for sarcasm instead. "What took you so long? I've been waiting here for hours!"

"Yeah. Sounds like you've had a rough day."

"You don't know the half of it," I exclaimed. "But... it's better now that you're here. I hope coming wasn't too much of an imposition." I didn't want him to think I wasn't appreciative that he'd come.

"Well you know Mr. Manetto. He sends me out to do his dirty work and I have to drop everything. It can really put a cramp in my style. You ready to go, or what?" He was playing along to keep things light, but in the back of his mind he thought I looked fragile and scared. It brought out those protective feelings in him that made him want to kill somebody. He didn't like feeling that way.

"Where are we going?" I asked. "I know you just got here, but I'd sure like to go home now."

He shook his head, raising his brow at me. "I think you know what we have to do first."

"Yeah, I figured as much, but I still had to ask." I smiled and shrugged.

"I've booked a place for tonight. Hopefully, after we've retrieved the item, we can leave first thing in the morning."

"All right," I agreed. I scanned the crowd as we exited the airport, still anxious about being spotted.

"Have you seen any sign of the guy that followed you?"

"Yes, actually I did. He came looking for me at my terminal, but he didn't spot me, and then he left."

"What did he look like?" Ramos asked.

"He was medium height and had longish wavy dark hair. When I saw him he had on an alligator print shirt. I think he was trying to look like a tourist."

"Latino?" he asked.

"Yeah, I think so. There's something else you need to know." I was a little nervous about this part, but it was Ramos. I had to tell him. "The detectives were here too. They summoned me over the intercom to come to the service desk. That's when alligator shirt showed up. He recognized the detectives and figured they were looking for me. Now he knows my name."

Ramos glanced at me, his brows drawn together.

"No," I answered his unspoken question. "I didn't talk to the detectives, but I did 'hear' them. I just hid behind a plant to find out who had summoned me to the service desk."

"But you talked to them earlier?" he asked.

"Yes. They questioned me at the scene of the crime, like everyone who was there. Detective Fitch noticed a car following my taxi and decided to find out where I'd gone. That's why he came to the airport."

Ramos' step slowed. Dozens of images of a much younger Detective Fitch flowed through his mind.

"You know him?" I blurted.

Ramos glanced at me, cutting off all thoughts of the detective. "Yeah, I know him."

"How?" I asked.

He scowled, annoyed that I'd picked up something he didn't want me to. He'd never thought my mind reading would bother him until now.

"You don't have to tell me," I said. "It's just kind of weird that you know him."

"You're right," he agreed. "So I might as well get it out in the open. I used to live here. I grew up in Florida and spent some time here in Orlando and Miami."

"Oh," I said, stunned by his revelation. "So, is your being here going to be a good thing or a bad thing?"

He let out a mirthless laugh. "I'm hoping we don't stay long enough to find out."

Chapter 4

"We need to rent a car," Ramos said, guiding me toward the rental places. He surveyed the crowd, thinking that Carson's man was probably gone. It was time to get down to business and put Fitch out of his mind. Fitch may be involved, but Carson was the one Ramos needed to focus on. Carson may know my name, but he didn't know that Ramos had arrived to protect me. He smiled grimly. He was going to enjoy this.

I got the feeling that Ramos and Carson had a history, but couldn't pick up anything else from Ramos' thoughts. When he focused his mind on something, his thoughts seldom strayed. This made him good at his job, mostly because his feelings didn't get involved. He was different from anyone I'd ever met, and if I didn't know him better, I'd be scared to death. He was like a shark in a pond of unsuspecting sunbathers.

While Ramos made arrangements for the car, I decided to give Chris a call. He should be home by now, and was probably anxious to hear from me.

"Hey there," I said, when he answered his cell phone. "Did you make it home already?"

"Yeah, we just walked in a few minutes ago. How about you? Did Ramos make it?"

"Yes. He's here and we're at the car rental place. It sounds like we'll probably come home tomorrow."

"So where are you staying tonight?" Chris' voice sounded a little strained.

"I don't know. I think he said he'd booked a place, but he didn't tell me where. Do you want me to ask him?"

"No," Chris answered a little shortly. "So you're all right? Everything's okay now?"

"Yeah. I'm good." I decided not to tell him about the guy following me and the detectives showing up. I could save that for another time. There was silence on his end so I asked, "Do you want to talk to Ramos now?" I hoped that was what he was waiting for. Ramos had the car keys and was walking toward me, so now would be the perfect time. If that's what he still wanted to do.

"Yes. Put him on."

"Okay. Here he is." I covered the phone with my hand and smiled at Ramos. His eyes narrowed and his brows drew together. "Um... it's Chris. He'd like to talk to you." I guess I should have warned Ramos this was coming.

He scowled and took the phone. "Yes?" he said, his tone low and hard.

At that moment I really wanted to disappear. I hoped Chris wouldn't try and tell Ramos how to do his job. That would be bad. I also didn't want him to imply there was anything going on between us. That would be unbearable. I especially didn't want Chris to say the words, "my wife" this or "my wife" that.

Still, I listened as hard as I could. Hoping I could do some damage control if things went bad. Surprisingly, Ramos pursed his lips in amusement. In his mind he was completely agreeing with Chris that I was always getting into trouble. I was a handful… there was no doubt about it. Chris was at his wits' end. Ramos could hear the frustration in his voice.

"I'll make sure she comes back to you," Ramos said. "Don't worry." He listened to Chris ask him if he should come. "No. That's not necessary." Chris thanked him and asked to speak to me. Ramos handed me the phone.

"Hey," I said to Chris.

"Thanks for letting me talk to him. I feel better now." Chris' voice had lost that hard edge.

"Good." I smiled, relieved.

"Listen… call me later, okay?" he asked.

"Sure… and I'll see you tomorrow."

"Yeah… that's right." He hesitated before adding, "Love you."

"Love you too." We disconnected and I put my phone away. Relief swept over me to know Chris was handling this more calmly now. I was grateful for the way he'd talked to Ramos, and felt bad that I'd thought the worst of him. It made me love him even more. I knew he was worried, and I hated to put him in this position. Somehow, I'd have to try and be better so something like this didn't happen again.

I followed Ramos to the parking garage where the rental cars were kept. He was feeling sorry for Chris and was glad he didn't have anyone in his life he felt so deeply about. He did once, and it had nearly destroyed him… never again.

I probably wasn't supposed to know that, but it made sense in a way, and I wondered what had happened to make him so hard. Had the woman he loved left him, or worse, betrayed him? It had to be something bad.

He led me to a black sports car and I groaned. "Black? Why does it always have to be black?"

Ramos smiled. "You'll see." He was thinking about how we were going to break into the restaurant tonight and a black car was essential for a quick get-a-way.

"We're breaking in?" I said. "Are you sure we can't just make up some excuse to check the cleaning supply closet?"

"Yes. I'm sure." He opened the trunk and threw his duffle bag inside. I got my purse out of my carry-on bag and slung it over my shoulder, then put the carry-on bag in as well.

Sliding into the passenger seat, I couldn't help exclaiming. "Whoa! This is nice. Plush leather seats, a sunroof, all the newest gadgets, and the best part of all... the new car smell! I could get used to this."

Ramos settled into his seat and slipped on his dark glasses. Then he arranged the rear-view mirror and put on his seatbelt. The car seemed to mold around him like a second skin. He owned that car. How did he do that just by sitting there? He turned on the ignition and it rumbled to life. I felt a flash of pleasure roll off him. It made me excited to be there, and I forgot all about breaking into the restaurant.

We drove out of the parking lot, and a few minutes later, hopped onto the freeway. I loved how the car felt. Smooth and sleek, with a promise of freedom topped by total hotness. To my delight, Ramos opened the sunroof. Laughing, I pulled off my hat and ran my fingers through my hair. A rush of exuberance ran through me, and I raised my hands through the roof, feeling the air whip through my fingers. After being cooped up in the airport all day, this freedom felt exhilarating.

"Wouldn't it be fun to take this car on a drive along the coast?" I asked. "Especially on the road that goes over the ocean with the waves crashing and everything?"

Ramos glanced at me and shook his head. He was thinking how sexy I looked with my blonde hair floating around my face, and the sparkle of excitement in my bright blue eyes. "Babe... you shouldn't tempt me like that," he growled. "What would your husband think? I made him a promise, remember?"

"I... I didn't mean it like that," I gasped.

He narrowed his eyes, but a playful smile betrayed him. "Then be careful what you say to me. I don't have quite the same scruples that you do. You'd be wise to remember that." He was thinking it was partly true. There was a certain attraction between us, even though there was no way in hell he'd ever act on it. Still, it was best not to go there.

I huffed. "You know I heard all that, right?"

He pursed his lips. "Yeah, and it was a lot easier than talking about it." He glanced at me and shrugged. "I'm a bad guy, what can I say? You should be careful around me."

I rolled my eyes and sighed. "Fine, but I don't think you're as bad as you think you are." Before he could protest I continued. "So where are we going?"

"I need to check out the restaurant in order to make plans for tonight," Ramos said. "Do you have the address?"

"Um... no. But I remember the name. It's called The Blue Heron. Do you know it?"

He shook his head. "I may have grown up here, but I haven't been back for years." He was thinking a lot had changed, but it wasn't enough to keep him from remembering the past. Stepping off the plane and smelling the air had brought it all back. It didn't matter how long he'd been gone, a part of him would always know this place, and he realized he could never outrun his past. Good or bad, it had made him who he was today.

He huffed, pushing all thoughts of the past away. He had a job to do, and the sooner it was done, the better. "Let's see if our GPS system can help us out." He turned it on and started speaking to it. "Orlando restaurants. The Blue Heron."

A British-sounding voice responded with directions, and Ramos grinned with satisfaction, like he'd just performed a major accomplishment.

"You just love it when things work right, don't you?" I asked.

"I certainly do," he said. "Lots better than asking directions."

Ramos drove through traffic with expert skill, and we pulled across the street from the restaurant in record time. Over four hours had passed since I had been there, but yellow tape still marked it as a crime scene. "I guess they're not open for business yet," I said.

"Looks that way," Ramos agreed. "It might make it easier to break in later."

"Yeah," I agreed. "I think there must be a door that goes from the kitchen and out the back. At least that's where Warren was headed when he got killed."

Ramos studied the surrounding buildings, noting where the light poles were in relation to the parking lot. "I think we can sneak in the back without detection." He was thinking about where to park the car and the route we needed to take. Putting the car into gear, he drove slowly around the block. "There," he said with satisfaction. "We'll back the car into that alley and go through the back to the parking lot behind it."

"What about that fence?" I asked. "It "is" blocking the alleyway, you know."

"Yeah," he glanced at me, thinking *duh* in his mind. "We'll climb over it."

"You think I can do that? It looks kind of tall to me, but I guess if you brought a ladder, I could do it."

"A ladder?" Ramos smiled. He figured I was serious, but no way would he be caught dead carrying a ladder. "Don't worry about it. I'll help you over." He envisioned pushing my ass up the fence and his smile got bigger.

"Stop that," I scolded. "It's chain link. I can probably climb it just fine by myself."

"Good." He congratulated himself, thinking his little ploy had worked like a charm.

"You..." I almost said 'big lug,' but punched his arm instead. It was like hitting a rock. I shook my hand and groaned.

He raised a brow in cool disdain. "Are you done?" he asked.

I frowned and Ramos chuckled. He enjoyed teasing me. "Let's get to the hotel and have some dinner," he said. "I have some calls to make."

"Fine," I agreed, slightly miffed. He sure knew how to push my buttons. Because of that, I wasn't about to ask him where we were staying. Besides, the way we'd been communicating, it was almost easier to pick it up from his mind and not waste my breath.

Ramos directed his attention to the road, leaving me in the dark. How his brain worked continually amazed me. Most people thought of lots of things at once, but not Ramos. He was real good at compartmentalizing his thoughts. Right now he was thinking of which road to turn on, instead of our destination. It was starting to drive me nuts.

"We're going to The Carlton," he said, surprising me. "In case you were wondering."

"I was," I said, narrowing my eyes at him. "And you knew it too, didn't you?"

He shrugged. "It was a good guess. I imagine it's a little like how you managed to keep people in the dark about your mind reading abilities. Telling them you were guessing?"

"Hmm... I suppose you're right about that." I couldn't compete with Ramos, and it was probably best not to even try.

A short while later, we pulled into the drive of The Ritz-Carlton Hotel, and my jaw dropped open. When he said The Carlton, I had no idea he meant The Ritz-Carlton. This place was amazing, and I could hardly believe we were staying here. An impressive panther fountain gave way to palm trees that lined the drive to the hotel, which was set back beside the Grande Lakes.

As we pulled into the hotel's valet parking, Ramos popped open the trunk. A parking attendant rushed to serve us, and another attendant took our bags from the trunk. I followed Ramos inside to the hotel lobby and tried to keep my mouth shut. The elegant lobby was richly appointed with marble columns, Italian furniture, and a mosaic floor that gave it a Palazzo feel. I felt totally out-classed in my jeans and pink t-shirt.

"Welcome to the Carlton," the hostess said. "Do you have a reservation?"

"Yes," Ramos answered. "One of the executive suites. It's under Alejandro Ramos." He flipped open his wallet, showing her his ID.

"Very good," she answered, quickly tapping his name into her keyboard.

Alejandro? That was his first name? How come I never knew that?

"You are on the sixth floor, room six-seventeen," the hostess said. "Here are your keycards. Enjoy your stay. If there is anything you need, just let us know."

"Thank you," Ramos said. He pocketed the keycards and motioned me toward the elevators. The attendant followed with our luggage, so I couldn't ask any of the questions floating through my mind, like... if we were in the same room, what bed was he sleeping in? But since this was a suite, it had to have more than one bedroom, right?

In between all of these thoughts, my mind kept coming back to Ramos' first name. Alejandro. Hmm... was it for real? I realized I hardly knew anything about Ramos' personal life. If today was any indication, this trip might change that, and I couldn't help smiling. I'd always been curious about him, and how he had ended up with Uncle Joey. This could get interesting.

We exited the elevator, following the numbers to room six-seventeen. Ramos keyed it open and stepped inside, holding the door for me. He tipped the attendant and brought our bags in himself. "This is a one-bedroom suite," he explained. "But you can take the bed, and I'll sleep out here on the couch."

"Are you sure?" I asked, suddenly nervous. "Maybe we should get two rooms."

"Look, I'm fine on the couch, and you can lock the bedroom door if it makes you feel better. Go on... take a look around. You'll find there's plenty of room. Don't worry about me. I have my own bathroom and everything."

The living room held a couch, end tables with lamps, a coffee table with fresh flowers, a chair, flat screen TV, and sliding doors that opened onto a balcony. The scent of fresh flowers along with a few potted plants made the room seem refreshing and pleasant.

On the other side of the room, double doors opened into the master bedroom. A king-sized bed sat in the center with a chaise-lounge, dresser, flat screen TV, and another private balcony. I couldn't resist opening the sliding balcony door and admiring the lakefront view. It was breathtaking, and the weariness of the day fell from my shoulders.

With a sigh, I turned back into the bedroom and found a walkin closet on the other side of the room before coming to the bathroom door. The luxurious bathroom was done in gray marble with a tub, shower, separate toilet, and double sink. Red rose petals were spread along the floor to the jetted tub over a lush rug. Wow, did I ever want to take a bath in there.

I turned back to the living room and found Ramos out on the balcony talking on his phone. While he was occupied, I rounded the corner to find the other bathroom. It was marble too, but didn't have a shower or tub, only a sink and separate toilet. It looked like I'd have to share the shower, but that was probably all, and it was only for one night. I could do this.

But was it fair to make Ramos sleep on the couch when he was paying for the room? The couch wasn't very big, and the bed was huge. On the other hand, he'd made the arrangements. He had to know he'd end up sleeping on the couch, so I couldn't really feel too bad about that. Besides, he could have gotten two rooms.

Feeling better, I picked up my carry-on bag and took it into the bedroom. Thank goodness I kept all my make-up in my bag, along with my toothbrush. Plus, my mother always taught me to keep an extra change of underwear for emergencies, so that was covered. I only wished I had more clothes to wear.

The sliding door opened, and Ramos ended his call, so I hurried into the living room. "That was Manetto," he said. "I needed to fill him in on our progress." At my nod, he continued. "Are you hungry?"

"Sort of," I said, feeling more unsettled with Ramos' close proximity than I wanted to admit. I mean seriously... we were sharing a hotel room, and he was... well... Ramos. "What do we need for tonight?"

Ramos grabbed his bag and set it on the chair. Unzipping it, he pulled out some nicely folded black clothes, black gloves, and a black cap for me to hide my hair. "I think I have everything here we need." He handed me a long-sleeved black shirt. "Your jeans are dark enough, and I don't think your shoes will matter that much."

I glanced at my gray running shoes with the purple stripes. "Um... yeah," I agreed. "They're dark enough they should be fine."

"We've got lots of time before we hit the restaurant. Why don't we go grab some food and get you anything you might need for the night?" He was thinking I probably didn't have pajamas, or whatever else a woman needed to survive, so we might as well get it now.

"Okay," I said. "Just let me fix my hair and I'll be ready to go." I hurried into the bathroom and pulled off the pink t-shirt, straightened my white one, and then ran a comb through my hair. After putting on some lip-gloss, I was ready.

"You don't think I need my hair-hat anymore do you?" I asked Ramos.

"No. I'm sure you'll be fine without it."

We drove in companionable silence until we came to a Walmart, and I begged Ramos to stop. "This will work great for getting what I need to survive," I explained.

Ramos pursed his lips at my use of his thoughts, and pulled into the parking lot.

"You can stay in the car if you like," I said sweetly. I didn't really want him hovering over me while I bought the necessary toiletries. He was thinking that was a good idea, as long as I didn't take too long. "I'll be quick," I promised. He grunted and I hurried inside.

I looked through the pajamas first, happy to find a set with an oversized t-shirt and capri-length bottoms, knowing it was important to keep my modesty just in case I ran into Ramos in the room with them on. No need to tempt fate.

Nearby, I found a table with swimming suits on sale and sighed, remembering the amazing pool at the hotel. I could probably go for a swim in the morning before we left if I had a suit. I quickly rummaged through them until finding a one-piece in my size. It wasn't the cutest in the bunch, but it had a halter top that I knew couldn't expose too much of me like some of the others. I never bought a swimming suit without trying it on first, but because I was in a hurry, I had to make an exception this time. For that pool, it was worth it.

Next, I had to find a blouse or shirt that wasn't so touristy to wear home tomorrow. I mean, how could I be staying at the Ritz-Carlton and fly in a private jet with this frumpy, touristy t-shirt on? It was unthinkable.

I spied a table with print tees on it, and found a Lady Gaga one that I was tempted to buy, mostly because it reminded me of her song titled "Alejandro." I picked it up and started singing under my breath "Ale-Alejandro, Ale-Alejandro." Smiling, I turned to take it with me and bumped into a solid chest.

"Oof!" I exclaimed, springing back.

Ramos stared down at me, his eyes narrowed.

"Aa! You scared me." Realizing he'd heard me singing his name, my face flamed red with embarrassment, so I went on the defense. "What are you doing in here? I thought you were waiting in the car."

"I was, but you were taking so long, I thought I'd better come in and check up on you." He took the Lady Gaga tee from me and studied it.

"Um... I was just singing that Lady Gaga song, you know, the one about Alejandro, mostly because I guess that's your name and I never knew that, and this shirt reminded me of it. Have you ever heard that song?"

"Are you going to buy it, or what?" he asked, focusing his thoughts on me.

He wasn't cutting me any slack, and it made me a little angry. I was about to tell him no when a thought of his came through that he was... embarrassed? Flattered? "Of course I'm going to buy it." I pulled it from his hands and threw it over my arm with the rest of my stuff. "I have to get one more thing." I raised my brow in a challenge. "You going to follow me, or what?"

He snorted, but wisely moved out of my way. "I'll wait over there." He motioned toward the closest cash register.

I nodded, and a bit rattled by our encounter, hurried to another rack of shirts. I still wanted something a little nicer to wear and quickly scanned the rack. Finding a jewel digital print tee, I held it up and admired the gold and silver tones over a white background in jewel shapes. It even had cute cap sleeves. With the right necklace and earrings this would look amazing paired with my jeans, plus it was in my size.

I grabbed it and marched over to the jewelry. After a few minutes' search, I found just what I was looking for. Gold and silver chains highlighted with geometric shapes and earrings to match! Now all I needed was a pair of metallic sandals to complete the outfit.

Glancing toward the cash register, I noticed Ramos looking through the magazines, so I high-tailed it over to the shoes for a quick look. One good thing about Orlando is the great selection of sandals. The only hard part was deciding whether to get the gold ones or the silver ones. I went with the silver, figuring they would go with more of my clothes.

On my way to the checkout stand, I passed a display of sunglasses and paused to grab a pair. I found cute white-rimmed ones with gold speckles on the sides that matched my outfit perfectly. I slid them on and smiled. Yup, they made me look good.

I rushed back to the cash register, hoping Ramos wasn't too upset with me for taking so long. I got in line and smiled at him, feeling his relief at finally being able to leave. The person at the cash register was grateful we were leaving too. Ramos' cold expression and watchful eyes made him nervous, especially since he looked like he was ready to kill somebody.

As the cashier rang up my purchases, Ramos' brows lifted in disbelief at all the stuff I was buying. He could understand the pajamas and shirts, but the jewelry and sandals? He took a deep breath and let it out, then noticed the swimming suit and sunglasses. He glanced at me, thinking there wasn't enough time to go swimming.

"Have you even seen the pool?" I asked. "It's awesome. Even a fifteen minute swim would be worth it."

He glanced away with a smile and shook his head. I opened my purse to get my credit card, but he stopped me. "I got this."

I took a breath to object but closed my mouth instead. Ramos was thinking that I'd better keep my mouth shut if I knew what was good for me. I chuckled and moved out of his way. I'd probably tested his patience enough for one day, and we still had some breaking and entering on the agenda.

That thought sent a chill down my spine. But I would be with Ramos. What could go wrong with him there? At least I knew he had my back.

We got in the car, and Ramos pulled into traffic. "I know a place that serves the best fish tacos I've ever had. You game?"

"Sure," I said.

"I don't know if it's still there, but ever since I got off the plane, that's what I've wanted to eat. Crazy how a place can trigger things like that, isn't it?"

"For sure," I agreed. "How long has it been since you've been back?"

He sighed. "I don't know, about fifteen years. I was eighteen when I left, and I swore I'd never come back. But it doesn't seem so bad to be here this time." He was thinking it was true as long as he didn't try too hard to remember why he'd left.

Since he was thinking that, I decided not to ask him any more questions about his past. Not when he felt such bitterness and pain. Something bad had happened to him here, and although I was curious, now was not the time to talk about it.

"There it is!" he said. "I can't believe it's still here." Ramos grinned like a kid. I'd never seen him like that. It was a little disconcerting.

"Sweet!" I said, trying to match his enthusiasm. We pulled into the small parking lot surrounding what looked like an old fast food joint that had been remodeled into a Mexican restaurant with a big sombrero hat on top. The word "Hector's" glowed in neon lights above the building. The place was crowded with people, and we hurried to the back of the line.

The only bad part about this idea was that I hated fish tacos. But there was no way I could tell Ramos that. I'd have to suck it up and eat at least one. That should work since I could use the excuse that I wasn't very hungry, which was mostly true. Hopefully it wouldn't kill me.

When it came my turn to order, I got one fish taco, some fries, and a drink. Ramos was thinking I was nuts to only get one but didn't say anything. He ordered five, thinking that after I tasted mine, I'd want at least one more. I tried not to shudder and took my cup to the drinks machine.

We found a small table near the back and settled in to eat. Ramos dug in, closing his eyes in pleasure with the first bite. He swallowed and glanced at me. "These are even better than I remember." Noticing I that I hadn't started eating mine, his brows drew together. "Aren't you going to eat it?"

"Of course." I smiled brightly. Unable to put it off any longer, I took a small bite. A burst of cilantro and lime with a tangy sauce coated my tongue. I chewed, surprised that I couldn't taste that fishiness that always repelled me. I took another bite, but the same great flavors came through, leaving me a little shocked. "This is really good." I finished it off like a starving person.

Ramos smirked. "Good thing I got an extra one for you." He pushed it toward me.

"I guess you could tell I usually don't like these," I confessed.

"The thought had crossed my mind," he agreed. "But you probably already knew that."

I nodded and took a bite of my second taco, savoring the flavor almost as much as Ramos had. Who would have thought I'd ever like these? Chris would be so surprised. A pang of remorse hit me in the chest. How would he feel knowing I was sitting here enjoying myself while he was probably worrying about me? I checked the time. It was after eight. I should have called him before now.

"What's wrong?" Ramos asked.

"I promised Chris I'd call him, and it's getting late."

Ramos nodded in understanding. "It's not too late. Let's get back to the hotel and you can call him there." He was thinking I needed some privacy to talk to my husband, and he didn't especially want to hear what I had to say.

"Sounds good. Thanks Ramos."

We finished up and got into the car. Ramos flipped on the radio to some salsa-type music, which surprised me. It wasn't his usual fare, but with the flavor of the tacos still burning my mouth, it seemed to fit.

"What time are we going tonight?" I asked.

"Around one or so," Ramos said. "Do you mind if we drive around the restaurant one more time? I want to see what it looks like now that it's getting dark."

"Not at all," I agreed. When we arrived, the crime-scene tape was gone. "They must have cleaned the place up to be ready to open tomorrow."

"Yeah," Ramos said. "It's a good thing we're going in there tonight. No one will suspect if we leave the cleaning supply closet a little messed up from looking for the thumb-drive."

I nodded and Ramos continued to drive around the block, slowing to check out the fence. He was thinking it might be a little too tall for me to climb over if we had to leave in a hurry, and he didn't want me to get stuck. "I'll take you back to the hotel and you can call your husband while I visit the hardware store for some wire clippers."

I couldn't hide the relief in my voice. "Sounds good."

Ramos dropped me off at the hotel with my purchases, and I hurried to our room, eager to call Chris. "Hey sweetie," I said. "How's it going?"

"Pretty good. How are you? Where are you staying?"

Guilt flooded over me, but I couldn't really lie could I? "You'll never believe it, but I guess Uncle Joey has connections or something because I'm at the Ritz-Carlton." He didn't answer right away.

"Wow," he said.

"Yeah, I know. Pretty crazy, huh? But anyway, I've got my own room and everything, so that's good." That wasn't exactly a lie.

"Um... good." He said it like he didn't expect anything less, so why did I bring it up? Or was that just my guilty conscience speaking? "So," he continued, "Did you get the thumb-drive out of the cleaning closet?"

"We drove by the restaurant a couple of times and it's shut up tight, so Ramos thought later tonight would be a good time to get the thumb-drive."

"You mean break in?" he asked.

"Yeah."

"You and Ramos are going to break into the restaurant?" he asked, his voice edged with incredulity. "Wait... no. That's a bad idea. If he wants the thumb-drive, he can do it without you."

"Yeah, exactly," I said, trying to reassure him. "He's going while I wait."

"At the hotel," he clarified.

"Um... probably, unless he needs me to drive the car."

"Shelby..." he sighed.

"Chris... I'll be fine. Don't worry so much. This is what Ramos does, and he's very good at it. I'll be home tomorrow and we can get back to normal." Oops, maybe that wasn't the best thing to say since our 'normal' wasn't like anyone else's normal.

"Yeah... okay," Chris said. "I'll try not to freak out. It's just..." he paused. "Well, let's just say I'll be glad to have you back where I can keep an eye on you."

"Right, because otherwise I get into so much trouble."

"I didn't say that."

"It's okay," I relented. "This isn't what you signed up for." Suddenly, I needed to know how he felt. "Chris... are you ever sorry you married me?"

"What? You're joking, right?"

"No, I'm totally serious," I said.

"Shelby... of course not," he answered. "I love you. I couldn't imagine my life without you. Sometimes you drive me crazy, but I can live with it. I just worry about you. Wouldn't you worry about me if our roles were reversed? If I was the one who could read minds and had to work for a person like Manetto?"

"Well... yeah," I said. When he put it that way I could totally understand his feelings. "I get it. It's just that sometimes you seem more annoyed with me than anything else. I really don't blame you. I just wish you'd cut me some slack. I really am doing the best I can." My eyes filled with tears. "Today... a man I was trying to help died. His last thoughts were about me. He felt bad he'd involved me, and then just like that, he was gone."

I sniffed and wiped my eyes. "I feel bad about it, but with everything else that's happened, I've had to push it to the back of my mind. Without you here, it's going to be hard to sleep tonight." I needed his comforting arms around me.

"Babe... I'm so sorry. I wish I were there. Don't cry... it'll be all right. After you get home tomorrow, I'll have something special planned, and tomorrow night... I'll make it up to you. I'll always be there for you, Shelby. Don't ever forget that. Okay?"

"Okay," I said.

"I'll do better, I promise. You're worth whatever I have to do. Just... don't give up on me either, okay?"

"I won't," I smiled through my tears. "I mean, if you think about it, if I hadn't been protecting you from Kate... I never would have met Uncle Joey. So... in a sense, this is all your fault."

He chuckled. "Fine. I take full responsibility."

"Good. I'm glad that's settled. Now I don't feel so bad about staying in this gorgeous hotel room." I fell back on the bed. "I'll miss you though... but I'll try to get over it."

"Fine. Just call me if you need me... I'll keep my phone on all night."

"Thanks Chris. I'm looking forward to tomorrow," I said.

"Love you babe."

"Love you too." We disconnected and I kicked off my shoes, then laid back and stared at the ceiling. It had been a long day and I was exhausted. Hopefully, stealing the thumb-drive from the restaurant later would go smoothly.

It was great to talk to Chris. He grounded me, and right now I needed that. I enjoyed being with Ramos, maybe more than I should, and that worried me. Not that anything would happen between us, but I had to admit, I was attracted to him. I could totally get why women fell for the "bad boy" types. That element of danger held a certain appeal. It was like throwing caution to the wind, which for me was not an option. Not when I already had a wonderful man in my life.

Chris loved me. Besides being ruggedly handsome and a great husband, he was stable and loyal. He was the perfect partner for me in every way. With our two great kids, we were a family that belonged together. We just needed to have a little more fun, and not be so serious all the time.

Thoughts of how we could accomplish that brought a smile of anticipation to my face, and I looked forward to getting home tomorrow, especially when he was planning something special. I'd have to get all dolled up and wear something out of the ordinary, but it would be worth it to see the look on his face and hear him say some of my favorite words... "Oh baby, oh baby."

Chapter 5

"Shelby. Wake up."

I opened my eyes, shocked that I had fallen asleep. Ramos stood over me, dressed in black and ready to go.

"What time is it?" I rose to my elbows.

"Two in the morning," he said, walking to the door. "Your black shirt is on the bed. I'll wait out here for you."

"Okay. Thanks."

The door clicked shut and I sat up, yawning widely and stretching my arms. I changed into the black shirt and visited the bathroom. After brushing my teeth, I pulled my hair into a low ponytail and slipped on the black cap. I looked kind of pale, but at least the dark circles under my eyes came in handy for a change.

I grimaced, thinking about how I'd told Chris I wasn't going with Ramos, but what he didn't know wouldn't hurt him, right? Besides, I needed to see that closet in order to find the spot where Warren had visualized hiding the thumb-drive. Otherwise, going through the closet from top to bottom might take too long and be too much of a risk.

My stomach twisted with anxiety, and I wished I'd bought some antacid at the store when I had the chance. That was definitely something I needed to survive, and I had totally spaced it. Oh well, not much I could do about it now.

I joined Ramos, and he quickly surveyed my appearance before giving me his nod of approval. "We're taking the stairs to the lower parking level. I don't want anyone to see us."

"Okay," I said.

He checked the hallway and then beckoned me out. I followed him to the stairwell and tried to keep my footsteps from echoing too loudly off the walls. How did Ramos manage to be so quiet? We made it to the parking garage, and it was a relief to climb inside the car without anyone spotting us.

As we drove away, the soft music from the radio kept us company, and I tried to focus on the words of the songs to keep my nerves under control. It wasn't long before we pulled off the road, and Ramos backed the car into the alleyway by the fence. He cut the engine, and in the sudden silence, I took a quick breath and clenched my fists. This was it.

"Babe... chill," Ramos said. He was thinking he'd be amused if he weren't a little insulted as well. "We'll be fine. You don't need to worry." He grabbed a bag from the back seat and opened it. "Here are your gloves. Under no circumstances should you take them off."

I opened my mouth to say "as if" but shut it before I could. I mean... I may be an amateur, but I wasn't stupid. I pulled on the gloves and glanced at Ramos, who pursed his lips to hide a smile.

He pulled on his own gloves and glanced at me. "You're not so nervous now, are you?" he asked.

"Nope. Now I'm just mad."

"Good." He grinned, reaching up to turn off the inside light of the car. He opened his door and got out, setting the bag on the seat, and proceeded to empty the contents. He handed me a small flashlight that was attached to a lanyard. "Put that around your neck," he instructed, doing the same with another one.

Next came an eight-inch compact bolt cutter, which he put in his back pocket, then a sheathed knife that he clipped to his waist. Last, he pulled out a gun. He put a clip of bullets into it and stuffed it into the waistband of his jeans.

"I sure hope you have the safety on," I said, only half joking.

He huffed and shook his head. "Let's go."

I gulped down my fear and scrambled out, shutting the door as quietly as I could. I followed Ramos to the fence, where he efficiently cut the links in a line from the bottom up, and rolled the sides open wide enough to allow us to slide through. He left the bolt cutter by the fence, thinking he would pick it up on our way out. Grabbing the fence with his fingers, he swiftly slid his body feet first through the opening and crouched on the other side.

That didn't look too hard, so I tried to slide through like he did, but only got about halfway, and had to turn over on my stomach and push myself backwards until I cleared the chain links. I stood up, and my black clothes were covered in a layer of dirt. Not only on the front of me, but the back as well.

Ramos' brows rose in amazement, and he wondered how anyone could get so dirty so fast. Even my chin had dirt on it. I rubbed the dirt off my chin, then slapped at my knees and chest where most of it seemed to be.

Ramos just shook his head. "Come on, we gotta move. Stay behind me." He glanced toward the restaurant, looking for the best route, but the path to the back door was pretty much out in the open. I hoped no one was watching right then, because even with our black clothes on, we were sure to be spotted.

At the door, Ramos took a couple of picks out of his pocket. "Shine your light on the lock," he whispered. I flipped it on and within seconds, he had the door opened. We hurried inside and Ramos checked the nearby wall for an alarm system, ready to disable it. Not finding one, he shrugged and glanced at me. "I don't like this. We'd better be fast."

A soft overhead security light enabled us to see where we were going, and after passing through the kitchen, we found the hall with the cleaning closet. It was dark in the hallway, so Ramos switched on his flashlight and opened the door.

I glanced inside, but it looked so different from Warren's visualization, that I had a hard time figuring out what I was looking at. "Can we turn on the closet light?" I asked.

"I think so. This hallway has no windows so we should be okay," Ramos said.

I flipped the switch and breathed a sigh of relief, recognizing some of what I was looking for. "His attention was on this part, where all the brooms and stuff are." I moved a few long handles out of the way and found an aluminum dust mop. "I think this is it," I said. It was lightweight and the color matched what I'd seen in Warren's mind. "Is the thumb-drive taped to it somewhere?" I asked.

Ramos took the mop and examined it. "No, but look... it comes apart." He twisted the top off and shone his flashlight down the tube. "There it is. It's taped inside." He reached his index finger in and tugged it out, ripping off the tape with it.

As he examined it, the hairs on the back of my neck rose, and I clamped my fingers around his arm. "Someone just came in," I whispered, panicked. "He's thinking his guys won't be here for about ten minutes, but he doesn't want us to get away. He's going to wait by the door and ambush us when we leave. No... wait. He's coming this way."

Ramos flipped off the light. "Keep this and stay in here," he said, slipping the thumb-drive into my hand before stepping into the hallway and softly closing the door.

My heart raced with panic and fear. I couldn't hear any thoughts with the door shut, and the darkness terrified me. In the silence, my heavy breathing seemed too loud. What was happening out there? What if Ramos needed my help? Maybe I should open the door a crack so I could hear what was going on. I stuffed the thumb-drive into my jeans pocket and placed my hand on the doorknob, ready to pull it open.

The sharp blast of a gun firing had me jerking away from the door with a little scream. Two more blasts followed, and I backed into the furthest corner of the closet, crouching as low to the ground as I could. I covered my ears while several more shots sounded. Then it stopped, leaving a profound silence that scared me to death.

I sat as quietly as I could, afraid to move. Was Ramos alive? I swallowed. I should go out there and see if he needed me. What if he was lying on the ground bleeding to death? As I rose to my feet, the door flew open and I cringed back.

"We need to leave." Ramos said. He grabbed my arm to help me up, pulling me out of the closet.

"Are you okay?" I asked.

"Yeah." He was thinking the other guy was dead and his buddies would be here any minute, unless the cops got here first, which was a definite possibility with all the gunfire.

He held onto my arm, leading me out of the hallway and through the kitchen to the back door. I tried to keep my attention focused on getting out, but couldn't help glancing at the body as we passed. I recognized the bald head before I caught a glimpse of the snake tattoos. "That's the guy who killed Warren."

"Yeah. I figured that." We made it to the door, and Ramos slowed to glance through the glass for signs of movement. "Can you run?" My legs were a bit rubbery, but I nodded anyway. Ramos grabbed my hand and pushed out of the door at a running crouch. I did my best to keep up with him, pleased to find that my legs were working after all. It also didn't hurt that Ramos was holding my hand.

We got to the fence, and Ramos pulled it up so I could crawl under it. As I stood, he came through, grabbing the bolt cutters with one hand, and my hand with the other. He pulled me forward until we got to the car, then he let go of me. I scrambled to the door and jumped inside. Ramos threw himself in and started the engine.

Without the car lights on, he pulled the car forward and turned onto the deserted street. About thirty feet further on, he flipped on the headlights and settled back in his seat. As I pulled on my seat belt, I heard sirens approaching and glanced at Ramos, my eyes wide with concern.

"Don't worry," he said. "I got this." He turned onto another side street, cruising slowly until we came to a main road, and pulled onto the street.

"There's enough traffic here that we won't be conspicuous," he assured me. "The freeway's not far. We'll be back to the hotel before you know it."

I let out my breath and my shoulders sagged with relief. We'd made it this far, but I couldn't totally relax until I was safe and sound in my room.

"Where did you put the thumb-drive?" he asked.

"It's in my pocket."

"Good," he said, his voice tinged with relief. He was thinking it was close... closer than he liked. That guy had been watching the restaurant. It was a good thing he was alone, or we might not have made it out. Ramos figured Carson was covering all his bases, and he shouldn't have underestimated him.

Ramos shifted in his seat and cringed, thinking the open bolt cutter in his lap had moved awfully close to his... "Can you put this in the back for me?" he asked, picking it up by the handle.

I took it and snickered. "Snip, snip." I latched it closed before dropping it on the back seat.

Ramos exhaled. "Right." With the excitement he'd momentarily forgotten I could hear everything he was thinking.

"Anything else you need me to put away?" I asked.

"Nope." He was thinking he'd have to get rid of the gun, but the lake behind the hotel would work well for that. *Shit. Did Shelby hear that?* "I think I must be tired or something. I'm usually better at controlling my thoughts."

"It's okay," I said. "I'm just glad you didn't get hurt."

His thoughts immediately centered on the pain in his side he'd been trying to ignore. He was pretty sure it was a splinter and not a bullet wound. It would hurt a lot more if it were a bullet wound.

"You got shot?" I asked. Dread washed over me.

"No! I've been shot before, and this isn't what it feels like. I'm sure it's just a splinter."

"How can you be sure?" I asked. "Do you feel blood running down your side?" I was starting to freak out. "Maybe we should pull over and take a look at it, especially if we need to stop the bleeding."

"No. I'm fine. It's nothing." He clamped his mind shut and concentrated on driving, not liking that I could hear his every thought. He was fine. Okay? No more questions. It wasn't a big deal. He could take care of himself. He didn't need anyone's help.

I took a deep breath and let it out slowly. The last thing I wanted was Ramos pissed off at me. "Well," I said, trying to be positive, "At least that's over with."

"Yes," he agreed. "And I'll have you home tomorrow, just like I promised your husband."

He didn't sound very happy about that, but I figured it was because he'd gotten hurt. I kept my mouth shut, but kept my mind open for any signs of Ramos passing out or something. I worried the rest of the way to the hotel, but Ramos didn't even break a sweat, so I figured he must be all right. Still, it was a relief to pull into the parking garage.

I got out of the car, my legs a little stiff, and took my time straightening up. I watched Ramos carefully for any signs of his injury, but he didn't even flinch when he got out of the car. He grabbed his gear from the back seat and popped open the trunk, putting everything inside, along with the gun. While he did that, I took off my gloves and threw them in too. I listened brazenly to his thoughts, but they were closed off as tight as a brick wall.

We moved to the staircase, and I worried that with his wound, Ramos couldn't make it up six flights of stairs. "We can probably take the elevator, don't you think? I mean... I doubt that anyone will be getting on at this late hour."

He narrowed his eyes and his mental barrier dropped. His side hurt like hell, but there was no way he'd let me baby...*shit! Not again.*

I couldn't help it, I laughed. But I kept my mouth shut, so it mostly came out of my nose and I tried to cover it with a cough. I held my hand over my mouth so he wouldn't see me smiling, but I couldn't stop snickering. The more I tried to make it sound like a cough, the funnier it seemed, until I finally just gave up and let it rip.

"Sorry," I said in between snorts. "I know it's not that funny." I giggled. "I don't know what's wrong with me." I took a deep breath to hold it in, and another laugh escaped. The look of disbelief on Ramos' face made me laugh even harder.

He shook his head at my antics and motioned me toward the elevator. "Come on. If I didn't know better I'd think you were drunk." We got in, and he pushed the button for the sixth floor. He was thinking it was a good cover if anyone got on with us, but I was probably right that we wouldn't see anyone else.

"You bet I'm right," I chortled, and laughed again.

Ramos closed his eyes, trying to stay annoyed at me. He knew that sometimes when people were under a lot of stress, they cracked, like I seemed to be doing right then. Even knowing that, he found it attractive... with another shock, he realized I'd heard that thought. What had happened? Where was his focus? Maybe it was all the blood he'd felt running down his side that had his guard down.

"What?" I gasped, my laughter forgotten. "You're really bleeding?" I glanced up at him, my chest tight with concern. "You should have told me the truth before now. Maybe we should take you to the hospital."

His smile confused me. Then he started laughing, and I realized I'd been had. I was ready to smack him, when the elevator opened on our floor. I got off first and marched to our room with annoyance, his laughter trailing quietly behind me. He had the keycard, so I had to wait for him to let me in.

He took the card from his pocket and leaned against the door to swipe it, still smiling. This close, I noticed the fine sheen of sweat on his brow, and alarm swept down my spine. He fumbled with the key card, and I put my hand over his to guide it through the slot. Grabbing his arm, I pushed the door open and steadied him as we walked inside.

"Come on," I said, pushing the door closed, and leading him toward my bathroom. "You don't want to get blood on the couch."

"I'm not bleeding that much," he protested, but let me lead him all the same.

"Uh-huh," I said. "We'll see about that. Take off your shirt and let me have a look." I motioned him toward the sink in the bathroom and watched him peel off his shirt with a soft grunt of pain.

Ramos in a tight fitting t-shirt was one thing, but Ramos in the flesh was a whole different story. Hard, lean muscles defined his abdomen and chest, swelling along his wide shoulders and long arms. I glanced away and swallowed, turning my attention to his side where he lifted his arm to get a better look. My breath caught to see the ugly red mess a bullet had made out of his skin as it passed through. Blood oozed from the jagged edges, leaving a trail of red running down his side, and I started to feel woozy.

"See," he said. "The bullet just grazed me. No big deal."

"You said it was a splinter. That's lots worse than a splinter." Feeling lightheaded, I quickly sat down on the floor and rested my head on my knees, then closed my eyes to fight the sudden nausea churning my stomach.

"I'll be damned. You really can't stand the sight of blood," Ramos said.

"I didn't used to be this bad," I said softly, keeping my eyes shut. "But ever since people started getting shot and dying around me... like the first time I met you... I haven't been the same." I felt horrible that he was the one bleeding, and I couldn't even look at his wound, let alone help him.

"It's okay, I can handle it," he said. "Do you think you can get my first-aid kit out of my bag for me?"

"Yes," I said, relieved to do something useful. "Where is it?"

"My bag..."

"Oh... right. I'll be back." I didn't trust myself to actually stand up, so I kind of scooted across the marble floor toward the bedroom. Ramos chuckled, and just hearing that made me feel a little better. If he could laugh, it wasn't too bad, right? By the time I got to the living room, I felt well enough to stand and managed to find Ramos' bag beside the couch. I rummaged through it, feeling kind of funny looking through his personal things. Having no luck, I decided to take the whole bag into the bathroom. Maybe he could find it easier than me.

I stood straight with the bag in my hand and faced the bedroom, knowing I had to go back in there but unable to move. I took a few deep breaths to steel myself and wondered if maybe it wasn't just the sight of blood that made me woozy. It was probably more like a combination of Ramos' bare chest plus the blood. It was enough to make any woman worth her salt swoon a bit. And what was I doing? I was standing out here instead of going in there to enjoy the view. That was pretty stupid. Instead of dreading it, I should look forward to going back in there. That's the spirit. Go me!

I strode in with my head held high and found Ramos at one of the sinks, wiping at the blood with a washcloth. Thoughts of pain with lots of swearing came through, so I put up my shields, relieved to have the feelings of wooziness leave me. I took a moment to study his broad back and noticed several scars. Of course, keeping his profession in mind, it probably came with the territory. It was still a fantastic-looking back, broad and long, tapering nicely to his hips with lots of muscles and not an ounce of fat. Yup, very nice.

"Are you going to stand there all night?" he asked, holding the washcloth over his wound so I wouldn't freak out.

"Oh... sorry. Just admiring the view." Damn! Did I just say that out loud?

He glanced at me through the mirror, his lips pursed, and an eyebrow raised. "Well... when you're through, I could use my first-aid kit."

"I couldn't find it, so I brought the whole thing," I said, my face heating with embarrassment.

"It's in the side pocket."

"Oh... okay." I quickly unzipped the pocket and pulled out a larger than normal container for a first-aid kit. Then I realized Ramos wasn't a normal kind of person when it came to stuff like this. I set it on the spacious counter by the sink Ramos wasn't using and opened it up. "What do you need?" I asked.

"It's okay," he said tiredly. "I can do it."

"No. I'm fine now. I want to help." The way he had to twist around to get to the wound couldn't be easy. Surely I could put a bandage on him.

He sighed. "You sure? I don't need you fainting on the marble floor and ending up with a concussion."

"I promise if I start to feel woozy, I'll sit down."

"All right," he agreed. "I've washed it out with water, so I think some hydrogen peroxide, followed by anti-bacterial ointment and a couple of butterfly bandages should take care of it."

"Okay. I can do that." I thoroughly washed my hands and dried them. Then found a small bottle of hydrogen peroxide, the ointment, some gauze, butterfly bandages, and tape. Last came a package of cotton balls. I pulled it open and then liberally doused a cotton ball with the hydrogen peroxide. I held it up, took a deep breath, and glanced at Ramos.

"I'm ready," he assured me. "But are you?" He was still skeptical that I could handle it.

"Sure, piece of cake," I said, wanting him to have a little more confidence in me.

Ramos raised his arm and turned so his side was to me, then pulled the washcloth away. Without all the blood, the wound didn't look quite as bad as before, and not as deep either, but still pretty ugly. I saturated the wound with the hydrogen peroxide, and Ramos caught his breath from the sting, making his muscles ripple. I pulled away, hating that I was hurting him. "Don't stop," he said. "It just stings a little."

I took a deep breath and tried to ignore his pain as I finished up. Satisfied that the wound was thoroughly clean, I gently applied the ointment until it was completely covered. With blood still seeping out, I quickly applied three butterfly bandages to pull the skin together, then doubled the gauze bandages and put a layer of tape over the whole thing so the blood wouldn't ooze through and make a mess.

"There," I said, pleased with my handiwork. "How does that look?" I glanced up to find Ramos watching me through the mirror.

He grunted, his gaze shifting to the bandage. "It'll do. Do you mind if I change in here?" Ramos asked. "I want to wash up a bit." He was thinking there wasn't a shower to rinse off the blood in his bathroom.

"Sure, take your time." I straightened and noticing his grimace, added. "I have some aspirin if you need it."

He nodded toward the first aid kit. "I think there's some pain reliever in there."

"Okay." I backed out of the bathroom and started to close the door. "I'll be out here if you need me."

"Um... Shelby... thanks. I know that was hard. I'm glad you didn't faint." He smiled.

"Me too." I smiled back and closed the door. A minute later, I heard the water running and decided to get out of my dirty clothes while I had some privacy. I found my newly purchased pajamas and slipped them on, leaving my clothes stacked on a chair.

I grabbed a pillow from the bed and went into the living room, closing the bedroom doors behind me. There was a spare blanket and pillow in the closet next to the other bathroom, so I got them out and made a comfy bed on the couch. I was too wired to sleep, even though it was close to four in the morning, so I turned on the TV and flipped through the channels.

I found the Disney channel, and since it made me feel closer to my family, I settled in to watch "The Little Mermaid." Somewhere during the part where Ariel was singing, "wandering free... wish I could be," my eyes got heavy, and I finally relaxed, sinking into quiet oblivion.

Light poured onto my face, waking me from a deep sleep. I cracked my eyes open to find Ramos pulling the curtains away from the balcony doors. He was dressed in jeans, a white button up shirt, and a blazer, with his hair nicely tousled and looking ready for the day. He glanced in my direction and noticed my frown. "Time to get up," he said, by way of explanation.

"What time is it?" I asked.

"Seven-thirty."

"Ugh." I sat up and ran my fingers through my hair, knowing I probably looked awful, while Ramos looked like a walking GQ ad. Sometimes life just wasn't fair.

"I thought you'd like to go for a swim before we checked out," he said. "We can order breakfast at a poolside table."

"Oh... okay. That would be nice." Thoughts of a morning swim in that gorgeous pool brightened my mood. Maybe life was fair after all. "What time do we need to check-out?"

"Eleven. But that should give you plenty of time for a swim."

"I guess you can't... I mean with your wound. How's it doing anyway? Did you get any sleep last night?"

"It's fine," he assured me. "Just a bit sore is all... and yes, I slept for a few hours." He was thinking that since I was zonked out on the couch, he'd ended up sleeping quite well on the bed.

"Good," I said. "Oh... I never gave you the thumb-drive..."

"I've got it," he said. "I took it out of your pants pocket. It's safe."

I nodded, then remembered the other thing. "What about the gun? Do we need...?"

"All taken care of."

"Wow, you've been busy," I responded. Ramos just nodded and raised his brows. He was keeping it professional and me in my place. "Then I guess I'll go put on my swimming suit and grab a towel." I hurried into the bedroom, locking the door behind me. While it was nice of Ramos to accommodate my desire to go swimming, he was almost acting like we were strangers, and he was just doing his duty. Of course, in a way, wasn't that what he was getting paid the big bucks for?

I found the bag with my new swimming suit and pulled off the tags, determined to enjoy my morning. I slipped it on, hoping I wouldn't look too fat. Luckily, it fit me pretty well, and the turquoise and purple print was actually quite flattering.

I washed my face and brushed my teeth, then found a plush white bathrobe hanging in the closet. It enfolded me in soft luxury while covering me up nicely, and made the trip to the pool less intimidating. After running a brush through my hair, I opened the door, ready to go.

Ramos was on his cell but quickly ended the call when I came out, thinking that it was a good thing we were going home today. Not that he didn't like being with me, but... he needed to get me home to my husband where I belonged.

Oh... now it made more sense. He was right, too. Ramos and me... well, there was no Ramos and me. Which was true, but on the other hand, that didn't mean we couldn't even talk to each other. The last thing I needed was to feel awkward around Ramos.

"Do you have a girlfriend?" I asked.

"No," he answered, surprised.

"Would you like to have a girlfriend?"

"Absolutely not."

Wow, that was pretty forceful. I opened my mouth to ask him why, but he raised his hand like he was going to smother me. "No. We are not going to talk about my love life. Ever."

I shrugged and smiled. "Okay." That seemed to break the ice between us, and things went back to normal.

We arrived at the pool, and I was surprised to see how many people were already there. I listened to their thoughts and realized that most of them had come for their morning laps before heading for the golf course. I wondered if they realized how pampered they were. But maybe it was just me never knowing how the top one percent lived, and now I was ruined forever. We found a table and ordered breakfast.

Ramos suggested I take my swim while we waited for the food to arrive.

The water was the perfect temperature, and I swam several laps until I was tired enough to get out, which for me, was about ten minutes. I glanced toward our table, and Ramos did a chin lift, thinking that our food was there and I should get out to eat. It was his way of waving me over without the waving part.

I chuckled to myself and obediently got out, drying off with a towel before wrapping it around my waist. The food was delicious, and while I enjoyed it, I was starting to get that homesick feeling in the pit of my stomach. Almost like if I didn't leave soon, I would miss my chance. I knew it was irrational, but part of me just wanted get out of town.

Ramos wasn't quite finished eating, but I'd had all the food I wanted. "Hey, is it all right if I go? I've got to shower and get ready, and I don't want to make you wait."

He studied me. "You've had enough of this place, huh?"

"I guess you could say that, although it's really great." I didn't want him to think I didn't appreciate it.

"Sure, here's a keycard. I'll be up soon."

"Thanks." I slipped on my sandals and bathrobe and headed back to our suite. It didn't take long to shower, and I enjoyed putting on my new shirt and jewelry. The only thing that marred my outfit was the dust and dirt on both sides of my jeans. But after shaking them pretty hard, I got most of it out.

I wanted to look good for Chris, so I took some extra time to blow-dry my hair and put on my make-up. Soon, I was looking fine, all packed up and ready to go. Ramos frowned when I came out, but he was thinking I looked good, so I tried not to be offended. "Is your side hurting you?" I asked him. "Do you want some aspirin?"

"No. I'm fine." He was thinking he'd be glad if I just forgot he'd been wounded. My 'mothering' bothered him. He was a grown man and could take care of himself.

I sniffed, but decided to leave him alone. He thought he didn't like my concern, but I knew better. Deep down, having someone care about him scared him. Big tough Ramos. He punched the button for the main floor in the elevator and glanced at me with narrowed eyes, wondering why I was so quiet. At that moment, I was sure glad he couldn't read my thoughts. He wouldn't like it one bit.

"I called the pilot. He'll be ready to go when we get to the airport."

"Great." I sighed, relieved. "I'll be glad to leave Carson and his goons behind. Especially after last night. You don't know how much hearing all those shots scared me. I was kind of freaking out in that closet imagining you getting shot. Which I guess you did, but at least you didn't die. It was close though... you even thought so."

"That's true." Ramos smiled, thinking I talked a lot when I was stressed. "You did well last night. I'm glad you stayed in the closet. It made my job a lot easier."

"Yeah, me too." I didn't dare tell him I almost came out so I could 'hear' what was going on.

We exited the elevator and I waited a short distance away while Ramos paid for the room. I wasn't sure I wanted to know how much it cost, but my curiosity got the best of me. That was probably a mistake, because I could hardly contain my astonishment at the one thousand plus price tag. For one night? Especially when we were hardly there. Well, at least I swam in the pool.

An attendant asked if he could carry my carry-on bag for me, and I sharply refused him. Ramos had already spent enough money, and I was certainly capable of carrying my own bag. The attendants' brows rose in surprise. He was thinking that was stupid since it was part of the service the hotel offered, but maybe I didn't know any better.

He took Ramos' bag and car keys and hustled out the doors to give the keys to the valet attendant. Ramos glanced at me, his brows drawn together in a frown. "What's the matter?" he asked.

"Nothing," I said. "Just a little surprised at how much the room cost. Uncle Joey's paying for it, right?"

"Yes." But he was thinking it was his choice to stay there, maybe because he wanted to show off for me.

"You did?" I asked.

"Well... you liked it didn't you?"

"Yeah."

"Then don't worry about the money," he said. "Even if I had to pay for it myself, it was worth it to see the look on your face when we drove up. Admit it, you were excited to be here."

"Um... well... yeah. It was pretty great."

"Just look at it this way, after what you'd been through yesterday and last night, you deserved it." His eyes sparkled with charm.

I raised my brows and shrugged. "When you put it that way, how can I disagree?"

Ramos smiled his approval as the car arrived. This time, I let the attendant put my bag in the trunk and open my door for me. I slid into my seat and slipped on my new sunglasses, happy to look better leaving than I did coming.

As we drove away, my cell phone rang, and I realized I should have called Chris before now. "Hello?"

"Mrs. Nichols, this is Detective Fitch. We spoke yesterday at The Blue Heron restaurant?"

"Oh, yes, of course."

"I'm so glad I got a hold of you," he said, relief in his voice. "We have a break in the case and could use your help."

"How can I help you?"

"You saw the man who killed Warren Pearce, and we just found someone who we think could be him. We need you to stop by and identify him."

"You mean like in a line-up?"

"Actually, no... at the morgue. He was found shot dead at The Blue Heron restaurant last night. It won't take more than a few minutes. We just need an eyewitness verification that this is the same guy who allegedly killed Warren."

"Well... I'm just leaving for the airport, but I suppose if it didn't take long..."

"I can meet you at the morgue in a few minutes. Here's the address." He rattled off the address and I repeated it for Ramos. "See you soon." He disconnected.

"Damn!" I said. "That was Detective Fitch. He needs me to identify the guy you killed last night."

Ramos swore under his breath. This was a complication we didn't need. "I guess you'll have to do it."

"He said it wouldn't take long."

"Yeah, well, let's hope for the best." Ramos turned on the GPS and repeated the address. "I'd say to forget it and run, but I don't want Fitch to get suspicious."

"True, and don't forget what happened yesterday. He noticed a car follow my taxi, and was suspicious enough to find out that the taxi took me to the airport. He also knows I missed my flight, and he tried to track me down. Do you think he's thinking that I'm more involved in this than I've said, or that I'm just in danger? He sounded pretty relieved when I answered the phone."

"I don't know," Ramos said. "It could be a little of both. You'll just have to read his mind to find out."

I nodded. "Thank goodness I can do that. What are you going to do? Do you want to come in with me?"

"No. I'll just wait in the car." There was no way he wanted to talk to Fitch. Although after all these years, Fitch probably wouldn't recognize him.

"So how do you know him?" I asked.

"Like I told you, I grew up here. We met." Ramos closed his mind up tight. Whatever had happened, he didn't want to talk about it.

Needless to say, we drove the rest of the way in silence. The morgue wasn't too far from the police station. Ramos pulled into the parking lot and found a space to wait. I didn't get out right away, and he could tell I was nervous.

"Don't worry," he said. "You'll be fine. There won't be any blood."

"Ha, ha." I gave him my best glare, but my sunglasses probably spoiled it.

"Maybe you could act like you're going to throw up or something, so it will be okay if you leave in a hurry."

"That's a good idea, especially since it will most likely be true. I know... I'll just keep my dark glasses on, so it will soften the shock." I couldn't seem to move my arm to open the car door.

"I know you don't want to go in there," Ramos sympathized. "But the quicker you get this over with, the faster we can go home."

"You're right," I nodded. "Okay. See you in a few." I took a deep breath and opened the door.

Chapter 6

I passed through the front doors of the morgue, grateful to find Detective Fitch waiting just inside for me. "Mrs. Nichols," he said. "Thanks for coming."

"Sure," I said, relieved he was there. I couldn't imagine waiting around in a morgue for very long. "Just so you know, this is a new experience for me, and I'm a little nervous."

"I understand," he answered. "I'm sorry to put you through this, but you were the best eye-witness we had and it will really help our case." He was telling the truth that I was the only one who got a good look at his face, even though there were others who had seen the snake tattoos.

I followed him through a set of double-doors and down a long corridor. A room with glass windows took up the whole right side of the corridor. I glanced inside to see a scrubbed-down sterile room with lots of stainless steel, from cupboards and sinks, to gurneys and instrument holders. There was nothing cozy about this place, and an involuntary chill ran down my spine.

Fitch pulled open the door and followed me through. At least there were no bodies on display, but there was the definite distinctive odor of formaldehyde and alcohol. All along one side of the wall were drawers like filing cabinets, only big enough to hold a body. I shivered, even though it wasn't any colder in here than in the hallway. A man in green scrubs washing his hands in the sink quickly dried them and moved to greet us.

"We're here to ID the gunshot victim from last night," Fitch said. "The one with the snake tattoos."

The attendant immediately glanced at me and then looked away, not liking this part of his job. He was thinking he hated it when the wife or family member had to ID the corpse. He hoped I'd hold it together and not make a scene like the last lady. He grabbed a list and scanned it, looking for the drawer number that held the body. Oh yeah, the guy with the multiple gunshot wounds. At least none of the shots were through his face or head, so it shouldn't be too gruesome for me. Still, he expected it would be a shock.

"This way," the attendant said. He made sure he had the right drawer number and pulled it open.

I swallowed my fear and stepped forward to stand beside Detective Fitch. Once the body was mostly out, the attendant nodded at us before he gently lowered the sheet covering the head and face.

The blue-gray color of his skin surprised me, until I realized I still had on my sunglasses and took them off. Even without the glasses he was about the same color, just not so dark. Detective Fitch pulled the sheet lower to show me the snake tattoos on his arms. It also exposed huge crisscross stitches from the autopsy and several ugly bullet holes in his sunken chest. "It's him," I said, wrinkling my nose and swallowing. The smell was starting to get to me.

"You're sure?" Detective Fitch asked.

"Yes. I'm sure."

Fitch nodded at the attendant and steered me away while the attendant replaced the sheet and pushed in the drawer. Even prepared as I was, my legs went a little rubbery, and Detective Fitch took hold of my arm to steady me. He moved me toward a chair and, feeling lightheaded, I quickly sat and managed to put my head between my legs so I wouldn't pass out.

The buzzing in my ears drowned out all sound, then slowly receded until I could hear Detective Fitch telling me to breathe slowly in and out. I listened to his voice, following his instructions until the dizziness passed and I could sit up. Wow, that was embarrassing.

"I'm so sorry," I said. "I had no idea it would affect me like that."

"It's no problem," Fitch answered. "No need to be embarrassed. You just take your time. When you're ready, the only thing I need from you is a signed statement, and you can go."

"Oh... okay. What kind of a statement?"

He took a paper out of his jacket and put it on a clipboard the attendant handed him. "It just says that you identified this man as the same man you saw at the restaurant." He handed it to me, and I looked it over before signing and dating it at the bottom of the page.

"Thanks," he said. "I think that's all, but I'll call you if I need anything else. Thanks so much for coming in. Are you okay to leave?"

"Yes," I said, more than ready to get out of there. I stood, grateful my legs didn't wobble, and headed for the door.

"If you want to wait a minute, I'll walk you out," Detective Fitch offered. "I just have to sign these papers."

"No, that's okay. I'm fine now." I gave a little wave and pushed open the door, eager to escape this sterile, awful place. With each step closer to the outside doors, my pulse quickened with anticipation. Walking out into the humid air and sunshine felt like being released from a cold, dark cave. I stood still for a moment to clear my head before closing the distance to the car and Ramos.

"Babe... you look terrible. Are you okay?" Ramos asked.

I quickly sat in the car and pulled on my seat belt. "I've been better. Remind me never to do that again."

He chuckled and shifted the car into first gear. As we drove by, the morgue doors flew open, and Detective Fitch waved to catch our attention. He was holding my new sunglasses in his hand and hurried toward the car.

"Dang," I said. "I must have dropped my sunglasses." Ramos braked, and I quickly rolled down my window.

As Detective Fitch reached me, I heard Ramos cursing in his mind. He was hoping Fitch wouldn't look at him too closely. The last thing he needed was for Fitch to recognize him. He held his breath and kept his face lowered.

Yikes! With rising panic for Ramos, I pasted a big smile on my face, hoping to help him by keeping all of Fitch's attention on me. "Thank you so much," I gushed. "I can't believe I left my sunglasses. They must have fallen when I nearly fainted. That was so nice of you to bring them out to me."

Fitch nodded and handed me my glasses, taking a quick look at Ramos. For a split second he froze. His eyes squished together and his breathing stopped. What the hell! "Ace?" Fitch asked, his tone incredulous.

Ramos let out his breath and shook his head in surrender. He glanced at Fitch, piercing him with a hard gaze. "Fitch."

"It is you," Fitch said. "I'll be damned! I never thought I'd see you again." He glanced at me. "So you're with Ace?"

"That's not his name," I said. "It's Ramos. And yes I'm with him. He's a client. Remember how I told you I have a consulting agency? We're working on a case."

Fitch was speechless for a moment, but quickly rallied. He didn't think for a minute Ace could be a client of mine, and came to the conclusion that if he was here with me, it had something to do with the body inside the morgue. "Ace, I mean... Ramos... don't tell me you're mixed up in this."

"Okay," Ramos replied. "I won't. If you'll excuse us, we have a plane to catch."

"Wait." Fitch's mind raced over the events of the last few days. "Before you go, there's something you need to know." He was thinking that if Ramos was involved with Carson in any way, it was time he knew the truth. He scrambled to think of a place to talk. "Can you meet me at Joe's Island Bar? You remember that place? I can take an early lunch and meet you there. It will only take a few minutes of your time, then you're free to leave."

Ramos raised his brows. "You're not going to arrest me?"

"No. Of course not," Fitch said. He was thinking about the guilt he had carried for so many years and hoping he could somehow make up for it by telling Ramos the truth. "It will be worth it to you, I promise."

Ramos sighed in contemplation. That time in his life was so painful, he wasn't sure he wanted to revisit it. "Does it have anything to do with that body in there?"

"Yes," Fitch said.

"All right," Ramos agreed. "We'll meet you there."

"Great," Fitch responded.

"Don't make me wait." Ramos pulled away, barely giving Fitch time to move out of the way.

"What was he thinking?" Ramos didn't waste any time contemplating Fitch's motivations. He preferred staying focused and methodical.

"Well," I answered, "he was thinking about telling you the truth, whatever that means, and hoping that would make up for all the guilt he's had to live with all these years."

"Guilt about what?" Ramos asked.

"You, I guess. How come he called you Ace?"

"It's the name I went by on the streets. My gang name."

"Oh," I said. "What happened between you and Fitch? It must have been something pretty bad."

Ramos pursed his lips. "I'd rather not talk about it."

"That's okay," I quickly agreed. "How about thinking about it? If it's easier, you could just do that."

He shook his head, but his lips tilted in a small smile. "Not a chance."

"Oh come on, if we're meeting up with Fitch, don't you think I should know? What if he starts thinking about it? I'll find out anyway. Wouldn't it be better coming from your perspective?"

"Shelby, stop. Until I know what he has to say, I'm not going there, and that's final."

I didn't say anything, hoping he'd feel guilty for leaving me out like that. After several minutes had passed in silence, I wondered if guilt was an emotion Ramos even felt. His thoughts were locked up tight as a drum, so all I could do was guess, which I didn't like to do because I always made up things that were lots worse than the truth. Of course, in Ramos' case, it really could be that bad. Now, I was more curious than ever to know what had happened to him.

We came to a busier part of town, and Ramos pulled to the curb. He put the car in park and killed the engine. The sign for Joe's Island Bar was half a block down the street, but Ramos made no move to get out of the car. He was thinking this was a mistake, and maybe we should just leave. We had what we'd come for, and looking into the past could bring nothing but trouble.

I waited for him to start the car, but he didn't do it. I felt his indecision and vulnerability before the wall he'd built around himself cracked open. Buried deep under a layer of guilt was a pain he hadn't been able to shake, not for fifteen years. Maybe it was time to face what had happened all those years ago and put it to rest. If Fitch had something to tell him about the past, maybe it was time to listen.

"You heard that, right?" he asked me.

"Uh-huh," I said.

"I've never talked about this with anyone." He leveled a hard stare at me. "In fact, if I could, I'd leave you here and not involve you. But it would help me to know what he's thinking."

"Ramos," I said earnestly. "I'm your friend. Whatever you need, I'll help you."

He sighed and gave a rueful laugh. "I hope you don't live to regret that."

"You mean I might die?"

"No... I didn't mean it like... you're teasing me, right?"

"Yeah," I said. "Mostly." Ramos didn't exactly know how to take that, so I covered it with a laugh. "You know, lots of times what we think could happen in any given situation is lots worse that what really does happen. So maybe talking to Fitch won't be half as bad as you think it will be."

"Um... actually I think I've got a pretty good idea, and I think it is bad." At my crestfallen expression he continued. "Although you could be right."

"Might as well find out," I said. "What have you got to lose? You already feel bad enough as it is, it probably couldn't get any worse, right?"

Ramos just grunted and opened the car door. He waited for me to join him, thinking that sometimes it wasn't easy being around me. He didn't like that I was picking up on his feelings and starting to sound like his conscience. He didn't need anyone telling him what he should or shouldn't do.

I refrained from pointing out that I could hear him. Mostly because underlying all those thoughts, he was thinking that having feelings made him weak. He had to stay cold and calculating, otherwise he could make a mistake, and that was unacceptable.

Joe's Island Bar had a full-sized bar surrounded with plenty of tables and chairs. It had a Caribbean flair with a thatched roof over the bar and lots of potted plants and flowers. Somehow Fitch had beaten us there and eagerly raised his arm to get our attention. Ramos scanned the few people in the restaurant and those sitting at the bar, taking note of anyone whom he thought could be a potential threat. Finding things to his liking, he motioned me toward the corner table where Fitch sat.

A waiter stopped by to get our order and soon left, leaving us alone to talk. Fitch's nerves were ready to snap, and he was thinking he hoped he'd done the right thing in talking to Ramos. He knew the guy in the morgue was linked to Carson and whatever had gone down at the restaurant. Now with Ramos here, and my proximity to Warren's murder and subsequent connection to the guy in the morgue, it looked like we were both involved. He also wondered what kind of life Ramos had led for the past fifteen years and hoped he wasn't involved in anything illegal.

"I can't believe you're here in Orlando," Fitch said. "I always wondered what happened to you after that night." From his thoughts, I caught a quick flash of a much younger Ramos with a gun in his hand standing over the body of another man, whose eyes were open and glassy in death.

I caught my breath and Ramos glanced at me, his brows drawn together. He turned his attention back to Fitch and replied, "You let me go. I always wondered about that."

"It's in the past. It doesn't matter now," Fitch said, thinking it was his fault Ramos had killed BJ. He couldn't change what had happened then. It was time to focus on the present and what kind of person Ramos was now. "What have you been doing since then?"

Ramos shrugged. "I guess you could say I'm a security specialist."

Fitch's brows drew together. Usually when someone said that it meant he was ex-military and used his skills as some type of bodyguard or hired gun. "You ever work for the government?"

"No. My contracts are all private."

The muscles around Fitch's eyes tightened. He was thinking this didn't sound so good, and it gave him a bad feeling. "Is that why you're here?"

"Maybe," Ramos said, thinking he didn't like where all this questioning was headed. Why did Fitch want to know about the kind of life he lived now? Why would he care? "What did you want to tell me?"

Fitch was beginning to regret his decision to involve Ramos. Maybe this was a bad idea, but he didn't think he'd ever have another chance to make things right. "I think this case might have some bearing on what happened to you fifteen years ago when your brother was shot."

"My brother?" Ramos tried to keep his cool, but I caught that inside he felt a swirling mass of regret, guilt, and a small kernel of hope. Fitch hadn't said Javier was killed... only shot. Did that mean he might still be alive? "What happened after I left?"

Fitch cringed and took a deep breath. He had to play this right. There was too much riding on this to make a mistake now. "I told you."

Ramos dropped his head and closed his eyes. Without looking up he spoke. "You told me you thought he was dead." He met Fitch's gaze. "Is he?"

Fitch looked away, this was it, but it was too soon. He didn't know enough about Ramos to trust him with the truth. "I'm sorry, Ramos. He didn't make it." He was lying. Ramos had a brother and he was alive. This was huge. It took all of my concentration to keep from reacting. Fitch hated lying to Ramos, but he had to know Javier would be safe... even from his own brother. He'd worked too hard to protect him.

"But there is something I can tell you." He held up both hands like he was surrendering. "I don't want to know anything about why you're here. I'm just passing along some information." He waited for Ramos to acknowledge this before he continued.

"All those years ago, you were helping me with my investigation, and I let you down. I feel responsible for what happened to you and Javier. But BJ wasn't the one behind the whole thing like we thought. He was reporting to someone else and just following orders. The guy behind it all had a source in the police department. That's how they knew you were helping me. That night was a set-up."

"Wait a minute," Ramos said, trying to understand. "Everything pointed to BJ, and now you're telling me he wasn't behind it?"

"That's right," Fitch said. "Think about it. There was no way he could have known you were working with me. Unless someone told him."

"Then who was behind it?"

"Carson," Fitch said. "I've been trying to nail him for years, but I've never been able to do it. We know the guy with the snake tattoos is his man, and that he's somehow involved in all this, but we can't prove anything. I was hoping if you knew anything about Carson you would help me. I want to bring Carson down for everything he's done."

Ramos was reeling from the fact that Carson was the reason his brother was dead. He glanced at Fitch. "You're asking for my help?"

"Yes," Fitch said.

Ramos shook his head. If he wouldn't have helped Fitch the first time, his brother might still be alive. He should have done things his own way. "Things have changed. I don't think you'd like the way I help."

"What's that supposed to mean?"

"Let's just say that sometimes there's a better way to bring about justice. I don't exactly trust the court system or the cops. You can understand why."

Fitch swallowed his dread. Did Ramos have something to do with the murder last night? Had Ramos killed Carson's man? This hadn't gone how he'd hoped, and he should have kept his mouth shut. Had he just opened a can of worms here? "Yes I understand, but I can't look the other way if something happens to Carson. I won't let you go again."

Ramos' smile didn't reach his eyes. "If something happens to Carson, it won't be me. I've learned a few things over the years. I don't get caught. Thanks for the tip. If I find out anything that will help you, I'll let you know."

Fitch knew he'd lost. Ramos had that same cold, hard look in his eyes Fitch remembered seeing just after Ramos had killed BJ. That day had changed Ramos' life forever. That's why he'd hoped telling him about Javier could somehow make up for it. But now? How could he put Javier in danger with Ramos mixed up in who knew what? It would make Javier a target all over again. He couldn't do it, at least not now.

"Shelby," Fitch glanced at me, hoping maybe I could give him something. "Is there anything you know that you haven't told me? Do you have any idea why they were after Warren Pearce?"

"Sorry," I said, shrugging. Ramos was practically yelling in his mind for me not to say anything. I couldn't help thinking about the thumb-drive and how it probably had all the evidence on it Fitch would need to take Carson down. How hard would it be to give it to him? Of course, it also might have something bad on it about Uncle Joey.

Fitch stood and pulled out a business card. Ignoring Ramos, he handed it to me, knowing I was more reasonable and likely to talk. "If you think of anything, please give me a call."

"Sure," I said, taking the card.

Fitch glanced at Ramos, regret in his eyes. "Ramos."

"Fitch," Ramos said. They locked gazes, and I was surprised to feel a measure of regret coming from both of them.

Without another word, Fitch turned on his heel. Ramos watched his progress out of the bar until he lost sight of him on the busy street. He turned his attention to me, his eyes raised in a question.

I wasn't ready to tell him about his brother. Not when Fitch had wanted to, but didn't. I needed to know what had happened first. This was a secret that had far too many implications to reveal lightly. Ramos deserved to know his brother was alive, but would it do more damage than good? How was I supposed to know? It put me in a terrible spot.

Ramos was already thinking of how to exact revenge on Carson. He didn't care if Carson was one of Manetto's associates. Once he told Manetto what he wanted, he was sure Manetto would agree with him.

"Ramos?" I asked. "Can you tell me the story now? I'd like to know what happened."

"I guess," he said, annoyed. "I'm sure you picked up quite a bit."

"Yeah," I nodded. "And if you want my help with this, it's something I deserve to know." He'd already been thinking how valuable my help would be, but wasn't so sure I would agree to it.

"All right," he gave in. "I'll tell you, but not here." He signaled the waiter and settled the bill. As we left the bar and walked to the car, he continued. "Since I'm revisiting the past, we might as well drive by the old neighborhood."

Several miles later, Ramos turned into a small run-down neighborhood with shabby houses and brick buildings. Ramos slowed as we passed one house and said casually, "I used to live there." He was thinking not much had changed in the old neighborhood, but it didn't bother him like he thought it might. With both his mother and Javier gone, it was like it had been someone else, and not him, who'd lived there.

We continued down the street, passing a small park with several children playing on a playground. "I remember that place," he said, thinking the equipment was much nicer now. We came to a business district with shops and gas stations, and Ramos pulled to the curb across the street from a garage with a sign above it that read "Rodolfo and Sons Full-Service Garage."

"It's still there..." Ramos couldn't believe this place had survived all these years. "I used to work there. Of course, it was called BJ's Garage back then." His thoughts returned to how it looked before, with the chop shop hidden in back, and all the junk cars and parts lying around the yard.

"It's why I have such an appreciation for nice cars." He glanced at me, a smile on his face. "I used to steal them, and we'd fix them up in the chop shop or take them apart to sell. I started working there when I was fifteen."

"What happened?"

"It was good for a while. My friend and I stole a lot of cars. BJ taught us everything. He was like a father to us. Besides stealing, we played a lot of poker. That's how I got my name, Ace. BJ stands for Blackjack, and my friend was Spade. There was a crew of about ten of us back then. We were tight, and BJ ran a smooth operation.

"Just after I turned seventeen, I met a girl at school. I didn't apply myself much in school, but I wasn't ready to drop out. I liked learning things. Lisandra was new, and thought I was hot stuff, but she was also a good girl. I told her to leave me alone, that I was no good for her, but she wouldn't do it." Ramos clenched the steering wheel as the familiar pain flooded over him.

"She looked at me and saw something no one else did." He shook his head, still amazed that she hadn't thought he was a lost cause. "She told me I was smart, and I could go to college and do something with my life... be somebody. Because of her, I did better in school, and the summer before our senior year, she spent all of her free time helping me get ready for the college entrance exams.

"I kept working for BJ, but Lisandra wanted me to stop. I cut back as much as I could, but BJ and the others put a lot of pressure on me, so I kept doing jobs for them, just not as many. I told BJ I was quitting, and he said he was fine with it, as long as I did one more job for him. I should have been suspicious, but I trusted him. He said he understood that I wanted a better life."

Ramos hit the steering wheel with his palms. "Can you believe that? I was so stupid back then, because I believed his lies. I thought he cared about me." Ramos let out a deep breath and pursed his lips to get under control.

"Anyway," he continued. "BJ always found the cars for us to steal, and this time was no different. But it turned out the car I stole belonged to a rival gang member. We returned the car, but things got dirty between us for a while.

"It was a few days after this that Lisandra came to see me. I'd told her never to come to the garage, but my test scores were back, and she was so excited to show them to me that she couldn't wait. That's what I thought at first, but later I found out she'd called the garage, and BJ had told her to come and surprise me. She was just outside the garage when it happened." Ramos took a deep breath and slowly let it out. Anger burned in his chest, and he took a second to get under control.

"Just at that moment, the rival gang drove by and spotted her. I was standing inside the garage right by that window when I noticed the car slow down. It didn't make sense until I caught sight of Lisandra running toward the garage. As I ran to the door, I heard two gunshots and the car peeling out. When I reached her, she was lying in a pool of blood. One bullet went through her neck and another hit her in the back. She didn't have a chance. She bled out and died right in front of me, and there was nothing I could do about it."

From his mind I watched the whole thing as he remembered it. I saw him gather her in his arms, and the anguish and pain seeping from this memory was so raw that I couldn't stop the tears from streaming down my face. Saying I was sorry seemed so inadequate. "She was beautiful."

He glanced at me in surprise, stunned to realize I'd seen her in his mind. It lessened the pain to know I understood exactly what he felt, and he nodded in agreement. "Yes she was."

After taking a deep breath, he continued. "Fitch was one of the first cops to arrive. He was assigned to the gangs back then and took an interest in me. Mostly because he knew I would want revenge against the gang that did this, and he wanted me to work with him instead. Of course, I wasn't about to cooperate, or tell him what had happened, but everything changed later, when I overheard BJ thanking someone on the phone for taking the bitch out. I wanted to kill BJ right then, but something held me back. It was like Lisandra was there, telling me to do the right thing.

"I called Fitch and told him I'd do whatever he needed to take BJ and his whole operation down. Fitch was ecstatic and eager to use me any way he could. I dropped out of school, and for two months, worked my way into BJ's trust, so I could learn more about how he did things. I was able to give Fitch information about the cars: who we sold them to, and where they came from...everything I could find out.

"Things were going great for the first little while, but then BJ started taking an interest in my little brother. I told Javier to stay away from the shop, but BJ started giving him money for running errands and doing odd jobs. Javier was only twelve and wouldn't listen to me. He said that if I was at the shop, then it was all right for him to be there too.

"I kept him away as much as I could, but BJ acted like he was doing me such a favor that I didn't want him to get suspicious about me. It was hard enough to act like his friend when all I wanted to do was kill him, so I let it go, thinking that BJ was going down and soon enough it wouldn't matter anymore.

"Fitch told me he was close to putting all the pieces together and was just about ready to make some arrests. The day before the arrests were to happen, BJ asked me to meet with him at the shop. It wasn't unusual, but I was uneasy about it, so I called Fitch. He didn't think there was anything to worry about, but decided to put a wire on me and listen from a car as backup in case I got in trouble.

"When I got there, BJ talked to me about a delivery he wanted me to make the next morning, but he seemed distracted. When I turned to leave, he pulled a gun on me. He was furious and told me he knew all about my betrayal, even after he'd trusted me with everything he had. He couldn't believe I would turn on him after everything he'd done for me. So I told him he'd made a big mistake when he'd had Lisandra killed, and he deserved a lot worse than being caught by the cops.

"He raised his gun to shoot me, when Javier shouted out and rushed at him. He'd been there helping BJ, and I didn't know. BJ fired his gun, hitting Javier in the chest." Ramos closed his eyes in pain and remorse. He took a few deep breaths and softly continued his story.

"Enraged, I tackled BJ. His gun went flying and we fought. I gained the upper hand and pounded on him until someone pulled me off. It was Fitch. I stood there, stunned by what had happened. Fitch ran to check on Javier and I hurried to kneel beside them. When I asked Fitch how he was, he told me he didn't think Javier was going to make it and called for the paramedics.

"By then, BJ was groaning, but I didn't care anymore. I picked up his gun and stared him in the eyes while I put a couple of bullets in him. Fitch yelled at me to stop, but it was too late. BJ was dead, and I'd killed him. I'll never forget the look in Fitch's eyes, like he was disappointed in me and that I'd ruined everything. With sirens in the background, I thought he would arrest me, but instead, he told me to drop the gun and get out of there. He said that he didn't ever want to see me again. That's the last time I saw him, until today."

Wow! I shook my head, trying to clear the images coming from his mind. Seeing everything as he remembered it gave me one of the biggest headaches I'd ever had. I didn't know if it was because of the story itself or because of my empathy for what Ramos had gone through. Even my chest hurt. I could probably put up my shields to lessen the pain, but then I wouldn't know what Ramos was thinking, and right now, that was more important.

"So, you haven't been back to Orlando since then?" I asked, trying to recover my wits.

"Yeah," Ramos said. He was thinking that he'd like to know where Javier was buried, so he could put some flowers on his grave. Then he was going to kill Carson and everyone in his organization.

"Ramos, you can't," I said, alarmed. "Fitch won't let you go this time."

"Who says he'll catch me?" he growled.

"There's got to be a better way to take Carson down. Sometimes killing someone is the easy way out... at least for them. I mean... wouldn't ruining him be better? Hey, I know... you could get someone else to kill him, maybe with the information on the thumb-drive. You could figure something out what would ruin him, or give someone else a reason to want him dead. That could work, right?"

Ramos drew his brows together and pursed his lips. He was thinking that what I said made sense, and could work as long as Carson still died in the end, although he hated the idea that it wouldn't be him pulling the trigger.

A plan began to take shape in his mind. Carson had his hand in a lot of things. Besides running drugs, a big chunk of his business was done through bookmaking and gambling. Carson's poker skills were legendary He was best known for his high-stakes poker games held in private locations throughout the city., and he proved it by winning lots of money and wagers that compelled people to do his bidding. That might just be the best way to get to him and beat him at his own game. He narrowed his eyes, glancing at me with interest.

"How well do you play poker?"

Chapter 7

"Poker?" I gasped. "I don't know anything about poker."

"Hmmm..." Ramos was thinking that it wouldn't take long to teach me.

"Wait... you're not thinking that I'm going to play poker with Carson are you?"

Ramos' mouth curved into a big smile. "What kind of a question is that? Especially coming from you?" He started to chuckle, then his whole body shook with unveiled mirth. "That's really funny."

I glared at him, crossing my arms and drawing my brows together. "Not to me."

Ramos stemmed his laughter and got under control, turning serious with a shake of his head. "I know it's a lot to ask, and you don't have to help me. It's probably dangerous, and I know you want to get home. I shouldn't have asked."

"Just..." I closed my eyes in consternation. I knew Ramos was going to attempt to take out Carson whether I helped him or not, but he might survive the encounter if I helped. "Tell me what you need, and let me decide."

"Okay," he agreed. "I should probably talk to Manetto first anyway. I know Warren hacked into Carson's computer, but I don't know exactly what kind of information he got from him."

Ramos started the car, checking the time. "Let's go somewhere else." He'd been there long enough, and now that he'd shared his story, he didn't care if he ever saw this place again.

We drove down the street and took a few turns toward a lake Ramos was remembering nearby. Since I had no idea where we were, it didn't really matter to me where we went. If I was going to help Ramos, that meant I wasn't going home to Chris. What was I going to tell him? How was he going to take it? I knew one thing for sure. He was not going to like it.

With a sigh, I glanced out the window and noticed several huge Banyan trees lining the road. They were on the side of the lane bordering a small lake, and Spanish moss hung from them, dipping serenely into the water. It was a beautiful sight, and it swept me away from my worries for a moment.

Ramos pulled into a small parking area and stopped the car. "I always loved this place," he said. "There's a trail right over there with a bench that looks out over the water. Do you want to sit there for a minute while I call Manetto?"

"Sure," I agreed. It felt good to get out of the car and stretch my legs. Coming beside the bench, I wasn't quite ready to sit down, so I followed the trail around the lake. Ramos got out too, but stayed close to the bench while he talked on the phone. I caught snatches of his one-sided conversation but didn't want to stay and eavesdrop.

Part of me hoped Uncle Joey would tell Ramos to forget about Carson and bring me home, but I couldn't count on it. Uncle Joey had Warren hacking into Carson's computer files for some nefarious reason. For all I knew, he'd probably be grateful if Ramos took him out.

I sighed, walking further down the trail. It was beautiful here, even if it was a little swampy. I didn't think I'd ever get used to the humidity, but the plants and trees were pretty, especially with the blossoms on them. To my right, the water near the bank surged in widening ripples, and I glanced out to see what caused it. Just a few feet away, something moved, and the hairs on the back of my neck stood on end. Another ripple sent my heart racing, and I yelped. Was that an alligator? A jolt of panic sent me racing back down the trail. I didn't stop until I found Ramos and hid behind him, soft gurgling noises coming from my throat.

"What's wrong?" Ramos tried to look at me, but I stayed behind him. Every time he moved, I did too.

"An alligator!" I squeaked. "Up that way!"

Ramos shook his head and spoke into the phone. "I'll call you right back." He disconnected and glanced over his shoulder at me. "You're fine Shelby. There's no alligator." His tone sounded a bit condescending and put me on the defense.

"Maybe not now, but there was." I straightened, peering around Ramos at the trail. "Why do they have trails if there are alligators here? They should post it on a sign or something."

Ramos pointed to the trail sign that said to watch for gators. "They don't usually attack people. And as long as you don't feed them, it's okay."

"That makes me feel so much better," I said sarcastically. I dropped my arms from Ramos' waist and took a deep breath. "Do you mind if I wait here for you to finish?"

"No, that's fine. I'm basically through anyway."

"What did he say?"

"He said to go ahead, especially if you're here to help me." Ramos glanced out at the lake, unsure of my response. "If you don't want to, I'll understand."

"No, I'll stay," I said. He'd put his neck on the line for me. I couldn't do any less for him.

"Good." Ramos breathed a sigh of relief. "We were just putting a plan together. I think it's going to work. Manetto's going to send Nick Barardini to help us out. He's the computer expert. He'll be here tonight. I just need to call Manetto back and settle things up."

"Sure, go ahead," I said. Ramos got back on the phone, and I sat on the bench to wait. Between getting startled by an alligator and hearing Ramos' story, I was starting to feel like an emotional wreck. Not only that, but I had to call Chris and tell him I wasn't coming home just yet. Of course, now that Nick was coming I wouldn't be alone with Ramos, so that should make Chris feel better, right? Plus, Chris had always wanted me to learn how to play poker, and now I would. That made two things to be positive about. Maybe it wouldn't be so bad after all.

Ramos got off the phone and sat beside me on the bench. He was feeling good that things were working out for him, but a little sorry for me since I had to tell my husband I wasn't coming home tonight. He bet Chris wouldn't like it, but maybe it was time he learned to trust me a little more. Ramos didn't know anyone who was as good a person as me, and he would watch out for me. Chris should cut me some slack. Maybe he should talk to him...

"You know I can hear you." I interrupted his thoughts. "Don't worry about Chris. I can work it out. He won't be too upset when he understands how important this is to you."

"Wait," Ramos said. "You can't tell him about what happened to me. You have to keep this to yourself."

"But..."

"No," he said. "I don't want anyone to know besides you. Manetto doesn't even know."

"What did you tell him?" I asked.

"Only that I just found out Carson killed someone close to me. That was a good enough reason for Manetto, and that's all anyone needs to know." He was thinking that he didn't want anyone's pity or judgment, and he didn't have to explain his reasons. It was his life, and any mistakes he'd made were his own. "Will you do that for me?"

I sighed. "Yes. I will." This was another secret I had to keep. I still hadn't decided what to tell Ramos about his brother. I wanted him to know the truth, but Fitch had a point. Ramos was in a dangerous business that could put Javier at risk. Still, I felt in my heart that he needed to know. I just had to pick the right time and hope he wouldn't be too upset with me that I'd kept it from him.

"Thanks," Ramos said, startling me out of my thoughts. He'd never thanked me for anything before.

"Wow." I smiled. "It feels good to be helping you for a change. Especially since you've saved my neck so many times."

"This should make us even."

"Ha! Hardly, but it will help."

Ramos nodded toward the lake. "We have a few minutes. Do you want to see if there really is an alligator down there?"

"Maybe. But only if you go first."

"All right, let's go."

"No," I said, shaking my head. "I meant that I'll stay right here, and you can go look for him by yourself. If it's safe then I'll come."

"You are such a chicken," he said, standing up.

"Wait!" I stopped him. "Before you go, give me the car keys, just in case you don't come back." I couldn't stop the smile that spread over my face.

He narrowed his eyes. "No way. You'll just have to wait here and hope for the best."

"All right," I groused. "I'll come."

I made sure to stay about three feet behind Ramos. We came close to the spot and I slowed my steps. Something rustled in the bushes. Ramos yelled and lurched back, scrambling away from the water. I screamed and nearly wet my pants. Ramos strutted toward me, barely concealing a self-satisfied smirk.

"What?" I said. "You bum!" Yikes. Had I just called Ramos a bad name?

His shoulders shook with laughter, and I relaxed. My lips twisted in a frown, but before I could say anything, a loud splash sounded behind him. We froze as an alligator poked its head around the bush, and started toward us with amazing speed. I yelped, grabbing Ramos' arm, and we both sprinted for the car.

"Did you know it was there all along?" I asked, catching my breath, and opening the car door.

"Sure," he said.

"Yeah, right." He was lying, but what the heck? It was kind of funny. As I put on my seatbelt I smiled, remembering Ramos' face. "You should have seen the look on your face. I didn't know your eyes opened that big." I was still chuckling when I glanced at him. The grim line of his lips tightened before turning up in a self-deprecating smile.

"Just don't tell anyone." He glanced at me, thinking that it would ruin his reputation if it got out that he'd been sca... no... startled by anything, even if it was an alligator.

"Another secret? Geez Ramos, you're taking all the fun out of life. But okay, if you insist." Had Ramos almost said scared? Oh wait... he'd only thought that, so I probably better not say anything.

"What are you smiling at?" he asked.

"Nothing," I said, innocently. "So where are we going now?"

"Manetto had Jackie book a vacation rental house for us. I thought we'd go find it and get settled, maybe buy some food and stock up the refrigerator. Nick will be getting in tonight, and we can start making plans."

"Oh." Reality came crashing back in, and my stomach clenched. "How long do you think this is going to take?"

"Not long," Ramos hedged. "Once Nick gets here and we figure out what we can do with the information on the thumb-drive, I'll have a better idea. Probably two or three days tops." He was trying to be positive.

"Three more days, huh? I guess I'd better call Chris. I just wish I knew what to tell him."

"Tell him that Manetto asked you to stay for a couple of days to take care of a small matter. No big deal."

"Ha," I said. "Chris is already upset with Uncle Joey. I'm afraid Chris might call him up and tell him off. That would be bad."

"You really think he'd do that?" Ramos thought Chris was smarter than that.

"I know! Me too! But where I'm concerned, Chris doesn't always think straight."

"I get that," Ramos said. If he were in Chris' shoes, he probably would have taken Manetto out by now. "You just have to let him know that I'll take care of you. I won't let anything happen to you."

"I think that's part of the problem."

Ramos glanced at me, his brows arched. "He has a problem with me?"

"No, that's not what I meant." I probably should have kept my mouth shut. "I'm his wife," I tried to explain. "That means he feels responsible for me. Like he should take care of me." I didn't add, "not you," but Ramos heard it all the same.

He nodded. "I get that." He was thinking that he enjoyed being my protector and spending time with me. Maybe more than he should...

"I think I'll just tell him that Detective Fitch put a lot of pressure on me to stay for a few days, so it's his fault. I mean... that's kind of true. If Fitch hadn't told you about Carson, we wouldn't be staying. Right?"

"Shelby... you can't lie to your husband." Ramos wouldn't like it, so he knew Chris wouldn't either.

I ducked my head, feeling ashamed. Ramos was right, but he also wouldn't let me tell Chris his secret either. Not that I would when it came right down to it. But if I could tell him some of it... then it hit me, this wasn't Ramos' problem. I probably shouldn't even be talking about it with him. This was between Chris and me.

"Listen." I smiled apologetically. "Don't worry about it. I'm sure Chris will be fine, and if he's not, we'll work it out. We always have. It'll be okay."

"Oh, okay. Good." Ramos could see what I was doing, and he realized he needed to back off. He was getting too involved, too close. He swore he'd never do that again. He kept himself apart for a reason, and he needed to remember that. "I know you just heard all of that," he said, surprising me with his candor. "You're just the first person I've ever told about my past, and it's brought out feelings I haven't had for a long time. I do care about you, Shelby, but it will never go beyond that. I respect you and your family too much. What you have is special. I wouldn't want to ruin it."

"Thanks Ramos," I said, touched that he'd talk to me about it.

He chuckled in a self-deprecating way. "I don't know what's gotten into me. It's like I've never opened up so much in my life, and now I can't stop."

I laughed with him. "It's good for the soul. When you hold things in for so long, they have a way of becoming bigger than you ever dreamed, and sometimes not dealing with hard things can hold you back from really living. Now maybe you'll find some peace."

"No," he shook his head, his voice going hard. "Not until Carson is taken care of. He's the reason my brother is dead. He ruined my life, Shelby. Someone's got to stop him."

"There is that," I agreed, half-heartedly. Maybe now was the right time to tell him Fitch's secret. "What if your brother isn't really dead?"

"What?" He glanced at me, his eyes wide with astonishment. "What are you saying?"

My heart raced with trepidation. Maybe I should have told him before now. He seemed a bit unhinged. Would he be mad at me? "Um... well, you see, I'm not sure... I mean when we were at the bar... it all happened so quickly..."

Ramos swore under his breath, barely missing a car on the side of the road. He pulled to the curb and killed the engine, turning his body to loom over me. "What did you hear?"

I flinched back and took a deep breath. "That's why Fitch was asking you all of those questions about what kind of life you were living now. He was trying to decide if it was safe to tell you about Javier. To tell you he's alive. The reason Fitch didn't was because he didn't want Javier to be a target because of you again. Because of the kind of life you lived and what you did."

Ramos froze for a moment, then slumped into his seat, his head falling back against the headrest, and his breath rasping in and out with shock. "He's alive? All this time I thought he was dead." He straightened, looking at me, his eyes full of vulnerability and hope that it was true. "You're sure about this?"

"Yes. I think that's the real reason why Fitch felt so guilty."

"Where is he? Where's Javier? Is he here in the city? We need to find Fitch and make him talk."

"No," I said, panicking. "We can't do that... at least not yet. Involving Javier in your life could be dangerous for him, unless you want to forget about Carson."

Ramos' gaze jerked from mine like I'd slapped him. He lowered his face, and for a moment, I thought maybe he'd consider it. "You're right," he conceded. "We can't risk it." He ran his fingers through his hair, something I'd never seen him do before, thinking about the consequences to Javier. He glanced at me, and my chest tightened the moment his eyes turned hard and cold. "Maybe when it's over."

"Yeah. That's probably best," I agreed. My heart filled with sadness, and I felt tears gather in my eyes. I blinked them away and cleared my throat. "We'd better get going. Are you okay to drive, or do you need me to take over?"

"I'm good," Ramos replied. He glanced at me, and a smile tugged at the corners of his mouth. "I'm really good."

I smiled back, hoping he didn't notice that my lips were trembling.

The drive to the rental house gave me time to get my emotions under control. For just a moment, I'd had a small hope that maybe Ramos would give up going after Carson and let Fitch handle it. I thought the gift of his brother's life might change that, or at least make him think about it. But it never even crossed his mind. Not once.

Too much had happened to Ramos to change him, and I needed to accept that. If it got out that Ramos had a brother, would it put Javier at risk? I knew Ramos had to have enemies. Would Javier become a target? Had I done the right thing? I guess it all depended on how Ramos handled it.

I glanced at Ramos, opening my mind to his thoughts. He was still in shock that Javier was alive. Ramos' yearning to see Javier nearly overwhelmed me. He wondered what he looked like, calculating that he was now twenty-seven years old. What kind of life did he lead? Had he finished school and gone to college?

Ramos surmised that Fitch must have stepped in and taken care of Javier and their mother until she died a few months later. If so, he owed Fitch a great deal more than he'd ever dreamed. Once Carson was out of the way, he'd have a long talk with Fitch and find out everything he could about Javier, and if there was any way he could help him, he'd do it. Whatever Javier needed, Ramos would be the big brother Javier had lost all those years ago.

Hearing those thoughts quieted my doubts. Ramos may be a killer, but he still cared about his brother. I hoped it was enough to keep Javier safe.

We entered a nice residential neighborhood not far from the resorts, and Ramos pulled into a driveway. "According to Jackie," he explained, "this is a three bedroom house with two master bedroom suites. That means you can have one all to yourself. The best thing about it is the price. For the cost of one night at The Ritz-Carlton, we get five nights here." He smiled widely, clearly in a good mood. "It even has a swimming pool." He was thinking that would make me feel better for not getting home sooner.

"It will help," I said, unable to hide my discontent.

A woman got out of a car parked across the street, and came toward us with a big smile. "Alejandro Ramos?" She had beautiful long brown hair and eyes, straight white teeth, and her accent was perfect. She was thinking how hot Ramos was and disappointed he had a wife.

I blinked in surprise, but gladly played along as she introduced herself and opened the house to give us a brief tour. I may not have any claim on Ramos, but thoughts of him with her made me a little nauseated. How crazy was that?

The house was bigger on the inside than it looked, and had a nice open feel with vaulted ceilings over the cozy living room and kitchen-dining area. Two large bedrooms were located on the third floor with their own bathrooms, and the third bedroom was on the main floor across the hall from a bathroom and laundry room. All of the bedrooms had their own wall-mounted flat screen TVs. Just off the kitchen was a small computer room with internet access and printer. Between the kitchen and dining rooms, a sliding door opened onto a deck with a hot tub and swimming pool that took up most of the backyard. I had to admit it was pretty fantastic.

A sick pang went through me to realize that my family would have been much more comfortable in a home like this than at the resort hotel where we'd stayed, and all for about the same price. Why hadn't I checked out vacation houses? Sometimes I really wished there was such a thing as a 'do over.'

The woman handed Ramos the house keys and her card with instructions to call her if we needed anything and strutted away, casting an alluring smile at him over her shoulder. Ramos enjoyed the sway of her hips and the way she'd smiled at him with a clear invitation. And now he had her number... The tapping of my foot caught his attention, and he turned to me with a guilty flush. "Um... which room do you want?" he asked.

"I'll take the best upstairs bedroom," I answered curtly, even though the rooms were pretty much the same.

"That's what I thought you'd say. I'll take the other one, and Nick can stay down here."

My smile didn't quite reach my eyes, and I really wanted to tell him he wasn't thinking that at all, but I had no claim on him, so I shouldn't be upset. It was stupid of me to even be thinking that way. I had a husband of my own... which reminded me. "Um... I should probably give Chris a call."

"Oh, yeah," he agreed. "While you're at it, I'll run to the store for some groceries." He was thinking I needed some privacy for this and was more than willing to disappear for a while, especially since he'd basically promised Chris he'd have me home by now. He didn't really want to talk to Chris and explain why. That could be awkward. He was happy to let me break it to him and not be around in case Chris wanted to talk to him again. "I'll be back soon. Be sure and lock the door after I leave."

He bolted out, shutting the door behind him before I could call him a coward like I wanted to. Annoyed, I grabbed my bag and hiked up the stairs to my room. Dropping my bag on the bed, I opened the curtains over the window to watch Ramos back out of the driveway and take off down the street.

"Damn!" I yelled in frustration, finding it hard to believe that if I hadn't nearly fainted, and dropped my dark glasses for Fitch to find and return, we'd be on the plane for home by now. It was crazy to think how that one little thing had changed everything else. And now I had to make this call to

Chris. Of course, if we hadn't talked to Fitch, Ramos wouldn't know his brother was alive, so looking at it that way, maybe it wasn't so bad.

Only... how was I going to explain all of this to Chris so he wouldn't be upset? I sighed. I was the coward. It couldn't be half as bad as I thought. Chris would understand. He was a great guy. And if he didn't, he could always fly back out here and stay with me. This place was great, and there was plenty of room... that was a good compromise, right?

I picked up my phone before I chickened out and placed the call. "Hi honey," I said in my usual cheerful voice.

"Hey," he answered, relief in his tone. "I'm glad you called. I was beginning to think something had happened."

"Actually... it has."

"What? What do you mean?"

"Oh... it's nothing really. Except that I have to stay a couple more days, but that's not too bad. I should be home by the weekend for sure. I hope you're not too upset. I know I am, but it couldn't be helped. You know I'd be there if I could. It's just... things happen, and sometimes it's out of my control..."

"Shelby," he interrupted, his voice a low rumble. "What's going on?"

"Um... well, I got a call from Detective Fitch," I explained, grabbing on to the first excuse I could think of. "He needed my help with something, and one thing led to another, and now it looks like I have to help Uncle Joey and Ramos take care of some business here, but like I said, it won't take long at all."

"Really? Are you serious?" His tone had gone up a whole octave. He wasn't taking this very well.

"Look, if you want, you can come and stay with me. I've got my own suite and everything. It could be fun." I heard Chris sigh and could imagine how his eyes were shut and he was rubbing his forehead. I grimaced, realizing he'd probably been doing that a lot lately.

"You know I can't do that," he said. "Not when I've just taken two weeks off work. I can't clear my schedule that quickly."

"Oh, right," I said. "Bummer."

"Bummer? I'll tell you what's a bummer. I've got reservations for dinner and tickets to a play tonight, all because I wanted to surprise you with something fun. Remember that?"

"You do? Oh Chris, I feel horrible." Hot remorse washed over me. "But you have to know I'd rather be there with you than stuck here."

"I don't get it. What's so important that you can't come home? Tell me so I can understand."

Now it was my turn to sigh. How much could I tell Chris about Ramos' secret? I had to tell him something so he'd understand better. Maybe keeping it vague would work.

"Okay, I'll tell you as much as I can, but keep in mind that it's pretty complicated. Detective Fitch called this morning and needed me to identify the body, so I went to the morgue and dropped my dark glasses. When Fitch brought them out to the car, he recognized Ramos from when he knew him fifteen years ago. Fitch told Ramos that Carson was the person responsible for something that happened back then, and now Ramos and Fitch need my help to bring Carson to justice." I paused for breath, hoping Chris wouldn't ask too many questions.

"What? That doesn't make any sense. What body? You already talked to Fitch about Warren."

"Oh... it wasn't his body. It was the guy who killed Warren, you know, the guy with the snake tattoos. When we went to the restaurant last night to get the thumb-drive, tattoo guy tried to shoot us, and Ramos shot back and accidentally killed him. Um... in self-defense."

"You went to the restaurant with Ramos?" Chris asked, his voice tightening with tension. "Yesterday, you told me you weren't going to go."

"Huh... I did?" I swallowed, realizing he was right. "Well, it worked out okay. I mean we got the thumb-drive and were on our way to the airport this morning when Detective Fitch asked me to identify the body. If Fitch hadn't seen Ramos in the car, I'd be on my way home by now. But unfortunately he did, and now I have to stay and help them catch Carson."

Chris huffed. "You and Ramos are helping Detective Fitch catch Carson. That doesn't sound like something Ramos would do."

"You're right. Normally, it's not. But like I said, they knew each other a long time ago and Fitch has been trying to catch Carson all these years, and now with our help, he can. See? It makes perfect sense."

"No... actually... it doesn't," Chris said. "But besides that, why do they need your help? What can you do... unless... oh no." Chris caught his breath. "Does Ramos know about you? Did you tell him you could read minds?" I didn't answer right away and Chris moaned. "Shelby...what have you gotten yourself into now?"

It was a relief to answer that question and not the first one. "To tell you the truth, I'm not really sure. All I know is Uncle Joey's sending Nick Berardini to crack the thumb-drive, and we're going to use the information from that to get Carson. And... I might have to play poker."

"Poker? What has that got to do with anything?"

"Well... it looks like Carson has some kind of professional poker games going on, and Ramos thinks we might be able to use my mind reading abilities to back

Carson into a corner and catch him or something. You did want me to learn how to play poker didn't you? So now I will. That's good, right?"

"No! I never wanted you to learn poker. Look... this is getting out of hand." He paused to rein in his frustration. "Is Ramos there? I think I'd better talk to him."

"Ah... no. He skipped out to get some groceries, and then he's got to pick up Nick from the airport. Jackie got us a nice vacation rental home for a few days, so we have a kitchen and everything. It made me mad to think we could have stayed in a place like this for about the same amount of money as the hotel. It would have been so much better, but what do you do?" When Chris didn't answer, I continued. "I can call you back when he gets here if you want."

"Yeah... sure... fine."

"Chris, I'm really sorry about this. I wish I were on my way home. Are you sure you can't come? I can call my mom and see if she can watch out for Savannah and Josh for a couple of days. I really do have my own suite."

"I'll check my schedule tomorrow and see how it looks."

"Really? That would be great!" I said, bouncing on the bed.

"Don't get your hopes up." His warning hit me like a bucket of ice water. "In the meantime, I really need to talk to Ramos. Got that? As soon as he gets back, call me."

"Okay," I agreed. Sensing that he was kind of disgusted with me, I needed to keep him on the phone until he wasn't so angry. "How are the kids? Is everything okay at home?"

"Yeah. Everything's fine."

"Will Savannah and Josh be okay on their own while you're at work?"

"Of course," he said. "It's not like they're little kids or anything, I mean Josh will be a freshman in high school for Pete's sake."

"You're right. I'm sure they'll be fine," I quickly agreed. "Hey, do you think you can change the play tickets to Saturday night? I'll make sure I'm home by then, and I'd really like to go."

He huffed. "You don't even know what play it is."

"I don't really care about that. All that matters to me is being with you. Heck, we could go to a baseball game or a soccer match, and I'd love every minute of it if it meant spending time with you."

"Hmm... maybe I'll get season tickets and take you up on that."

I chuckled and relief loosened the knot in my chest. "Sounds good to me."

He sighed. "You know I don't like this. Not one bit."

"I know."

"I'd ask you to tell me what happened last night at the restaurant, but I'm not sure I can take it right now. It makes me want to call Manetto and tell him off, but that probably wouldn't be a good idea either. I just feel so helpless, and I don't like it."

"I promise I'll be fine. Ramos and Detective Fitch won't let anything happen to me." I knew I was stretching it about Fitch, but if Chris thought Fitch was involved, I knew he'd feel better.

"I still want to talk to Ramos when he gets back."

"Yeah... I'll tell him."

"Okay." He let out his breath on a deep sigh. "The kids are hungry. I guess I'd better get us some dinner."

"Oh, sure," I said, a pang of guilt rolling over me. "I've got some coupons on the fridge if you want to use them."

"Yeah, I see them," he answered. "Don't worry, I got this."

"I know. I'm just a little homesick. Tell the kids I love them, okay?"

"Sure. Just call me later," he said.

"I will. I love you."

"Love you too," he answered, and we disconnected.

Chapter 8

I flopped back on the bed, feeling bad about this whole mess, but glad that I'd gotten through to Chris. He wasn't real happy about me staying and would probably use this to get me to do whatever he wanted for the rest of my life. I wouldn't ever be able to object to anything because he could always say, "Remember Orlando...and how you stayed there with Ramos?" I'd probably feel guilty enough to cave in every time.

I did feel bad, but maybe not as bad as I'd sounded. I was sad not to be with Chris, but as I glanced around the luxurious room and checked out the bathroom with the jetted tub, I remembered the hot tub and swimming pool in the backyard. Yeah, I was sad, but since I was stuck here, and it wasn't costing me a thing, I might as well enjoy myself. I couldn't remember the last time I'd been away from my husband and kids for this long. It was a little weird not having to be responsible for anyone else; weird and kind of nice. Did that make me a bad person?

I glanced down at my clothes. Since I was staying for a few more days, I'd need more things to wear, but that could wait until I found out what the plan was for taking down

Carson. If it got too complicated, I might need to buy a dress and heels and maybe some other nice stuff.

I wandered into the bedroom across the hall for a closer look. It was nice, but didn't have the jetted tub like mine. Still, I didn't think Ramos would care. A prickle of unease ran down my spine, and I checked my door knob, sighing with relief to find it had a lock. Not that I was worried about Ramos... or Nick, it was still nice to know I could lock my door.

Downstairs, I roamed into the kitchen and opened the fridge. It was empty, and I wished Ramos would have waited for me to go shopping with him. I needed a diet soda something fierce. I was also looking forward to cooking. After two weeks of eating out, I was tired of it and ready to cook up something nice and healthy. Ramos hadn't seemed too concerned about picking up supplies, so maybe he could cook as well. That was one thing Chris didn't do, and the times he had tried were disastrous, so I always did the cooking. But seriously, I didn't mind... much.

I didn't know how long Ramos was going to be, so I rolled up my pants and sat in the shade by the pool with my feet dangling over the edge. The yard was private and fenced in on all sides with lots of flowering hibiscus bushes, ferns, and tall trees for shade. It was pleasant, but starting to get hot. The water was calling to me for a swim, but I didn't want to have to re-do my hair and make-up. I could wait until later tonight with the pool light on and the starry black sky as a backdrop. Just imagining it brought a smile to my lips.

The sliding doors opened, and Ramos popped his head out. "Hey, do you want to help me put the groceries away?"

"Sure," I said. "As long as you got me some Diet Coke."

He grinned. "You know I did."

As we put the groceries away, I was impressed with all the fruits and vegetables Ramos got, as well as the eggs, pasta, and fine cuts of meat. It looked like he really did know how to cook.

"So, how did your talk go with Chris?" he asked.

"It went about like I expected. He's not too happy that I'm still here, and I think he's a little confused about why. Mostly because I had to tell him we were helping Fitch catch Carson, since I couldn't explain the real reason. I figured if Chris thought Fitch was involved, he wouldn't think my part would be dangerous, although he had a hard time believing you would work with a cop, and he didn't get the poker thing at all."

Ramos shook his head and grunted, thinking that it was no wonder Chris was confused. That was a lot to take in. "So what did he say?"

"He wants to talk to you."

Ramos swore under his breath and raised his brows. That was one conversation he was hoping to avoid.

"Yeah, exactly," I said. "Now you know how I feel, but don't worry. I'm sure he doesn't expect you to explain anything. Plus, you're intimidating enough that all you have to do is tell him you'd take a bullet for me and he'll be fine."

"Is that all?" he asked, his lips twisted in a wry smile.

"Uh-huh." I smiled sweetly. "But you don't have to talk to him until later tonight." I finished putting the drinks in the fridge and closed the door. "So what is the plan anyway?"

Ramos checked his watch. "Nick should be arriving in a couple of hours. Once he has a chance to look at the thumb-drive, we'll know how to take Carson down. That means we'll have to wait until he gets here to come up with a plan."

"So the poker part isn't a sure thing? Dang! I wish I wouldn't have said anything to Chris about that. The only reason I did was because at one point he was thinking about me learning how to play and winning a lot of money in poker tournaments. I thought he'd be happy that I was finally going to learn. Only when I mentioned it, he wasn't too thrilled. That's when he wanted to talk to you."

"Hmm... yeah. You probably should have left that part out," Ramos said. "In fact, maybe it's best if we tell Chris as little as possible."

I narrowed my gaze at him. "So now you've changed your tune? Before you were saying I shouldn't lie to my husband, and now you're saying I should."

"Hey, that's not what I'm saying at all." Ramos didn't like that I'd thrown his words back at him. "Telling him as little as possible is not lying to him."

"But in a way, it is," I reasoned. "Not telling the whole truth is kind of like lying."

"So you want to tell him the whole truth now?" Ramos glared at me.

"No." I crossed my arms in front of me. "I'm just trying to prove a point. That what we choose to share isn't so cut and dry all the time." My heart started to pound, and my chest ached. The last few days had been rough, and the stress was starting to get to me.

"And let me tell you something," I continued. "The fact that I can read minds puts me in a real bind. You don't have any idea how hard it's been for me to know stuff, and not know what to do or say about it. I swear, after today I've about had it. I think if I could quit right now, I would! Got that?" Once I stopped speaking, I realized I'd raised my voice, and worse, my eyes were filling with tears. Embarrassed, I blinked them away and turned toward the fridge and opened it. "Where's my Diet Coke?"

"Um... I think it's on the bottom shelf." Ramos hadn't missed my tears and it made him uneasy. He didn't relish talking to Chris, but he hated upsetting me more. Hoping to diffuse the situation, he moved behind me, opened the door wider, and bent down to look inside, nudging me aside. "Here it is." He opened the box and pulled out a can, glancing at me with a worried smile. "It's not cold yet, but there's an ice dispenser right here in the door. Let me get you a glass."

By now I was completely out of his way, and he opened the cupboard doors until he found a glass. Putting it under the ice dispenser he asked, "Crushed or cubed?"

"Um... crushed," I answered, sniffing.

"Good choice," he said. He filled it up with ice and set it on the counter, then popped open the can and began to pour.

Hearing the familiar sizzle calmed my nerves, and the care with which Ramos filled the glass increased my shame. What had just happened? Had I nearly broken down and cried in front of Ramos? What was wrong with me?

"Here you go," Ramos said.

"Thanks." I took the glass and gulped down a few swallows, feeling better and more in control. "Mmm... this tastes different. It's... good. Wait, is this diet?"

"Yes," he said, hurriedly. "I just got the kind with vanilla in it. I thought maybe you'd like it. Is that okay?"

"Um... yeah, actually it's really quite good." I drained the glass and smiled. "I like it. Can I have some more?"

"Sure."

I held out my glass, and Ramos poured the rest of the can into it. "Thanks."

"No problem." Ramos watched me take another drink, thinking he'd just averted a disaster. He also thought it was a good thing my drink wasn't anything stronger, the way I was guzzling it down. Then he wondered what I would be like if I got drunk. Probably best to keep that from happening, since in that state, who knew what I'd blurt out?

I raised one of my brows and pursed my lips. Ramos just chuckled, not intimidated in the least. "We should probably eat something," he said. "I'm sure that will help you feel better." He opened the refrigerator and pulled out a package wrapped with white paper. "How does fresh salmon sound? I can make a great lime-mustard sauce to put on it, and there's a grill outside. We can eat it with rice. I've also got ingredients for a green salad."

"Sure," I said, just now realizing how empty my stomach felt since we'd only had drinks at the bar. "Sounds great. I'll make the salad and cook the rice while you grill up the salmon."

He grunted his agreement and I got busy. I concentrated on the familiar tasks and felt the stress leave my shoulders. With the rice cooking and the salad done, I got the table ready just as Ramos came in with the salmon. It smelled heavenly, and we quickly settled down to eat.

Everything tasted wonderful, and I shared an appreciative smile with Ramos. He returned my smile, thinking he could get used to this arrangement. Sharing a meal with a beautiful woman did wonders for his digestive system.

I blushed. "Are you trying to embarrass me?" A quiver of guilt at the intimate nature of our dinner rushed over me, but I did my best to brush it away.

A self-satisfied grin spread over his face. "I'm glad you're feeling better. For a while there you had me worried. All I can say is, it's a good thing I got the soda."

I huffed and shook my head. "I guess I got a little upset, but I'm fine now."

"Good." He checked his watch. "I should probably leave for the airport. Nick will be arriving soon. You'll be safe here, but you can come if you like."

"I think I'll stay. Maybe go for a swim or something."

Ramos nodded, thinking it would be good for me to take it easy and enjoy myself. Who knew when I'd get another chance? He took his dishes to the sink and began stacking them in the dishwasher.

"I can clean up if you want to go now," I offered.

"Um... sure." He finished what he was doing and turned to leave, grabbing his keys from the counter. "I should be back with Nick in about an hour." He started toward the door.

"Wait!" A sudden thought occurred to me, sending my heart rate into overdrive. "Nick can't know about me."

Glancing back at me, Ramos stilled as the implications of what that meant hit him. "No, of course not. Don't worry, we'll figure it out."

I let out my breath and nodded. Ramos opened the door and was gone, leaving me to worry about how we were supposed to do that. Remembering the few times I'd talked with Nick tightened my stomach. He was curious about me the first time we met, wondering exactly what I did for Uncle Joey and why I was so important to him. How was I going to keep Nick from finding out all he could about me?

I grabbed my cell phone and called the only person I knew who could take care of it.

"Shelby? Are you all right?" Uncle Joey asked.

"Actually, no. I'm worried about Nick being here."

"What? Why?"

"Because he doesn't know about me and what I do," I explained. "You know he'll try and figure it out, right?"

"Hmm... I see what you mean. We can't let that happen."

"Exactly," I said, relieved he was agreeing with me. "You know that Ramos knows, don't you? Given how curious Nick is, I'm sure he'll try and figure it out too. I just can't have one more person knowing. Especially Nick."

"Hey, Nick's not that bad," Uncle Joey protested.

"Yes he is," I said quietly.

"All right," Uncle Joey sighed. "What do you suggest?"

"Can't you just call him and order him not to ask any questions about me? Tell him what I do for you is off limits and that's all he needs to know?"

"Do you really think that would work?" he asked with a chuckle. "If anything, that would make him even more curious. No... we'll just have to give him another explanation for your involvement. Why don't you just tell him that you have premonitions? You've told other people that."

"Oh, yeah," I stammered, chagrined that I had made such a big deal about something so simple. "That should work."

"Good. Listen... Ramos told me you wanted to stay and help him, but you don't have to. I'm pretty sure he can take care of things himself if you want to come home."

I arched my brows in surprise. Uncle Joey was giving me an out? "Oh, that's okay. I'm fine to stay and help. Chris isn't real happy about it, but I don't mind."

"I can believe that," he snorted. "Just be careful. I want you back in one piece." Before I could respond, he continued, "So... how's the vacation house?"

"It's great," I said, warmed by his concern for my welfare. "In fact, I think I'm going to go take a swim in the pool."

"Good. Let Ramos know what we discussed, and call me if you need anything."

We disconnected and I sighed, somewhat surprised at the irony that Uncle Joey had actually helped me feel better.

Twice in two days. Who would have thought that possible? Chris wouldn't believe it.

Knowing the next few days were going to be stressful, I hurried upstairs to put on my swimming suit and go swimming. I was actually going to take Ramos' advice and enjoy myself.

I was swimming on my back when the sliding doors opened and Ramos stepped out. The sun was low on the horizon, sending hues of golden light through the sky. It caught Ramos in the face, outlining his chiseled features and making his skin take on a burnished bronze glow. I sighed in appreciation.

"Just wanted you to know we're back," Ramos said. "Nick's inside working on the thumb-drive." As Ramos took in my wet hair and welcoming smile, he gritted his teeth against a sudden desire to join me in the pool. Before I could answer, he disappeared into the house and slid the door closed with a thwack.

Hmm... I grimaced, what was that all about? Did I really want to know? Nope. I was going to pretend I hadn't picked up that Ramos' attraction to me was making him angry. Maybe it wasn't so bad that Nick was here after all, although I was hoping to have a minute alone with Ramos to tell him what Uncle Joey and I had discussed. Now that would have to wait for a better time.

I hesitated to get out of the pool just yet, mostly because I didn't want to face Nick. Or was it Ramos? Or maybe a little of both? Of course, when Nick found out I had 'premonitions' I was sure he wouldn't take it seriously. He'd probably think I was joking, which was just fine with me.

I swam a few more laps, then got out of the pool and dried off with the beach towel I'd found. I wrapped it around my waist and went inside. Nick sat at the table working on his computer, and Ramos stood behind him, looking over his shoulder at the screen. Both of them had frowns on their faces.

"What's wrong?" I asked.

"I got this," Nick said. "Ramos doesn't think I can break the code, but as good of a hacker as Warren was, I'm better. It would help if you'd quit looking over my shoulder, though." He said this to Ramos, who straightened and jerked away with a scowl.

"I'm going to go take a shower." I could see that now was not a good time to talk to Ramos. Besides, Nick didn't seem concerned about my presence at all. If it ever came up, I'd figure out what to tell him then.

I took my time in the bathroom, hoping Nick could get into the files before I joined them downstairs. More than half an hour later, I gingerly crept down the stairs to find them both much happier and I sighed, finally relaxing my shoulders.

Ramos glanced at me and smiled with cold calculation. My heart broke to find his feelings locked up tight, replaced by a much darker focus. Taking down Carson made him hard and unemotional. This was the Ramos that people were afraid of, and it usually meant someone was going to die.

"We found a way to bring him down," Ramos said. He was thinking how easy it would be to take all of Carson's money right out from under him, and then tell him why he did it right before he shot him between the eyes.

My eyes widened. What? That wasn't the plan. What was he thinking?

Ramos took in my alarm and pursed his lips, thinking that as much as he wanted to pull the trigger, he would have to come up with a different plan because of me. I heaved a big sigh, grateful he'd changed his mind. "Don't forget... that other thing." I was about to say "your brother" but couldn't in front of Nick.

"What other thing?" Nick asked suspiciously, not missing a thing.

"Oh... just that one of the police detectives knows Ramos, and would suspect him if anything happened to Carson." This was safe to admit without telling Nick the whole story.

Ramos grunted, shaking his head in disgust, but played along with me since it was true. "We're going to have to be creative about this. I was hoping there would be a way we could encourage one of Carson's associates to kill him so we don't get our hands dirty."

"I see," Nick said. "Maybe with this information that won't be a problem." Nick was thinking this little trip was getting more and more interesting. He relished this kind of work and looked forward to figuring out a plan. "From these files, it looks like Manetto was right. I think Carson was cheating him out of at least five hundred thousand dollars. Maybe more."

"Wow, that's a lot," I said. "Uncle Joey's not going to be happy about that."

"No, he's not." Ramos was suddenly worried that Manetto wouldn't let him kill Carson without getting the money first. That might be a problem. "I'd better call him." He picked up his phone and opened the sliding door, going outside to talk in private.

That left me alone with Nick, who focused on me for the first time since he'd gotten here. He'd caught an undercurrent that something was going on between Ramos and me, but there was no way he'd ever mention that. Still, it was an interesting development. He also wondered what I did for Manetto, knowing it had to be important since both Manetto and Ramos trusted me.

Of course, there was a lot he didn't know about Manetto's organization, and for now, he was okay with that. He'd learned from his father that in this business, it was probably best to know as little as possible, just in case the police showed up.

"It looks like Carson hasn't been sharing the profits with anyone like he should," Nick said, going back to the files. "If these numbers are right, Manetto's not the only one he's been cheating."

"That's it!" I said. "If we can get this information to everyone else he's cheated, they'll take care of him so Ramos doesn't have to."

"That should work," Nick agreed. "I have their names, so it would just be a matter of tracking them down and giving them a hard copy of these files."

Ramos came in, hearing Nick's last comment. Nick filled Ramos in about what he'd just told me. "Sounds good," Ramos said. "But before we alert the others, Manetto wants his money."

"I was afraid of that," I said. "How are we supposed to get it?"

"I'm going to have a little chat with Carson."

This did not sound good in so many ways. "Don't you think that's dangerous?" I blurted. "He could kill you."

"Relax Shelby," Ramos said. "As far as Carson knows, I'm just here on business. Nothing for him to be worried about."

"Yeah, until you tell him to pay up. Then what's going to stop him from killing you?"

"Babe," Ramos said, his voice low and level. "Give me a little credit. I know what I'm doing. I handle stuff like this all the time. It's my job."

"Oh," I stammered. "Yeah, okay." I could feel my face flushing with embarrassment.

"But I wouldn't mind some company," he said. "If you're up to it."

"You want me to go? But he knows who I am."

"Exactly." He was thinking this could work out great if Carson fell for it.

"Fell for what?" I asked, peeved that Ramos wasn't explaining anything to me. Ramos glanced at Nick, who was thinking my comment didn't make any sense. Oops. "I mean, what are you thinking?" I clamped my mouth shut and waited for Ramos to explain.

"Carson won't want to get on Manetto's bad side, and once he knows you're Manetto's niece, he'll leave you alone. We can trade the thumb-drive for the money, and then let the other people he's cheated take care of him."

"I guess that could work," I said, dubiously.

"How quickly can you make copies of the files?" Ramos asked Nick.

"All I need is a printer and some paper," Nick replied.

"There's a computer room with a printer just off the kitchen," Ramos answered, pointing the way. "It should have everything you need."

"I'll go check it out." Nick took his computer and disappeared inside.

Ramos checked his watch. "We can talk to Carson tonight, and I'll make the trade tomorrow. While I'm making the trade, you and Nick can deliver the copied files to Carson's associates. Nick can encrypt the thumb-drive so Carson won't know what's on it without a good hacker, and by the time he figures it out, it will be too late."

"I'd better go change then," I said, my voice sounding breathless and small.

I turned to leave, but Ramos caught my wrist and pulled me to face him. "Don't worry Shelby. I won't let anything happen to you."

I nodded and managed a weak smile. "I know." He gave my wrist a reassuring squeeze and I hurried up the stairs.

I hadn't bothered to fix my hair or apply any make-up after my swim, and now I regretted swimming at all. My hair was still damp, so I tipped my head upside down and blew it dry. Satisfied with my wind-blown look, I concentrated on my make-up, wanting to look extra-good. Being the "niece" of a mob-boss brought a lot of expectations, and I wished I had something nicer to wear, but as my wardrobe was limited, I just threw on the same clothes from this morning. Thank goodness for the jewelry. It saved an otherwise blah outfit.

Ramos noticed me coming into the living room and smiled appreciatively. He was thinking Manetto would be proud to call me his niece. I even out-did Kate, which was saying something. "Ha," I said. "You're just prejudiced."

"True," Ramos agreed. "But she still doesn't hold a candle to you."

I shook my head at his flattery while my heart flooded with warmth. Nick joined us, mumbling that he needed paper and envelopes for the copies.

"We're going to Carson's club tonight," Ramos told him. "I'd like you to join us. Maybe after, we can get the supplies you need."

"Sure, that sounds great" Nick replied. "But what do you need me for at the club?"

"It's simple, I need you inside, but close to the door to keep an eye on things," he answered. "I don't expect any trouble, but you never know. You have a gun?"

"Not with me. I couldn't exactly bring it on the plane," Nick replied. "But don't worry about me. I can take care of myself." He was thinking his martial arts training would come in handy, and he almost hoped he could use it.

"Where's the thumb-drive?" Ramos asked.

"I'll keep track of it," Nick said. "Let me get ready and we can go. Nick hurried to his room and returned wearing a nice blazer over a green striped shirt.

Ramos set the house alarm and locked the door behind us. We settled into the car with Nick taking the back seat. With shades of gray to the west, the black night held a bright full moon overhead. The stifling heat of the day had subsided, and the scent of night blooming jasmine filled the air. It would have been a perfect night if not for the reason we were out.

As Ramos drove into the downtown area of the city, my stomach fluttered with nerves. I didn't question how he knew where to go, just as I didn't want to think too hard about all that could go wrong with this little meeting. Before I was ready, we pulled to a stop in front of a building with a group of people standing outside waiting to get in. A big man guarded the door to the inside, letting people in for a fee.

Ramos turned to Nick. "Once we get inside, we shouldn't be long. Remember, Shelby is your first priority. If anything happens, get her to safety." Ramos wasn't taking any chances with me, and he wanted to make sure Nick knew that.

A valet came to park our car, and Ramos stepped out, handing him the keys. Nick got out of the back seat, but I couldn't bring myself to open my door. Ramos and Nick both had blazers on, so they looked good, but scanning the skimpy dresses and high heels of the women in line gave me a stomachache. I was woefully underdressed, and my confidence deserted me. I couldn't go in there to face Carson looking like this!

Ramos opened my door and extended his hand to help me out. I ignored it. "Babe." His voice prodded me out of my stupor, and I reluctantly took his hand. I stood as tall as

I could in my flat sandals, trying to bolster my confidence. Ramos arched his brow at me, wondering what was going on.

"I'm not exactly dressed for this," I said, under my breath.

He glanced at the women in line and squeezed my hand. Turning back to me, he held my gaze with measured confidence. "Don't let their clothes intimidate you. You look great just as you are. Besides, you have nothing to prove, remember? You're the niece of a bad-ass mob-boss who's got more clout than anyone in this puny city."

I couldn't help snickering, but went along with it just the same. "Damn straight!" I agreed. His smile lit up his eyes before he expertly tucked my hand into his elbow and led me to the door.

The big guy standing there frowned and held up his hand for us to stop. "You on the V.I.P. list?"

Ramos stared at him before replying. "The name's Ramos. Carson is expecting us."

The man paled, knowing Ramos' reputation, and dipped his head. He quickly opened the door for us and kept his eyes lowered as we passed him. Wow! That was kind of cool. It bolstered my confidence enough to strut through the door like I owned the place. Who cares if I'm not wearing a sexy dress. I'm with Ramos.

Inside, we walked down a short hallway to a second set of double doors. Another big man guarded this entrance, but moved to the side and opened the door for us with a polite smile. "Welcome to Club Metropol."

He ushered us inside, where we were instantly assaulted by loud music coming from a live band at the opposite end of the room. The place was packed with people, and Ramos turned to Nick. "Wait here," he shouted.

At Nick's nod, Ramos took my hand and pushed his way through the crowd. Without his bulk in front of me, I would have been lost. Bumping against people in the throes of drinking and dancing, with plenty of sexual undertones, turned my stomach, leaving me a little nauseous. This place was insane. Without my mental shields, I would have been a mess.

We broke through the crowd at the bottom of a set of stairs and I swallowed, sagging with relief. Ramos tightened his grip, giving me a few seconds to recover before we continued up the stairs. At the top, he placed my hand into the crook of his elbow while we took in the floor plan. This was a smaller space with a balcony overlooking the dance floor. A few tables and chairs placed nearby had a great view of the scene below. Here, the music wasn't as loud, and only a few people lounged in their chairs around the tables.

An older man sat at the table with the best view, looking over the crowd like a king seated on a throne. He was practically bald, with a long nose and a distinguished salt and pepper goatee that conveniently disguised a double chin. This was Carson. His cold blue eyes zeroed in on us, and the two men sitting beside him stood, bracing their feet in a protective stance.

As we approached, Carson heaved his bulky frame to a standing position, and a wry smile twisted his lips. He motioned his men to back off while he studied me with undisguised curiosity. His gaze travelled to Ramos, and a stab of discomfort pierced his calm exterior. He hoped Manetto didn't suspect anything, and that Ramos was only here to talk about their business arrangement.

The man standing behind Carson jerked his head toward me, and recognition flashed in his eyes. My step faltered. Damn! This was the same guy who had followed me to the airport. The man quickly leaned over to whisper my identity into Carson's ear.

My heart started to gallop, and my legs felt like rubber. My instinct to run turned my breathing shallow. Noticing my distress, Ramos patted my hand and kept repeating in his mind that I shouldn't worry, and that this was part of the plan. *I won't let anything happen to you. Pull yourself together. It'll be all right.*

Yeah, that was easy for him to say since he couldn't hear Carson thinking he wanted me to die a slow and painful death. All at once Carson put it together that it must have been Ramos who had killed Cobra. Cobra? The freaking snake guy was called Cobra? Wasn't that a G.I. Joe character? Did people really name themselves after cartoons? Unbelievable!

"Shelby," Ramos whispered into my ear, tugging on my arm. "Come on."

I hadn't realized I'd stopped. I swallowed and took a step closer to my doom. I trusted Ramos, I really did, but this was nuts.

Carson lost all pretense of friendliness, narrowing his eyes and turning his lips into a vicious scowl. He was seriously pissed off.

"Mr. Manetto is not real happy with you, Carson," Ramos said with cool disdain. "It seems you've been cheating him out of a lot of money."

I watched, fascinated, as all the bluster went out of Carson. "That's preposterous," he said. He was thinking that if Manetto knew the truth, he wouldn't have sent Ramos to talk to him. He'd be here to kill him. It gave him hope that maybe it was all a bluff, and he could work his way out of this.

"Please, have a seat and let's get this misunderstanding cleared up. Please, sit down." Carson motioned to the seats on the other side of the table, and Ramos pulled out my chair, nodding for me to sit. "Would you like a drink?" Carson asked.

"No," Ramos said quickly, sitting beside me. "But there is something you can do for us." He was thinking, *die,* and I nearly choked on my spit. Ramos ignored my throat clearing and continued. "Mr. Manetto is a reasonable man. He's not one to tolerate cheating, but he still values the business arrangement he has with you."

"But I haven't cheated him," Carson interrupted. "Whatever gave him that idea?" He flicked a disgusted glance my way. "This is because of her, isn't it? You can't believe anything she says. I knew the man she was with. Sure, he was trying to bribe me, but he had nothing. He claimed to have some information, but he made it up so I'd pay him. None of it was true. It's all lies!"

Ramos' mouth twitched. He was enjoying this. "You'd better not say any more until I introduce you, since I don't think you've actually met. Carson, this is Shelby Nichols, Manetto's niece."

I narrowed my eyes at Carson, giving him the most venomous look I could think of. Carson's brows rose, and sweat popped out on his forehead. "I have the thumb-drive," I said in a low voice. "Warren may have been stupid, but he was an amazing hacker. Uncle Joey suspected you'd been cheating him. Now he has proof. If there's one thing I know for sure about my Uncle, it's that he has no patience for double-crossers. Makes you wonder why you're still alive doesn't it?"

Sweat actually ran down the side of Carson's face. Wow, what a rush. I inhaled through my nose, smelling his fear, and realized I was enjoying this way too much. Now I understood how Ramos felt.

Carson leaned back in his seat and chuckled to cover his fear. "You think you can just walk out of here?" He held his arms out. "I've got my men everywhere."

Ramos smiled coldly. "And if anything happened to me or Shelby, do you think any of this would be left once Manetto got through with you?"

Carson sighed, deflated that Ramos had won this round. Then an idea popped into his head. "How much money are we talking about?"

"At least five hundred thousand," Ramos answered.

Carson swore in his mind, but none of it showed on his face. "That's a lot," he said. "Giving you that much money all at once could nearly bankrupt me. But I'll make a deal with you. I'll give you all the money up front, if you'll just let me try and win it back with a friendly game of poker. I'll spot you five hundred thousand to my five hundred thousand. At the end of the night, we take our winnings and call it good. What do you say? You could end up with a cool million if you take it all."

Ramos smiled, and my heart sank. Was he really going to make me play poker with Uncle Joey's money? What if I lost? I didn't even know how to play.

"What do you think, Shelby?" Ramos asked. He was thinking, *Go for it...jump on this...be excited...convince him you want to play so you can win all of that money, and that your Uncle will let you do it! This is our big chance. You can't lose! Come on! Hurry up!*

I smiled brightly, hoping Carson couldn't tell how much I was faking it. "Wow. You'd put up all that money just for a little game of poker?"

Carson shrugged his shoulders. "Why not?"

"And if I win, you'd let me keep it all?"

"Of course," he said, just now realizing it was me who'd play. "It would be a pleasure to lose to such a beautiful woman."

I smiled coyly. "Then it's settled."

Chapter 9

"Very good." Carson was thinking it was obvious I had no idea what I was getting myself into.

"Can we play Texas Hold'em?" I asked. "That's the only kind of poker I really know how to play."

"Of course," he agreed. "Whatever you want." He was thinking this was the best deal he'd ever made. He was good at reading people, and with my face showing every single emotion going through my pretty little head, it would be a cinch to win back all of his money. This was getting better and better. Glee fairly rippled over him, but his face was a mask of stone, showing nothing but a polite smile.

"Shelby, are you sure your Uncle will be okay with this?" Ramos interrupted, feigning unease.

I blew out a breath, sending him an annoyed frown. "You're forgetting that he sent me to take care of this problem, so it's my decision, not his. And I say we play."

Ramos sighed, letting his shoulders sag in pretended defeat, then straightened with purpose and pinned a no-nonsense gaze on Carson. "We'll want to play on neutral ground," he said forcefully. "And I'll be there as Shelby's bodyguard."

"Agreed," Carson said. "I know of several venues that will let us play a private game for a small fee." He took a pen and notebook from his jacket pocket and scribbled their names and addresses down. Handing it to Ramos, he continued, "Why don't you pick the place and let me know?"

Ramos nodded. "How soon can you get the money together? We're kind of on a time frame."

"Would tomorrow be all right?" Carson asked. "I can have the money and meet you at the venue by five o'clock. We can agree to call the game at midnight... unless one of us is out of money before that. Does that work for you?"

"Sure," Ramos said. "I'll check these places out tonight and let you know where the game will be in the morning. We can meet there and agree to the terms then."

"Good." Carson stood. "I shall look forward to it." With a gleam in his eyes, he turned his sugary sweet smile to me, and I wanted to gag. He thought he had it in the bag, and was so pleased with himself that he couldn't help letting his delight show.

We shook hands, and he held mine a little longer than necessary. He was thinking about bringing my hand to his lips for a kiss, but I quickly pulled it away, smiling demurely so I didn't offend him.

"See you tomorrow," I said. I turned my back, letting the smile fall from my face, and tried not to grumble. I didn't know how I'd be ready by tomorrow, but I'd give it my best shot. Beating him now became my number one priority, and since it was just going to be the two of us, I wouldn't have to divide my attention between other players. I couldn't imagine how I'd keep everyone's cards straight, but just his? Yeah, I could do that. Now all I had to do was learn how to play. With a name like Ace, Ramos had to be an expert, and with him teaching me, it couldn't be too hard, right?

I couldn't wait to get out of there and started toward the stairs with Ramos at my heels. I slowed at the top of the stairs, and he came beside me, placing my hand in the crook of his arm to escort me out of the club. He was thinking this was working out better than he'd planned, and that Carson was in for a shock when I bested him and won all his money.

"Are you sure I can do it?" I asked. "That's a lot of money. What if I mess up?"

"Trust me, you won't," he said.

How could I argue with that? I sure hoped he was right. We pushed through the crowd again, and I could feel the attention of Carson and his goons looking down on us from above like an itch between my shoulder blades. He was already making plans for the big game, and I caught something about a person he needed to call for a favor. He probably needed help getting all that money. Before I could hear more, we made it to the doors where Nick stood guard and pushed through to the other side and out of the club.

Nick followed behind, and waited until we were in the car before he spoke. "So, how did it go?"

"Good," Ramos said. "He didn't even ask for the thumb-drive. All he wanted was a chance to win the money back in a poker game."

"What?" Nick asked. "That could be bad. I heard that Carson always wins at poker. He's a professional player. You didn't take him up on it, did you?"

"Relax," Ramos said. "He's not going to win. He doesn't know about our secret weapon. Shelby's going to play against him. He thinks it's a joke. Is he ever in for a surprise."

Nick was more confused than ever. "Shelby's going to play him?" He turned his attention to me. "Are you that good?"

"Well, I'm sure once I learn how I'll be good at it." I glanced at Nick to find his mouth hanging open and his eyes bulging with alarm. I burst out laughing. "Sorry, Nick, but you should see your face!"

"I don't see what's so funny, unless you know something I don't know." His face darkened in a scowl. "So what is it?"

That sobered me up in a flash. "I get premonitions," I answered quickly, before Ramos could say anything. I glanced at him, and he frowned, but kept his mouth shut. "That's how I help Uncle Joey. I'm sure you've wondered about me. Well, now you know. Just keep it to yourself. This isn't something we want people to know."

Nick sat back in his seat, thinking I was nuts. He'd heard about people who thought they were psychics, but how could that help me win at poker? This was crazy. Psychics couldn't read minds. "What, so did you get a feeling you'd win if you played him or something?"

I huffed. "Yeah, something like that." I knew I wasn't helping, but I didn't feel like explaining it to Nick. Telling him I had premonitions was hard enough, and I didn't want him to figure out I really could read minds. That would be lots worse.

He didn't buy it and was thinking he'd better call Manetto and let him know something was going on between me and Ramos and we couldn't be trusted. He hated to be the one to tell him we were double-crossers, especially when it came to Ramos, but someone had to do it.

"Listen Nick," I turned in my seat to face him. "It's a little more complicated than that, but I can't explain it. You'll just have to trust us. Go ahead and call Uncle Joey if you want. He'll tell you it's true."

Nick's eyes widened. Either I was the best liar ever or there might be something to my story. Still, he wasn't going to take any chances. He'd call Manetto as soon as he could talk to him in private. "It's just a lot to take in," he said. "So what's next?"

Ramos raised his brows at me, but didn't question Nick's comment, and explained how he needed to find a neutral location for the game. He handed Nick the paper with Carson's suggestions. "We need to check those out, but also see if we can find something else. I'd be happier if we found a place Carson's never been before. The game starts at five tomorrow, so that doesn't give us a lot of time. Can you work on that? Manetto has a few contacts here. They might know where to look."

"Sure, I can do that," Nick agreed, thinking that would give him just the excuse he needed to talk to Manetto.

I glanced at Ramos. "You'd better call Uncle Joey first and let him know what's going on. Do you think he'll be upset?"

"No," Ramos said forcefully. "This is my operation. He'll be fine with it, but I'll call him as soon as we get back if that's what you want."

"I think that would be best," I said. Glancing back at Nick, I asked, "Do you know how to play poker?" He nodded, but he was thinking that he didn't want to be involved in any part of my downfall. Sheesh, talk about a confidence killer. "Since we're stopping for office supplies, maybe we should get a deck of cards and one of those dummies books on how to play poker. I could study that tonight at least."

Ramos started to chuckle. "I'll teach you how to play."

"She has a point," Nick spoke up. "It's one thing to know how to play poker, but another to actually have the experience. She's going to have to play all day tomorrow with one of us just to get the gist of the game, if she's going to even have a chance at winning tomorrow night.

Premonitions or not, most of playing poker is strategy." He ran his fingers through his hair in agitation. "I can't believe you're actually going through with this."

My heart sank. Was he right? Could I learn the strategy in time? "He has a point, doesn't he Ramos? Are you sure this is going to work?"

"Yes," he said, his voice firm with conviction. "With a little training and your advantage, it will work like a charm. Don't worry so much. What you can do is every poker player's dream. You'll be great."

"Okay," I said, somewhat relieved. If Ramos thought I could do it, then I might as well start believing it myself. Plus, it was lots better than thinking I would fail.

We found a store, and while Ramos and Nick gathered the things we needed, I found the "Poker For Dummies" book and slipped it onto the counter just before Ramos got out his credit card to pay. He glanced at me with his eyebrows all scrunched together, thinking it was a waste of money, but shook his head and paid for it anyway.

I smiled my thanks at him, and he rolled his eyes, thinking that I had a lot of nerve after he'd promised to teach me. I feigned offense and smacked his arm. It lightened my mood until I caught Nick's suspicious thoughts, wondering what was going on between us. Talk about ruining the moment. After that, I insisted on sitting in the back seat and perused my new book until we got home around ten p.m.

Ramos hurried out to the deck to call Uncle Joey in private, and Nick headed to the computer room to find information about the venues on the Internet. I needed to call my husband and dashed upstairs to my room.

"Hi Chris," I said, out of breath. "Sorry I'm calling you back so late."

"That's okay." His voice was gravelly, like he'd been asleep. "What's going on?"

Taking a deep breath, I plunged right in. "I'm scheduled to play poker with Carson tomorrow night, so I should be able to come home day after tomorrow. What about you? How are things going at home?"

There was silence on his end for a few heartbeats before Chris finally spoke. "Isn't Carson the guy who killed Warren?"

"Well, not technically, but yeah... his guy with the snake tattoos did. Oh and I found out his name was Cobra. Isn't that nuts?" When he didn't answer right away, I continued, "You know, like from the cartoon?"

Chris sighed heavily. "Where's Ramos? I really need to talk to him."

"Um... he's on the phone with Uncle Joey, but he might be off by now. Just a minute and I'll check." I hurried down the stairs, hoping I could hand the phone over to Ramos and he'd take care of this, because seriously... I didn't know what else to say.

Ramos was still out on the deck talking. "It looks like he's still on his phone, but we can chat until he gets done."

"Um... sure," Chris said.

"What did you guys have for dinner?" I asked, needing to start somewhere. Chris answered, and we ended up talking about the kids for a while. "You know, someday we'll look back on this and laugh."

"I sure hope so," Chris answered. "Are you going to be okay? I'm really anxious about this. Maybe I'd better catch a flight out there first thing in the morning."

"Yeah? I would love that, but you'd probably better talk to Ramos first." Hearing the sliding door, I glanced up. "It looks like he's done. Just a minute and I'll get him."

Ramos came in frowning. Manetto had brought up some things Ramos hadn't thought about, making it more complicated than he wanted, but it could still work. He just had a lot to do between now and the game.

As I came toward him, his gaze caught mine, and noticing the phone, he knew it had to be Chris. Sighing deeply, he took the phone from my hand.

"Yes?" he said, impersonally.

"Is Shelby going to be all right? Because if anything happens to her, I'm holding you personally responsible." Chris was speaking so loud I could hear him over the phone. "What have you gotten her into? She said something about playing a poker game with Carson. Won't that be dangerous? How can you let her do that?"

"She'll be fine," Ramos said, his tone harsh. "I have plenty of backup, and nothing's going to go wrong."

"Are you sure? Should I catch a flight out there in the morning?"

"No," Ramos said. "That's unnecessary. I won't let anything happen to her. You have my word."

More silence then, "You'd better mean that, because I'm holding you to it. Now let me talk to my wife."

Ramos handed me the phone with a shake of his head, and stormed back outside onto the deck. Yikes! "I think you made him mad," I said.

"Good." He paused to get under control.

"Chris, I know this is hard, but I'll be okay. I've got my super powers remember? I'll know if anything bad is going to happen, and Ramos can take care of it. I've been in worse situations than this, and I've come out fine."

"That's true," he agreed. "You've been awfully lucky. I just hope your luck doesn't run out anytime soon."

"Geeze! Lighten up. You're giving me the creeps. Everything will be okay, and learning how to play poker is bound to come in handy, right? Now quit worrying."

He sighed. "Okay... sure. Hey, Savannah's here, she wants to say hi."

"Sweet, put her on."

Talking to Savannah was like coming home and remembering what it was like to be normal. I didn't even mind answering all her questions about the friend I was helping, where I was, and when I'd be back, although I had to keep it light, without going into a lot of detail. It was easy to turn the focus back to her, and she chatted on and on about what she'd been doing the last few days. I enjoyed telling her all about the hair hat I bought at the airport, and she couldn't wait to see it and try it on herself. Finally, she put Chris back on. To my relief, he sounded more like his old self, and after I promised to call him the next day, we said goodnight.

Ramos was still outside sitting by the pool, and I quickly joined him, ready to do damage control. "Thanks for talking to Chris. Sorry he was so hard on you. He's fine now."

Ramos grunted, thinking he didn't like the way Chris had talked to him. He was good at his job, and Chris' accusations stung. He didn't deserve being talked to like that. He'd take care of me, and it made him mad that Chris didn't respect that. Of course, I was Chris' wife, so he had to cut him some slack. It almost made him feel guilty for even asking me to help him catch Carson. How stupid was that?

"What did Uncle Joey have to say?" I asked, wanting to change the subject. "What did he think about me playing poker with Carson?"

Ramos' lips turned up in a wry grin. "He thought it was great. He said it was something he'd like to see for himself, and wished he could be here just to see the look on Carson's face when you beat him."

"Really? So he thinks I can do it?"

"Shelby... of course you can. We'll go over it all tomorrow."

"I'd rather start tonight, if that's okay with you," I said. "I don't think I could sleep anyway."

He nodded. "Okay, but there's a few things I need to do first. Manetto doesn't trust Carson, so I need to have a backup plan in case things go bad."

"Couldn't Nick help with that?"

"Yeah, let's go talk to him." Ramos moved to stand.

"Wait." I put my hand on his arm, keeping him in his chair. "If you keep Nick busy, I think that would be best. I don't want him around while I'm learning the game. He might figure out I can read minds, and I really don't want him to know."

"Yeah... okay. But once you learn the basics, I want you to play him. It would be a good test."

Overwhelmed, I dropped my face into my hands. "Are you sure I can do this?"

"Yes, now come on." He grabbed my wrist and pulled me up. I followed him into the house just as Nick came into the kitchen from the computer room.

Nick was thinking that after talking to Manetto, he'd underestimated me. He couldn't figure it out, but Manetto didn't have a problem with letting me play poker with all that money, so my premonitions had to be real. Whatever that meant. "Manetto gave me some names to call for backup," Nick said. "Did he tell you?"

"Yes," Ramos said. "We have to assume that Carson's not just going to hand over the money," he explained to me. "So we need to expect him to do something, and have some friends around in case we need them."

"I got some names and phone numbers to call," Nick added. "They'll help us find the people we need as well as a place for the poker game. I'll go get started." Nick went back into the computer room and closed the door, leaving Ramos and me at the table.

Ramos opened the deck of cards. "You ready to play?"

At my nod, he began with the hand rankings, like a pair, two pair, and all of that, and I had to stop him to write it all down. I'd heard of them before, but I didn't have a clear picture about which ones were better, like the difference between a flush and a straight.

After that, he taught me the basics of Texas Hold'em. The flop, the turn, and the river were all new to me, plus I had no idea how to bet, raise, or fold. Ramos was patient, and I tried to soak it all in. It wasn't until he assigned monetary amounts to the chips that I panicked. "You mean this one chip will be worth twenty-five thousand dollars?"

Ramos took in my stricken expression and raised one eyebrow, thinking "duh." My eyes widened further, and he sighed before checking his watch. "You know what? Let's call it night. It's almost midnight and we're both tired. My side is bothering me and we've got a big day ahead of us. Sound good?"

"Your side?" That caught my attention. "Oh my gosh! You don't think it's infected do you? You'd better let me take a look. If it's infected you'll need to go straight to the emergency room."

"I'm sure it's fine."

"Maybe you need a tetanus shot."

"No. I'm up to date on all my shots," he said.

"At the very least, you should have gotten a shot of penicillin."

"Shelby stop!" He grabbed my arms. "I didn't mean it was bothering me that much. I'm fine."

We stared at each other until he finally let go of me. I sat back in my chair and crossed my arms. "Good," I bit out. "But I'm not going to bed until I see it for myself. I can at least put a new bandage on it."

"I already did," he said. He was thinking that he didn't need anyone to take care of him, and he especially didn't want or need that from me. Not right now.

"That's not what I'm..." I held my breath as it hit me. What was I doing? Had I just crossed that invisible line between us? The line that changed us from friends to something more intimate? Was he putting me in my place? But what if his wound was infected? Good friends still cared about each other, didn't they? "Did you get a good look at it? Are you sure it's not infected?"

He glanced up at the ceiling in frustration before pinning his gaze on me. "If I let you look at it, will you go to bed?

"Sure," I agreed.

His lips thinned, then with one quick move, he pulled off his shirt and turned so his injured side was facing me. I had to give him credit for putting on the bandage without help, because it looked pretty good... just like the rest of him. He didn't try to remove the bandage, but glanced at me with a raised eyebrow and a clear challenge to do it myself.

I knelt down beside him and started to peel off the tape. It was sticky and wouldn't come off very easily, but I just kept pulling. I could hear Ramos thinking that I should just rip it off, but for some reason, I took perverse pleasure in pulling it off slowly. Studying the wound, I could see he'd left the same butterfly bandages I'd put on, and they needed to be replaced, but the rest of it was healing nicely with no sign of infection.

"It looks pretty good," I said, relieved. "Where's your first aid kit? I need to put some more ointment on this and replace the bandages."

"You know what? I'd like to take a shower first. If you want to wait, you can put the bandages on then. Otherwise, I'll just do it when I'm done." He pushed back his chair and stood, gazing down at me as I knelt on the rug, his mind blank, but his eyes darkening. "You know what? Never mind. Go to bed Shelby. I'll see you in the morning." With that he turned on his heel and fled into the backyard, closing the patio door with a thwack, just like he had earlier.

I swallowed and stood, not exactly sure what had just happened, and realized my heart was beating a bit too fast. Scowling, I grabbed the poker book off the table and hurried up the stairs to my room, locking the door behind me. I hoped that if I concentrated really hard on poker and the upcoming game, it would help me forget all about Ramos and the way he'd looked at me with those smoldering eyes.

I threw myself into studying the book and got clear through the chapter explaining Texas Hold'em before the words started to blur and I fell asleep. I woke sometime after three in the morning to turn off my bedside lamp. Turning to my side, I punched my pillow, but my mind kept going over the terms of the game as I tried to remember the sequence of events, when to bet, when to fold, and how my mind-reading could possibly matter when so much of winning depended on the cards.

Between that and pushing away thoughts of Ramos, I tossed and turned for another hour. Finally, I decided I just needed to relax and forget about everything. Ramos was my friend, and nothing more. My worries about the game were based on the fact that I just didn't know enough about it, and once I had some practice, I was sure to get the hang of it. I had the whole day to practice, and losing sleep over it wasn't doing me any good. I finally drifted off to sleep, and the next time I woke, relief swept over me to find the sun shining through my window.

The clock read eight-thirty, and with so much happening today, my heart lurched with sudden anxiety. After a nice hot shower, I blew my hair dry and applied my make-up, knowing I would have to go shopping for something to wear to the poker game. But I had no idea what. I didn't want to wear a slinky dress like the women at the club, but I certainly couldn't wear the same clothes I'd had on yesterday... which turned out to be what I had to wear again today. What I wouldn't give for my suitcase!

Downstairs, I found Nick at the table putting copies of the printouts from the thumb-drive into envelopes to deliver to Carson's associates. He glanced up at me and murmured a quick good morning.

With my stomach a ball of nerves, I didn't feel like eating much, so I cooked a piece of toast for breakfast. I kept waiting for Ramos to come down the stairs, but soon realized he was gone. "Where's Ramos?" I asked Nick.

"He's checking out a couple of places for you and Carson to play tonight." Nick was thinking that this little poker game of mine was a lot more involved than I'd ever know, given the extra security Manetto insisted on having, and setting up the place for the game. He sure hoped it was worth it, and that I'd pull through for them. They were all counting on me.

I suddenly lost my appetite and knew today was going to be one of those Mylanta days, and I'd better get some soon. "What are you doing?" I already knew, but needed him to quit thinking about me and how incompetent and untrained I was at playing poker. He explained about the envelopes and that he'd be delivering them once the game started.

"We don't want them to get this information too soon, or you might not get to play Carson before they come after him." Nick smiled, tapping the envelopes on the table. "We also don't want Carson to find out what we've done before the game, so while you're playing is the perfect opportunity to deliver them."

"Makes sense to me," I said. "When do you think Ramos will be back?"

"About an hour or so," he answered. "He said we should play some poker and I could teach you all I know about the game."

"Okay," I said, eager to do something. "Let me get my notes." I ran upstairs for my book and notes. By the time I got back, Nick had the chips out on the table and was shuffling the cards.

We spent the next two hours playing. Nick helped me with the basics of the game, from how the blinds were set up, to who went first and when to bet. Once I got that down, he helped me with what cards were worth betting on, and which ones weren't. The only thing I didn't like were the little negative thoughts he kept thinking about me that I wasn't picking it up very quick.

"You should fold on anything in your hand that isn't good," he said. "Since you don't know what you're doing, that's probably best." He didn't think I could ever pull this off, and figured the only reason Manetto agreed was because I was his niece and I'd insisted. Manetto was blinded to this stupidity because I was family. He vowed then and there never to let any of his relatives get to him like that.

Ramos came through the door, and I happily threw down my cards. Nick had destroyed my confidence, and I couldn't take another minute of it. I lurched to my feet and glanced around for my purse. "I've got to go to the store," I announced. My stomach clenched, and I bent over until the pain passed. "Right away."

"What's wrong?" Ramos narrowed his eyes.

"Nothing a little Mylanta won't cure," I said. "Can I have the keys?"

Ramos studied me and realized I needed to get out of the house almost as much as I needed the medicine. "I'll take you." He turned to Nick. "I got it all set up for tonight and met with Carson to set the terms. I need you to let Manetto know how it's going. We're playing the game at Max's Club. Will you call Manetto and make sure it's good with him?"

"Sure," Nick agreed. "Oh, and while you're out, you might want to get Shelby something nicer to wear. Probably something that will distract Carson. She needs all the advantages she can get."

I had pulled the front door open, but turned with a gasp of indignation at his comment. That was just too much. I tried to push past Ramos, but he wouldn't let me get around him, grabbing my shoulders and holding me back. "Come on, Shelby, let's go. He didn't mean anything by it."

"Yes he did. He's been thinking... he's been... he said..." Damn, I couldn't say it out loud. "Oh, all right." I pulled out of Ramos' grasp and marched out the door, knowing I had to get a hold of myself and calm down.

I took a deep breath and got in the car, clicking my seat belt in place while Ramos started it up. Ramos wisely didn't say anything, and his mind was quiet, giving me the silence I needed. We pulled into the grocery store, and I grabbed two bottles of Mylanta and some Tums. I also found some flavored water and grabbed several bottles of that. The way my stomach was behaving, I knew I couldn't drink soda until I had some food in me, and this would taste better than plain old water. Plus I needed it with what I had to face today.

We got back to the car, and I opened the Mylanta and took a few swallows. Feeling better, I found a bottle of water and drank half of that. With my stomach starting to settle, I knew I needed something to eat or it would start up all over again. "Can we go back to that place with the fish tacos?"

Ramos allowed a small grin. "Sure."

I didn't know how far away it was, so I was surprised when we pulled up a few minutes later. It was just past eleven, but there was already a line. We placed our order and found a table. After devouring my tacos, I felt a lot better and sat back in my seat, finally ready to talk. "Nick thinks I'm stupid and that I'm going to lose all that money."

"That's not going to happen," Ramos said. He was thinking I was sweet and unpredictable, even though I could be pretty stubborn. There was more to me than most of the women he knew, and he liked that. "You're a lot of things, Shelby, but you're not stupid. You can do this. It's really not that hard. When we get back I'll show you how you're going to beat Carson at his own game. You're going to make him so mad. It'll be great."

"Okay," I said. "But I'm still nervous."

"I'm sure you are, but it'll all work out." He checked his watch. "We've got a little over five hours before the game starts, so we'd better get moving." I followed him to the car, feeling much better.

"We have to make one more stop before we head back," he said, thinking he had to be careful about how he said it.

"What's that?" I asked, curious.

"Well, Nick had a point. You do need something nicer to wear."

I chuckled. "I know that. I was thinking that earlier myself. So what do you suggest?"

"I'll show you." His eyes held a hint of excitement, so I knew it had to be good, which made me excited too.

A few minutes later, we pulled into the parking lot of this huge mall and followed the lane toward the main building. Palm trees lined both sides of the drive, and Ramos pulled to a stop in front of a glass-enclosed, circular, two-story entrance. A valet opened my door, and I stared up at the mall while Ramos circled the car to join me.

Inside we found more trees, several fountains, a breathtaking glass ceiling, and every store imaginable. I didn't know where to start. "What do you think I should wear?"

"I don't know," Ramos shrugged. "Something casual, but sexy, like a short dress and heels. Just something to keep Carson a little distracted. There." He maneuvered me toward a large Neiman-Marcus store. "They should have something here that would work."

"Okay, sure," I agreed, pursing my lips to contain my enthusiasm.

We found the dress department, and hardly a minute went by before an attendant spotted us and eagerly trotted over. She was young, probably a college student, and barely looked at me while I tried to explain what I wanted, instead staring at Ramos with undisguised admiration. She sent quick glances my way with an occasional head nod to show me she was listening, but her smile was all for him.

Ramos' phone buzzed, and he excused himself to take a call from Nick. I breathed a sigh of relief to have him gone, and the attendant finally turned her helpful attention to me. From her thoughts, I knew she was determined to find something I'd love just so she could see Ramos smile again.

I tried not to snicker at this turn of events and let her help me all she wanted. This time she listened when I told her I was going for the playful but sassy look that didn't reveal too much, but still looked feminine. I also wanted it to be comfortable since I'd be sitting in it for hours and hours.

After my explanation, she found the perfect dress. It was a blue floral-print georgette with a gathered split surplice neckline that didn't reveal too much, but just enough to be sexy. It was sleeveless and had a smocked waistband that wasn't a bit uncomfortable. The length was just right as well, hitting my legs a few inches above the knee. Even better, she thought I looked great.

"Do you have shoes?" she asked. I shook my head, telling her no, and her eyes lit up. "I know the perfect shoes to go with this dress. Follow me."

With the dress still on, I followed her to the shoe department, and she went straight to a pair of black leather zip-back sandals. My breath hitched at the price, then I realized they were Prada. I'd never worn Prada before, and my heart rate doubled just to try them on. The attendant also brought over a pair of Jimmy Choo's that were similar in style and price. I'd never worn those before either. Indulging myself in the moment, I tried them both on. No doubt about it, they looked great and gave me a boost of confidence, but I couldn't get over the nearly thousand-dollar price tag.

"Do you have anything else?" I asked the attendant. At her crestfallen expression, I continued. "You know, just to compare?"

"Sure. Let's look over here."

We came upon another pair that I immediately liked. They were dark paloma snakeskin suede sandals, which seemed kind of fitting in a way, and even better, they were on sale. They were still expensive, but at least they didn't cost more than the dress. I put them on and smiled. They looked just as good as the others, and more important, I still got a rush of confidence just walking around in them. "I'll take them."

"Great choice," the attendant said. "How about some jewelry?"

Wow, she was good. "Yeah, I probably need that too."

She grabbed the shoebox and led me across the aisle to the jewelry department. "I'm thinking silver and blue," she said. She went straight to a striking three-strand blue-beaded silver necklace with matching earrings. They were simple, but elegant, and set off my dress beautifully.

"Yes," I said, my eyes glazing over, knowing I had to have them.

"Okay then, let's get you back to the changing room." The attendant was glowing herself, thinking how satisfying her job was when she helped someone like me look so good. I tried to take that as a complement. Anticipation ran over her to see Ramos again, and she wasn't disappointed to find him sitting in the chair outside the changing room.

"What do you think?" she asked, gesturing toward me and hoping she'd pleased him.

He glanced at me and nodded, a slow grin spreading over his face. "Very nice," he said. The attendant followed me to the changing room and unlocked the door. Once I was inside, she wasted no time getting back to Ramos.

Shaking my head at her reaction, I quickly changed into my clothes, placing the dress on the hanger, and the shoes back into the box. I'd certainly enjoyed myself with this little shopping excursion, but now it was time to get back to business. An hour had passed, leaving me with only three hours to prepare for the poker match. My stomach clenched, and I took another swig of Mylanta before opening the door.

The attendant bagged my dress efficiently and scanned Ramos' credit card, paying special attention to Ramos' name. She sighed over it, thinking Alejandro was perfect, and bid us a fond goodbye, her gaze following Ramos all the way out the door.

"You do know she was totally into you, right?" I couldn't help asking.

He pursed his lips. "Yeah, I get that a lot." He threw a mischievous grin my way. "Especially when I'm with someone. It's like they gang up on me. I guess they just can't help themselves."

"Whatever," I said, rolling my eyes. He chuckled and we got in the car. "So, is everything set up for tonight?" I asked.

"Pretty much," Ramos responded. "Like I told Nick, we're playing at Max's Club, and I already met with Carson this morning to agree on the place. One of Manetto's friends suggested it, and since it wasn't on Carson's list, I checked it out. I hit it off real well with Max, especially when I mentioned we were playing against Carson. Turns out, he doesn't like Carson much, and was real interested when I told him about our agreement. He told me Carson wasn't known to cheat, but he wasn't to be trusted either.

"I asked him about hiring a few of his bouncers to keep a watch out on Carson's men, just in case he tried something, and he was very obliging. So we'll have extra people there to rely on if we need them."

"That's good to know," I said. "What about Nick? Will he be able to come at all? He talked about delivering the evidence of Carson's cheating to his associates during the game."

"Yeah. But that shouldn't take all night. Once he's done, he'll be back to help out as well. Right now, Nick's on his way to the club to meet with Carson's men. It's just a preliminary kind of thing where the location is inspected by both sides to make sure there's nothing set up that could be interpreted as cheating, or anything like it. After that's accomplished, we should be set to go."

I nodded, feeling a chill at the back of my neck. "Do you think it's all going to work out?"

"Yes," Ramos said. "Now all we have to do is get you ready. I've hired a professional dealer, so all you really need to do is play the game."

It sure sounded easy to him, but what if I messed up? What if I got mixed up between a flush and a straight and which was better? What if I didn't realize that what he had in his hand was better than mine until it was too late? What if Carson cheated? How would that go over if I accused him of cheating? I could imagine him pulling a gun and everyone shooting everyone. So much could go wrong.

"Shelby?" Ramos asked.

"Huh?" He nodded toward my hands and I realized I'd been clenching my purse. "Oh." I let go and smoothed out the wrinkles. "I guess I'm worried about tonight. Do you think I could take a cheat sheet? You know, with the ranking order of the poker hands so I don't mess up?"

Ramos let out a laugh. "Sure. That's a great idea. It would totally throw Carson off his game. He'd think you were a total novice, and then when you started winning it would drive him nuts. That's perfect."

"Okay, good," I said, going along with him, and not pointing out that I really was a total novice.

Sometimes I just didn't understand that competitive streak men seemed to have when it came to sports and games. It seemed to cloud their judgment. Ramos was so stoked about my ability to win, that I worried he knew what he was doing. Of course, worrying about it now didn't help, and I knew I had to change my attitude and quit worrying so much. If only I could convince my stomach, I might begin to believe it.

Chapter 10

Back at the house, we settled in at the table to play some poker. I grabbed a granola bar, and Ramos got me a soda with crushed ice. It was so sweet of him that I didn't have the heart to tell him it might upset my stomach. Of course, with the food we'd eaten earlier, I was feeling lots better, so maybe I could handle a soda.

It was also a relief to have Nick gone so Ramos and I could actually talk about how to use my mind-reading skills to play the game.

"Our strategy is to play cautiously," Ramos said. "I don't want you to bluff, and only bet when you have the advantage. If your first two cards are higher than his, then stay in. Fold if he has the good cards. It's as easy as that."

Ramos told me what a good beginning hand was, and what cards I'd have the best chance of winning with. "It's different with just two players. You're not going to get a lot of good cards, so you'll probably be folding a lot. Don't forget, if his cards are higher than yours, you should probably fold. But it won't hurt to stay in if his cards are bad, especially since he might try and bluff. That's the beauty of reading minds, you'll always know when he's bluffing."

"Yeah," I said, wishing I could match his enthusiasm. I sure hoped playing a few games would help me pick this up. It didn't matter so much now, but how was I going to handle it when it was a million dollars we were playing for? Just thinking about it frazzled my nerves.

We played a few hands, and pretty soon I started to get the hang of it. He showed me how to bet, check, raise and fold. "How much should I raise? I mean, what's high and what's low?" I asked.

"In this game, anything that's five thousand or below would be a low raise," Ramos answered. "Just make sure you never bluff, and always raise him at least five thousand or more when he's bluffing."

"Okay, I'll try and remember that."

"Let's just keep practicing," Ramos said. "That should help."

I used everything Ramos taught me, and it started to make more sense and get easier. I didn't know how hard Ramos was trying, but using his strategy, I was starting to get way ahead of him, and my stack of chips was growing.

"This is good, Shelby," Ramos said. "Now that you're ahead, you have an even greater advantage. At this point, when you have the nuts, bet big."

"Um... I don't think I have any nuts." I chuckled self-consciously.

"No, that's not..." Ramos burst out laughing. "I guess I forgot to tell you about that."

"Uh-huh," I said.

"When you have the nuts, it means you have a hand that can't be beaten."

"Oh, okay. So in that case I should bet big or raise him?"

"Yeah. He'll either fold, or if he has good cards, call, and you'll win the round. Or if you have the most chips, you could go all in and win the game. But remember, you can't do that until you have the most chips." Ramos demonstrated how that could work until it made sense to me.

Nick walked through the door and told us that everyone was satisfied with the location, and we were all set for tonight. A sudden fit of nervous tension ran over me, making my stomach hurt. As he came to the table, I reached for my bottle of Tums and took a few, hoping neither of them noticed. Ramos' brows creased, but before he could comment, Nick asked a question. "With both of them having so much money, how are we going to set up the game so one of them wins?"

"Carson and I agreed about that this morning," Ramos answered. "Since we want the game to end at midnight or earlier, we thought we would start the blinds at one thousand and double them every hour, so that by eleven o'clock the big blind will be worth sixty-four thousand dollars, and the small thirty-two thousand."

"That should work," Nick agreed. He glanced at me, thinking I looked a little pale, and decided not to tell me it would take a miracle for me to win all that money. "Does she know how to play now?" he asked Ramos.

"Hey... sitting right here," I said. "For your information, I could beat the pants off of you any time."

His eyes widened. "Okay then. That's the spirit."

"Go ahead," Ramos said. "Take my place and see how well you can do." He was thinking that all Nick needed was to get trounced by me. It was bound to convince him my skills were real and no laughing matter.

We played for a while, and I beat Nick most every time. I had to fold when his cards were better, but I was still doing lots better than him. He was starting to get frustrated with me, and I was starting to like playing poker. Winning carried with it a sense of power and control, and I liked that feeling... a lot.

"It's three-thirty," Ramos interrupted. "Time to stop. "I think you're ready." He glanced at Nick. "What do you think?"

"She beat me," he said. "I don't know exactly how, but she's got my vote. It's hard to believe you're not cheating; and you're not, right?"

"Nope," I said, glancing at Ramos. He grinned, thinking that while I was cheating, it was the best kind of cheating, since it couldn't be proven. He thought I'd do great, and I smiled back at him, starting to believe it myself.

"Better get ready," he said. "Can I fix you something to eat first? It's going to be a while before you get another chance."

"My stomach's too nervous to eat much. Maybe just a piece of toast and some yogurt. But I can fix it."

"How about you get the yogurt and start eating, and I'll put in the toast."

After gulping down my food, I hurried upstairs to put on my dress, first applying a liberal amount of deodorant so I wouldn't sweat too much. Once I had the dress on, I touched up my make-up and hair. Last, I slipped on my shoes and checked myself in the full-length mirror. I looked good, but it didn't help with the butterflies in my stomach. I couldn't remember the last time I felt this nervous.

I came down the stairs and into the living room, finding Ramos and Nick glancing up from their seats admiring my outfit and the way my dress showed off my legs. Although Nick was hoping for a little more skin to distract Carson, he thought my dress suited me. Ramos was thinking I had just the right amount of class and respectability to play my part.

He had no doubt that I would do well, and the expectation of getting even with Carson settled something inside of him, something that had been missing for a long time.

"You look great," Ramos said.

"Thanks," I answered. "So do you." He wore his standard dark blazer and jeans, but looked more formal with a gray dress shirt that set off his dark eyes perfectly, making it easy to get lost in their depths.

"Ready?" Ramos asked.

I took a deep breath and nodded, then grabbed my purse, making sure everything I needed was inside. "Now I'm ready," I said.

We arrived at the club thirty minutes early. Nick dropped us off, leaving to deliver his envelopes. The club wasn't crowded yet, but there were still a lot of people at the bar and tables. A dance floor fronted a stage at the opposite end and was set up for a live band that would be performing later. The rich mahogany wood bar and dance floor spoke volumes about how well the bar was doing and gave the impression of old money.

A man sitting at the bar noticed our entrance and hurried over, shaking Ramos' hand and ushering us into his office. Ramos introduced him to me as Max, the owner of the club, and three burly men whom Ramos had hired earlier quickly joined us in the room.

"I don't want Carson or his men to know you're working for me," Ramos explained. "Let them assume you work for Max, but keep an eye on them. If any of them leave, I want them followed. I want to know what they're up to. If they even look like they're going to pull their guns or come in shooting, take them out."

Ramos waited to see their nods before he continued. "Nick will be joining us later. Since I don't know how many men Carson will bring, that's up to you to find out and tell me during one of our breaks. One of you will be stationed inside the room with the poker game. Tell me immediately if you see anything suspicious."

"I'll be coming in and out as well," Max said. "I like to keep tabs on what's happening in my establishment."

After a few more words, the guards left, and Max ushered us out of his office and down a long narrow hall toward the back of the building. He opened a door into a beautifully furnished room. It was a comfortable size, reminding me of a family recreation room, with one poker table set up in the middle. Dark wood paneling covered the lower half of the walls, and the upper half was done in gold and tan swirls, giving it a Mediterranean feel. A dark wood bar spanned the back wall with five bar stools set in front. Drop lighting shone on bottle-filled cabinets and illuminated the beautiful blue-toned tile work on the wall behind.

A frosted glass chandelier hung from the ceiling directly over the table, sending warm light onto the surface. A leather couch and side tables with lamps were grouped along one wall, and two leather chairs with an oblong coffee table were grouped on the other. In one corner, with a potted ivy plant on top, sat an old-fashioned, black safe. Although there were no windows, the room was pleasantly lit, with paintings and plants strategically placed for maximum comfort.

The round mahogany poker table had a pedestal-type base and would easily seat six. A ring of cup-holders and a carved chip well lined the wine-colored felt gaming surface and was surrounded by a padded, faux leather elbow rest. Several wooden and leather rolling chairs matched the table and set it off beautifully.

Max introduced us to the man stationed at the bar, and the other man sitting at the table who was the card dealer for our game. “The bathroom is over this way,” Max said. He led me to a door beside the bar, thinking that from my pale face, I would probably need a place to escape more than once during the game.

He was right about that. I peeked inside to find a large marble countertop and sink, with mirrored wooden cabinets matching the outside room. It was spacious and classy with all the comforts one could hope for. Yes, I could definitely spend some down time in here.

Max’s phone chirped, and after checking the message, he excused himself. “Carson’s here. I’ll bring him back. Please make yourselves at home.”

Sudden fear tightened my stomach, causing my head to spin. The lights around me dimmed, and my legs lost their strength.

“Shelby?” Ramos caught me around the waist and pulled me against his side, walking me to the couch. We sat down together, and Ramos shoved my head toward my knees. “Take a deep breath,” he said. “Pull yourself together before Carson gets here.”

His words sent a rush of adrenaline through me. I couldn’t let Carson see me like this! “Let me up! I’m fine now.” He released my head and I sat up, pushing my hair out of my eyes. Taking a deep breath, I relaxed against the cushion. “Sorry. I’m okay now.”

Ramos studied me, his brows scrunched together, thinking that was close. He hadn’t expected that... not at all. “Just stay there. I’ll talk with Carson and keep him occupied until you feel better.”

Just then, the door opened, and Ramos left my side. He greeted Carson and kept him talking near the door long enough for me to get my equilibrium back. Two men came in with Carson, one I didn’t know, and the other was the same guy who'd followed me the first day, identifying me to Carson the night before.

Carson spotted me sitting on the couch. He was thinking I looked a little pale, and a small smile curved his lips. It was the impetus I needed to snap me out of it. What was wrong with me? I could do this, and more important, I couldn't let Ramos down. He was counting on me. Forget the money. Forget Carson. Do it for Ramos.

Almost like he'd heard my thoughts, Ramos glanced at me, worry tightening his eyes. I caught his gaze and smiled reassuringly, giving him a slight nod to let him know I could do this. The tension left him, and he nodded back, relieved. He was thinking that he'd forgotten to tell me that I could read his mind for help with the game if I needed to, since he had no doubt he'd be thinking what I should do.

I smiled at that, and stood as Carson approached. "Shelby," he said. "You're looking splendid." He took my hand and smiled, thinking the night might not be too boring since he'd have me to look at.

"Thank you," I said. "I'm looking forward to our game, although I've heard some things about you that make me nervous."

"Me?" He feigned surprise. "Like what?"

"Oh, just that you're really good," I said. "But I hope to give you a run for your money." He smiled, but didn't say, *"yeah, right,"* like he was thinking. Defensive anger swept over me, and suddenly, I couldn't wait to wipe that stupid smile off his face.

Ramos came to my side and cleared his throat, successfully pulling my attention away from my murderous thoughts. Max placed a silver suitcase on the table, flicking it open and lifting the lid. Seeing all those stacks of bills totaling a million dollars sent shivers up my spine.

Max glanced through it, totaling it up in his head. "One million dollars," he said. "Agreed?" he glanced at Ramos, then Carson, who both nodded their heads. "According to house rules, it will be placed in the safe until after the game is concluded." He clicked the lid closed and carried it over to the safe in the corner. Spinning the dial to the correct numbers, he popped the door open and placed the case inside.

"You may state the terms of your bet," he said, coming back to the table. "And the game will begin."

"Five hundred thousand per person to begin, winner takes all, game ends at midnight," Carson said.

"Agreed," Ramos said. "The opening big blinds start at one thousand to be doubled every hour to facilitate a clear winner by our midnight agreement."

"I agree," Carson said. "I would like a five to ten minute break at the end of each hour."

"Agreed," Ramos said. He stared at Carson who stared back like it was a staring contest or something. They were both thinking how great it was going to be to beat the other, and I had to work hard to keep from rolling my eyes.

"Anything else?" Max asked. No one spoke, so he continued. "Take your places, and begin your game."

I was kind of bummed that he didn't say "let the games begin," and then end with "may the odds be ever in your favor," but that was probably asking too much. Besides, I might have burst out laughing, and that would never do.

Ramos pulled out my chair, and I dutifully sat while he stood directly behind me. The dealer put a stack of chips in front of me and I watched Carson put them in his chip well and did what he did. The bartender came by, asking me what I would like to drink. I grabbed a bottle of water from my purse and handed it to him. "Could you put that in a glass with some ice?" I asked.

"Um... sure," he said. He smiled, but in his thoughts he was offended that I'd brought my own drink. Didn't I know this was a first-rate joint? He had plenty of vitamin water. All I had to do was ask.

Oops. Oh well, nothing to do about looking like a novice now. At least Carson was getting a kick out of it, thinking his suspicions were right that I'd never played professionally before. It made him happy and eager to show me up, and stick it to Manetto at the same time.

It made me mad, but also determined that he'd be singing a different tune when I got done with him.

The dealer began shuffling the deck, and I took the moment to quickly grab my cheat sheet and place it on the table. "Do you mind if I keep this out?" I asked Carson. "It's a list of the poker hands, you know, one pair... two pair. I just want to make sure I don't mess up."

"Um... that's fine." Carson smiled politely, but he was thinking that he could hardly believe it. Was I for real? Anyone else would have had that memorized. Wow, this was going to be a lot easier than he thought. He didn't think he'd have to put his other plans into action if it was going to be this easy.

Other plans? He had other plans? Uh-oh. Now I had to make sure I figured out what they were before the night was over.

"Ready?" the dealer asked.

I nodded, then glanced at Carson, and my eyes widened in surprise. Carson had put these little round dark glasses on. It made him look like a fat John Lennon. I coughed to hide the choke of laughter that bubbled up, and cleared my throat.

The dealer had already dealt the first two cards so I quickly glanced at them. A queen and a ten... that's good.

Carson had an ace and a jack. Yikes! He had the big blind and me the small, so I folded instead of calling.

Ramos was thinking a queen and ten were good, what was I doing? I wanted to look at him over my shoulder and roll my eyes or something. He should know that Carson's cards were better. Maybe listening to him wasn't such a good idea.

The next three rounds came and went with me folding every one because Carson's cards were still better. When was I going to get a good hand? At least Ramos had seen my puny cards and understood, but having him watch over my shoulder was not as helpful as I'd thought.

Carson was wondering if I knew how to play at all and thinking I should at least go one round without folding. How could I observe his playing style if I didn't do that? The first rounds were the best for observing your opponent when the blinds weren't so big. I wouldn't have that luxury later. The game of poker was a lot more than winning and losing. It was finding the subtle tells and nuances in your opponent. Deciding from their body language if they had better cards than you. Gaining that experience only came by actually playing the game. Did I even know I could go further than the first round?

I let out my breath slowly and settled back in my chair. He didn't think I could play, huh? Well, I'd show him. The next round my cards were high, and I called, going for the flop. I had an ace and a queen, and the flop showed a queen, a five, and a seven, giving me a pair of queens. Carson had a jack and a seven. With the flop, that gave him a pair of sevens, which wasn't very high, but he was so excited that I'd actually bet that he put in two thousand dollar chips.

I called, and the dealer flipped the next card. It was a ten of hearts, which didn't help either of us. Carson threw in another two thousand, expecting me to fold, but I called instead. The dealer flipped the next card, or river, and it was another ten.

Carson stared at me, trying to gauge if I actually had something. Since I hadn't bet before, he figured I did, but did I have a queen, five, or ten? On a whim, he decided to place another bet, only this time it was ten thousand. If I were playing as cautiously as it looked, I'd fold over that much money, whether I had the queen or not, thinking he might have another ten.

I pursed my lips, trying to make it look like I wasn't sure what to do. Since I had this in the bag, I decided to call and raise him, but I couldn't make it too high or he wouldn't take the bait. I threw in ten thousand, and then raised him five more. "Call and raise," I said.

I tried to keep my expression neutral. Carson thought I probably had a pair of queens or another ten, but just in case I was bluffing, it was worth it to find out, so he called me.

I flipped over my cards, showing him my queen, and there was absolutely no expression on his face. It was like he was made of stone. I made a show of looking at his cards and gave a surprised smile that I'd won the round. He was thinking I'd been lucky this time, but it wouldn't last. I wouldn't always have better cards than him.

The next few rounds went about the same. I folded twice, then won the next two, and at the end of the hour, my stack was slightly larger than his. It was a relief when the dealer called for a break. The concentration it took to play was intense, but almost worse was not showing any emotion. Holding back my smile was killing me, and I worried that I could keep this up for five or six more hours.

Carson said he needed some fresh air. He left the room with his two goons trailing behind. Ramos nodded at the security guard stationed at the door, and he followed them at a discreet distance. The dealer left as well, leaving the room empty except for the bartender and us.

I stood and stretched, grateful to move my arms and legs.

Ramos came to my side. “You’re doing real well,” he said, his voice low so that only I could hear him. “In fact you’re doing so well, you probably don’t need me looking over your shoulder all the time.”

“Thanks,” I replied. “Honestly, it bothered me at first, but after a few hands, I didn’t even notice. But feel free to tell me stuff like you did that one time about the possibility of a flush. I almost missed that.”

“Sure.”

“Oh, and I picked up something from Carson,” I whispered. “He has something planned in case he loses, but I don’t know what it is yet. I guess he’s waiting to see how things go first.”

“Good to know,” Ramos said. “Maybe I’d better check with our guys and see if they noticed anything. Will you be all right here?”

“Yeah, I’ve got to visit the restroom, so go ahead.”

The bathroom was a nice sanctuary, and I took my time, even making faces in the mirror to get it out of my system, and doing some leg stretches. When I came out, everyone had returned, and it looked like I’d kept them all waiting. Oops, I hoped I hadn’t broken a cardinal rule or something. As I passed the bar, the bartender asked if I wanted more water, and I told him to keep it coming. He smiled, thinking I was okay after all, and hoped I’d win all that money. It was easy to smile at him after that.

Max came in to check on us, and after finding everything satisfactory, he quickly left. As we settled down to play this hour, I wasn’t so nervous, and after a few hands, I felt like I was starting to find a rhythm to the game. I was winning more, and my stack was showing it.

By the end of the hour, Carson was getting frustrated. He couldn't understand how every time he had good cards I folded. It wasn't so bad when we got as far as the turn or the river, because he still won a little, but he was losing more often. Something wasn't right.

At the break, he left without saying a word to anyone, and I got worried that maybe I was playing a little too well. Was he going to do something rash? I still hadn't heard anything more about the plan he had in place, and it bothered me.

"What's wrong," Ramos asked.

I sighed and pushed back my chair to stand up. "Can we go outside and get some air?"

"Sure." Ramos guided me down the hall, opening the door to a blast of music from the band. "The walls are soundproof," he said loudly, noticing my surprise. He walked me through the crowd to the door, pushing it open to the sultry evening air. The sun was low on the horizon, and things were starting to cool off.

"Where's Carson?" I asked.

"He's back inside, listening to the band."

"Oh," I nodded. "I'm a little concerned about him. He's getting frustrated. Am I playing too well? Do you think I should lose a few hands?"

"Hell no," Ramos growled. "Don't change a thing. I'm enjoying this."

"Did you find out how many men he brought and what they're doing?"

"Yeah, I've got it covered," Ramos replied. "And Nick should be here soon, so don't worry about that. Just keep doing what you're doing. It's working great."

"Okay," I said, relieved. "I actually think I'm getting the hang of it. He keeps staring at me, but I hardly notice anymore. I have to say the hardest part is keeping a straight face, especially when I know I'm going to win."

"You're doing great," Ramos smiled, thinking how satisfying it was to watch Carson squirm. And I was playing my part better than he'd hoped. He really enjoyed watching me play and wished Manetto were there to see it. Maybe when we got back he could set up a game, just for the hell of it. He glanced at me, knowing I'd heard everything, and shrugged. "It might be fun."

"Yeah, you just want me to show off."

"And win some money," he added. "Don't forget that part."

"Hmm, there is that," I agreed. "As long as I get to keep it."

"Well, you might have to split it with me, since I'm the one who taught you how to play."

"Sure. I get ninety percent, and you can have ten. How does that sound?"

"Like I'll have to negotiate for better terms." Ramos checked his watch. "We'd better get back."

The next hour went by quickly. I made a couple of mistakes, but at the end of it, Ramos assured me I was still on track. Nick joined us during the break, letting us know he'd successfully delivered the information. He was impressed that I was doing so well and interested to watch the next round.

"Got anything more from Carson?" Ramos asked.

"No," I responded.

Ramos told Nick I had a 'premonition' that Carson was up to something, but I didn't know what it was yet. Nick nodded grimly, telling us he'd parked the car in the alley next to the employee entrance in case we needed to leave in a hurry. Ramos checked in with our hired guards, but they had nothing new to report.

"We'll just have to keep alert," Ramos said.

The break ended, and I went back to my chair with resignation. Playing poker this long was wearing me out, and I was ready for it to be over. With the fourth hour, we were now up to eight thousand for the big blind, and four for the small. That much money made things a little more difficult, and I had to really think about betting on some hands that I might not have at the beginning of the game.

After several hands, I'd won more than I'd lost, and I eagerly checked the clock. The hour was nearly over, but I was in a tight spot. My two cards were a six and ten, which were low, but Carson's were worse, with a four and nine. Since he'd placed the big blind, and me the small, I added four thousand to call.

Rather than raise me, Carson checked. He'd only done that once before, so I decided to check too. It made him think I didn't have anything, which was basically true except that my ten was higher than his nine. The flop came out with a five, a king, and an ace. Still nothing for either of us, but Carson threw in five thousand, so I called.

The turn was a lousy two. This time Carson checked again, wanting to see if I'd bet. I figured I'd check too, and Carson assumed I still didn't have anything. The river turned up a seven. Carson decided that since I'd checked, he'd play to get the pot, and bet ten thousand, thinking I'd fold because betting that much meant he had something.

I knew I'd won the round, so I called his ten thousand and raised him twenty-five. He threw down his cards, shocking me with an emotional outburst. He was thinking I was such an amateur that I didn't know when to fold. I didn't know how to play real poker, and it was messing up his game. His face turned red, and he took shallow breaths. Cursing loudly in his mind, he ran his fingers over his thinning hair, trying desperately to get under control.

Wow, he was really mad. The dealer was working hard to keep a straight face and pushed the chips toward me. He began shuffling the deck for the next round, thinking this was the best poker match he'd ever witnessed and that I was an amazing player. That brought a smile to my lips.

Just then, a bell sounded, signaling the end of the hour. I exhaled with relief and glanced down at my chips. With this big win, I had close to seven hundred thousand dollars, leaving Carson with only three.

Carson staggered over to the bar, calling his men to his side. He couldn't figure out what was going on. Was it something he was doing? Did he have a tell I was picking up on? He knew he sometimes widened his eyes, but that's why he wore dark glasses, so it couldn't be him. That left me. The only tell I had was that I pursed my lips a lot, but I did that whether my cards were good or bad, so that didn't seem to be it. No, I had to be cheating. He'd asked his men to watch me closely. Maybe they'd figured out what I was doing.

I stood, making my way toward Ramos, still listening in on their thoughts. Neither of Carson's men had anything to offer that would explain how I was winning, and Carson about lost it. He quietly told them to make the call to Esposito like they'd planned and have him show up before the next hour was over.

My breath froze. From the image in Carson's mind, I knew Esposito was a cop. I reached Ramos, taking his arm and moving behind him so he blocked Carson's view of me. "They're making their move," I whispered. "One of them is going to call a cop named Esposito to come within the hour. Is gambling here illegal? We can't let them make that call. Oh damn!"

"What?" Ramos asked.

"They just sent a text message to Esposito. We can't stop him now. What should we do?"

"You'll just have to win before the cops show up," he said. "How much time do we have?"

"Carson said before the hour was up."

"Then we probably have a little time." Ramos motioned Nick to his side. "We know their plan," he explained. "Carson has a cop on the take, and he's arranged for him to show up. I need you to watch the club from somewhere safe and text me when they get here."

"Okay," Nick agreed, and quickly left.

"Don't worry, Shelby," Ramos said. "We can still do this. You get the better hand, go all in."

I nodded, but didn't know if I could pull it off in time. The ten-minute break was up, and I made my way back to the table. Carson sat down across from me, his anger and frustration gone. He didn't want to lose, especially to me, but at least he'd get to keep the money, minus a small fee to Esposito and his men. He knew I was cheating. There was no other explanation, but how was a mystery. He'd find out though, and he couldn't wait.

What did that mean? He'd find out? It was almost like he planned to torture it out of me. At least that's how it sounded. What was he up to?

"It's your bet," the dealer said to me. "Sixteen thousand for the big blind, eight for the small. You play first."

I counted up the chips and slid them in, hoping my cards would be great and I could go all in on the first hand. The cards were dealt, and I got a seven and a two. Those were the worst cards ever! Carson had two tens and called, but I folded right away.

The next two rounds were just as bad, and my heart sank with each fold. Finally I got a jack and a ten. Carson had a queen and a four. I called, and the dealer turned the flop, showing an eight, nine, and a four. My heart raced. This was close. All I needed was a queen or a seven for a straight, and I'd win.

Carson put in ten thousand, even though he only had a pair of fours. He didn't care too much if he lost, since it didn't really matter anymore. I called, and the turn was a seven. Yes! I had it! I glanced at Carson, but instead of placing his bet, he folded, and I could have screamed. Carson was thinking he'd seen my pupils dilate and knew I was excited, so he'd folded. From my disgruntled expression, he figured he'd made the right choice.

I took the chips and waited for the next round. He'd read me pretty well, and it made me mad. Then I remembered my purse under my chair. With a smile I couldn't hide, I reached down and rummaged through my purse until I found my dark glasses and slipped them on.

Carson scowled. How had I known? It was almost like I'd read his mind. Now how was he going to know when I had a good hand? He breathed slowly in through his nose, telling himself it didn't matter. He was still going to keep the money. He just hated losing to a cheater.

What a dirtwad jerkface! Now I almost regretted that I'd talked Ramos out of shooting him. Maybe I could do it for him. I closed my eyes until I felt more in control, opening them when the dealer finished shuffling and dealt out the next cards.

A pair of aces! I kept my breathing normal, but was suddenly grateful I'd found my dark glasses. With the stress, I couldn't have kept my eyes from dilating for anything. This was good. Carson had a pair of nines. He called and I checked, wanting him to think I didn't have anything. He raised me ten thousand, hoping I'd fold, but I called instead. So far, so good.

The flop revealed a three, ten and jack. This time I bet ten thousand. He called and bumped me ten thousand. I called and the turn revealed an ace. That made three aces! It was the winning hand I needed!

Pursing my lips, I bet another ten thousand. Carson called and raised me ten thousand again. Narrowing my eyes at his bold move, I listened to him thinking that he needed to stall until the cops got there. He was hoping to make me waste all my time thinking about what to do next.

So not going to happen. I quickly called his bet, and the river turned a nine, giving him three of a kind. Carson was ecstatic. He thought he had it made. He'd raise whatever I did and win some of his money back.

It was my turn to bet first. This was it. "All in," I said.

"Huh?" he asked, surprised. He hadn't expected that. He studied the cards, trying to decide if I really had anything or was just bluffing. The cards weren't sequential enough to give me a straight, and they were different suits, so there was no way I could have a flush. I might have two pair, but his three nines beat any pair I had. He glanced at me to see if my pupils were dilated or if my lips were pursed more than normal.

Thankfully my dark glasses hid my eyes from him. I almost licked my lips, but stopped at the last moment. Just hurry up already!

He could either fold and keep the chips he had, or go all in and see my cards.

"All in," he said, pushing all his chips forward and thinking he'd call my bluff.

Relief swept over me, and I wanted to jump up and down and do a few victory laps. Instead I smiled, a nice big smile, and turned over my cards.

"Three aces takes three nines," the dealer said. "The winner of the match goes to Shelby."

"Woohoo!" I yelled, throwing my arms up in the air. I couldn't contain my elation and pushed back my chair to throw my arms around Ramos, who picked me up and twirled me in a circle. We were both laughing when Ramos' face turned serious.

"My phone," he said, letting me go and reaching into his pocket. "They're here," he whispered.

Chapter 11

"We have to go," Ramos said.

"What about the money," I asked.

"Won't do us much good in jail." He grabbed my hand and we started toward the door.

"Wait!" Carson shouted. "Where are you going?"

"Something's come up," Ramos said. "We'll pick up the money later."

He pulled the door open and we dashed down the long hallway. Just before we came to the outer door, it opened, and a detective pushed inside. Another detective along with two uniformed cops followed.

Seeing us, he quickly raised his gun. "Stop right there and put your hands where I can see them. Now!"

My heart pounded in my chest as I slowly raised my arms. What now? There was no way we could get out of this mess, and I hoped Ramos wouldn't try anything. The detective quickly cuffed Ramos while the other man patted him down, pulling out Ramos' gun and slipping it into his pocket.

Another cop came to my side and pulled my hands behind my back to cuff me. He motioned me to turn around, and marched me back to the room we'd just vacated. Inside, things were much the same as we'd left them. As we entered, both the card dealer and the bartender wore identical shocked expressions. Carson just looked bored, but inside he seethed with anger. Even though Esposito had gotten there in time, I'd beaten him, and he wasn't going to forget it. Ever.

Before anyone had a chance to speak, Max burst into the room, full of outrage. "What's the meaning of this?" he shouted. "You can't come charging in here like this without a warrant."

"I don't need a warrant," Esposito answered. "What you're doing here isn't exactly legal. Casino-style card games are not allowed for gambling over ten dollars in Florida."

"You've got to be kidding me!" Max said. "No one gets arrested for gambling in Florida."

The detective grimaced, thinking Max had a point. Good thing that wasn't the plan. "That's not why I'm here." He turned to Ramos and me. "You're both under arrest for the murder of Kato Ortega."

"What?" I asked, the blood draining from my face. "Who's that? This is all a big mistake."

Ramos shook his head, thinking that I needed to keep my mouth shut. The less I said the better, especially if these guys were on the take from Carson. Who knew what they were capable of? Things like planting evidence and tampering with a witness were only the tip of the iceberg.

"You have the right to remain silent..."

I couldn't believe this was happening. The cop kept reading us our rights as he led us down the hall and through the crowds to the exit. Everyone moved out of the way, and soon we were outside, standing beside a police car parked at the curb. Instead of making me get in, the detective kept walking me toward an unmarked squad car. He opened the door, put his hand on my head, and pushed me inside the backseat.

Esposito pushed Ramos in on the other side, and we sat together while they got into the front seat. I watched the other police car drive off with a sinking feeling in the pit of my stomach. Esposito's thoughts confirmed my fears. They weren't taking us to the police station. The charges weren't real.

I glanced at Ramos, letting the fear in my eyes do the talking. He'd come to the same conclusion as me, but it didn't scare him like it scared me. It just made him mad. Especially since they were scaring me. These guys were going to be sorry they'd ever messed with him.

The knot loosened in my stomach, and my lips turned up in a small smile. Whatever happened, it was going to work out. I had Ramos with me. He was like Rambo and Die Hard and all those tough guys combined. Only... he was for real. Somehow, we'd get out of this.

"If you haven't figured out who Kato Ortega is yet, I might as well fill you in," Esposito began. "His street name was "Cobra." Does that ring any bells?" Esposito watched me through the rearview mirror and caught my startled eyes. "Yeah, Carson was pretty pissed off that you killed him. But don't worry. He doesn't want you dead. He's got something else in mind."

He was thinking it involved the money and me... he was going to... pull over and let Ramos out. What? He did just that, pulling into a parking lot and stopping the car in a deserted corner. He opened Ramos' door and told him to get out, while the other detective hauled me out of the back seat.

Once I was out of the car, the detective pulled his gun and held it to my head. My knees nearly buckled, but I knew he wasn't going to pull the trigger, at least not yet, and that helped. He was thinking it was necessary to make sure Ramos didn't try anything.

Ramos scowled while Esposito took a small key from his pocket and unlocked his handcuffs. "Here's the deal. Carson will trade Shelby for the money. If you want to see her alive, I suggest you hurry back and get it. Call Carson, and he'll tell you where to meet for the exchange." Esposito stepped away from Ramos and waited for him to walk away.

Instead, Ramos turned to face Esposito, who instinctively took a step back. "If anything happens to her... if she is harmed in any way... know this, I will hunt you down and kill you."

Esposito swallowed. "Just get the money. She'll be fine." Ramos stared hard at him, leaving no doubt that he would do it. "I swear it," Esposito blurted. He was thinking that Ramos was the real deal. He could see death coming for him in those eyes, and it scared the hell out of him.

Ramos glanced at me, sending a glimpse of regret that this had happened, along with reassurance that he'd move heaven and earth to make it right. With that, he slipped away, and the detective holding me holstered his gun and helped me back into the car.

Esposito could hardly wait to get away from Ramos and jumped into the car, peeling out in record time. I looked out the back window, keeping my gaze glued on Ramos, but lost him as we pulled into traffic. Esposito was thinking Ramos was one scary dude, and he was sorry he'd let Carson talk him into this. The money had seemed worth it then. Now, he wasn't so sure.

We drove in subdued silence to our destination. From their thoughts, I knew they were taking me to Carson's house. He had the latest security installed and several men to watch the place. Esposito was thinking that he might have to stay and watch over me. Mostly to make sure Ramos didn't come after him. He didn't quite trust Carson, and he sure didn't want to get killed over this.

We pulled into a driveway and followed it to a gated entrance with an eight-foot wall that surrounded the property. After Esposito punched in the code, the gates swung open, and we followed the drive to a large two-story house. In the dark, floodlights illuminated the house and surrounding yard. The house was done in tan stucco with bar tile shingles and stately columns, giving it a Spanish hacienda feel.

An armed guard stood at the front door, awaiting our arrival. Pulling to a stop, the detective opened my door and helped me out, gentler than he had been previously. I bit back a smile, grateful to know that the wrath of Ramos was now in effect.

It had worked on these guys at least, but what about Carson? Some part of him must have lost it to think he could double-cross Uncle Joey and live to tell about it. If that was the case, it meant we were dealing with a desperate man who needed money more than life. Or he could just be plain stupid. Either way, this was a bold move. It made me cringe to think how Carson was going to take it when he realized that besides Uncle Joey, all of his associates had it in for him as well. Under these circumstances, his life wasn't going to last long. Because of that, this was probably the worst place I could be right now, and I sure hoped no one tried to blow up the house before I got out of there.

Opening the door, the guard ushered me inside, putting his hand out to stop Esposito from following. "I'll take it from here," the guard said. "Mr. Carson will be here shortly. You can go."

"If it's all the same, I'll wait," Esposito said, pushing past the guard to follow me inside. After Ramos' threat, he wasn't about to take any chances with my safety. The guard shrugged and closed the door behind us. With a frown, Esposito unlocked my handcuffs and motioned for me to take a seat on the couch.

Rubbing my wrists together, I gratefully sat, feeling the stress of the whole day come crashing down on me. It was after ten, and my purse with my phone and Mylanta were still at the Club. Everything I needed to survive was in my purse. It was stupid, but I sure hoped Ramos got it for me when he went back to pick up the money.

Esposito paced back and forth, unable to sit still while waiting for Carson to show up. He was thinking that he'd been in Carson's employment for several years now, and should be used to this, but this time he was filled with unease. Ramos and I had to be affiliated with someone bigger than Carson, and Esposito worried it could come back to haunt him. If Carson was in this much trouble, maybe Esposito should find Ramos and cut a deal to help him find me. He'd rather be on the winning side if things went bad, and he had a feeling things were going bad fast. Of course, dealing with Ramos could be worse. He had a feeling Ramos would just as soon shoot him, as work with him. Maybe it was just better to stay out of it and live another day.

I tensed at the sound of a car pulling up to the house, knowing it was probably Carson. The guard immediately opened the door to greet Carson and his two men. Carson frowned at Esposito, wondering why he was still there.

After taking in the look on Carson's face, Esposito wondered the same thing. "Just wanted to make sure nothing happened to her before you got here," he said to explain. "Ramos wasn't too happy."

Carson huffed, thinking everyone was so scared of Ramos, they forgot to be scared of him. "Uh-huh, well... now that I'm here you can go."

Esposito nodded and quickly left, taking my small sense of safety with him. Carson didn't have those same feelings of self-preservation, and it made me nervous.

Carson turned to his men. "You two should head out to the marina now and get everything set up. Text me when it's ready, and wait for me there. It shouldn't be too long before I get a call from Ramos, and I don't want to give him a chance to get there before we're ready." Carson was thinking about his boat, and his plan to use it in the exchange, but I couldn't get the full picture before his thoughts turned to me.

Two of the guards left, leaving one outside to watch the door. Carson took a seat in the wingback chair across from me and sighed. He wished things were different, but with his assets drying up, and people not making their payments, he didn't have money to lose. He needed that million dollars to stay in business and couldn't afford to let Manetto walk off with it.

He'd been convinced I'd never win it from him, and now look what had happened. This was all my fault. What had I done? How had I cheated him? He had to know. Somehow, he'd get the answers out of me. Even if it was the last thing he ever did.

Yikes! This was bad. I needed to make up something really good to tell him, but what? Something like a hidden camera inside the table that let me see his cards? That might work. He might even believe it. I mean, it made more sense than the truth, right? I'd hold out as long as I could, so that he'd believe I'd only told him under duress. Unless he tried to torture me, then I'd spill right away and hope for the best.

I was about to blurt that if he harmed me he was a dead man, but I figured that would backfire, because Manetto would never let him live after kidnapping me anyway, even if I came through it alive. On some level, Carson probably knew that, but he was too busy blaming me for the mess he was in.

"I know you cheated me," he began. "I just can't figure out how you did it."

"I didn't cheat," I said. "But I'll tell you how I won if you'd like."

"You'd tell me?"

"I might, if you call this off and let me go."

"Okay," he agreed. "You can go. Now tell me how you did it."

"Do I look stupid?" I blurted. "My uncle told me to never trust a liar, a cheat, or a scoundrel, and you're all three. So we have to make a deal. You want to know how I cheated, and I want to go home. What can we do to make that happen?"

"Nothing," Carson said. "Because I hold all the cards, and that means you're not going anywhere until you tell me what I want to know."

"Fine, I'll tell you," I said. "But you're not going to like it." I paused dramatically. "You have a huge, big tell."

"What?" His eyes widened in surprise. "No I don't. Now you're just making this up."

"No, I'm not. But if you don't want to know..."

"Oh, I want to know all right, and you're going to tell me the truth, not some stupid thing like me having a tell. I know what I'm doing and I'm an excellent poker player. So you'd better come up with the truth this time."

"Or what?" I asked.

"I'll break your thumbs." He lurched over to me and tried to grab my arm, but I jumped out of his way. Not wanting to chase me around the room, he went to the door and called for the guard to come in and hold me down.

"Fine," I said, as the guard came inside. "I'll tell you. Just sit back down and we'll talk like normal people."

Carson stared at me with narrowed eyes, but he could tell I was rattled, so he waved the guard away and resumed his seat across from me. He raised his brow, and I knew I had to tell him something, so I went with my next story.

"We had a camera set up in the table that allowed me to see your cards. That's how I did it. Whenever you had a good hand, or a better hand than me, I always folded. Think about it, I always knew when you were bluffing, and I always knew when I held the winning hand. Because I knew what your cards were. That's how we did it."

Carson pursed his lips. "A hidden camera?" He had a hard time believing that, especially since his men had gone over the room with a fine-tooth comb. He always checked for devices like that. How had he missed it? In order to see his cards, it would have been placed just in front of them, probably in the leather elbow rest. But how had he missed it? "If there was a camera, how did it get to you?" he asked.

"Um... well," I said. "I had a screen that I pulled down from under the table in my lap. I'd just glance down at it when you looked at your cards and that's how I'd see them."

"And the screen was hooked up under the table?"

"Yeah."

Carson snickered. "That's the most unbelievable lie I've ever heard. You just made that up. My men checked the table before the game and there was nothing under it. But I mostly know you're lying because you're blushing and chewing on your bottom lip."

I shook my head and frowned like he was the big liar. "Whatever."

"That's a huge tell of yours by the way. Whenever you have something, you always chew your bottom lip."

"But I also do that when I don't have something, so you can't always know if it's one way or the other." I knew that was true because he'd thought that during the game.

He narrowed his eyes. "Do I need to pull off your fingernails? Or are you going to tell me the truth?" When I didn't answer right away, he walked over to a desk in the corner, and opened the bottom drawer. He pulled out a box that looked like a tool kit. Bringing it over to the coffee table, he sat across from me and opened it up to show me all the nasty little devices inside. Most of the tools had sharp edges, and one looked like it could cut off a finger. It was enough to make me light-headed.

"Okay," I said, swallowing. "I'll tell you the truth." Besides Carson's cold smile, his calculating thoughts made me realize he wasn't kidding. "I'm a psychic."

"Huh?" That surprised him.

"Yeah. I just know things before they happen."

Carson was shaking his head. "I don't believe it."

"But you can tell I'm telling the truth, right?" I asked.

"Mmm... maybe." He studied me, wondering if it was true. It explained a few things, but not how I'd beat him so handily. Just then, his phone rang. He glanced at it, before holding it to his ear. "Yes."

I could hear Ramos talking in his thoughts, telling him that he had the money and was ready to meet. Lucky for me, he also told Carson that if I was harmed in any way, the deal was off. Carson glanced at me, thinking he hated to lose his boat, but this was the only way he could get his money back and kill us at the same time. "We'll make the exchange in one hour. Bring the money to the Titusville Marina, Dock A."

He ended the call, thinking it would take Ramos that long to get there from the club. If we left right now, we'd arrive in about forty minutes. Good thing he'd sent his men on ahead to set everything up. His plan was simple. He'd tie me to the boat to insure his getaway, and while Ramos untied me, BAM, we'd be dead. We wouldn't even know what hit us. He could hardly wait to push the button on the explosives. It was perfect.

"Time to go," he smiled at me. Glancing at the guard he said, "Bring the SUV around front."

The guard left, leaving me alone with Carson. I knew this might be my only chance to get away, but how? My hands were free. Maybe I should hit him over the head with a lamp or something. Because of his weight, he didn't move very fast. I glanced at the lamp. It was pretty big, but I figured I could still lift it up and smash him with it.

"Don't even think about it," Carson said.

I jerked my gaze back to him, and my eyes widened. He pointed a gun at me, and his eyes held a certain coldness that froze me in place. Like he was daring me to make a move, just so he could shoot me.

"That's what I don't understand," he said. "Your face shows everything. You're so easy to read. How could you beat me?"

"I told you..."

"Shut up," he barked. "I don't believe that. You were cheating. It's the only thing that makes sense. Besides, if you're a psychic, you'd have known the police were going to arrest you." His eyebrows lifted as he contemplated a new idea. "If you're a psychic, why don't you tell me what's going to happen to you now."

I swallowed and shrugged as if I didn't care he was waving the gun at me. "You're going to kill me."

"How?" he asked, practically screaming. He growled and raised the gun to my face.

"Don't," I said forcefully. "If you shoot me now, you'll never see a penny of that money you want so badly."

Defeated, he lowered the gun. "That's probably true. All right. I won't shoot you. In fact, I'll let you live if you're that good. Just tell me my plans for getting the money and getting rid of Ramos."

I sniffed. "After you get the money, you're planning on killing Ramos and me at the marina. You're going to blow us up on your boat. What I don't understand is how you think you can get away with it. You see... you're already dead. The minute you took me hostage, you signed your death warrant. Uncle Joey will come for you. He could be on his way right now. Make no mistake about it... he will kill you. There's no place you can hide from him."

He blanched and his breathing quickened. He was thinking that I was right, and he was a fool. His life here was over. The only way out now was to leave everything and run. He knew Manetto would come after him, whether I was dead or not. So it wouldn't really matter if he killed me now. He had nothing to lose, and it would sure feel good to pull the trigger.

As he raised his gun, the lights went out.

I dove for the floor seconds before Carson fired, feeling the couch jolt as each bullet hit the cushions. The door burst open with a crash, and more gunfire erupted. Then all went quiet.

"Shelby? Shelby!"

"I'm... here," I said, my voice straining against the sudden thickness in my throat. My ears were ringing, but I'd recognize that voice anywhere.

"Are you okay? Where the hell are you? Nick! Dammit! Get the lights back on! I can't find her."

The room suddenly flooded with light and I opened my eyes to find Ramos shoving the coffee table out of the way and kneeling beside me. Pieces of foam littered the floor, along with a slowly spreading pool of blood. I caught sight of Carson's open eyes before warm hands pushed the hair out of my face, and gently pressed against my shoulder to turn me over. "Are you hurt?" Ramos asked, searching for signs of blood.

I swallowed. "I don't think so." I pushed myself into a sitting position and glanced down to make sure I was okay, experimentally moving my legs and feet. Seeing no signs of blood, I relaxed and gazed up at Ramos. "He missed."

Ramos' shoulders slumped before he grabbed me, pulling me into his arms in a hug. "Damn it Shelby. I thought we were too late." He held me close, nearly crushing me to death. "Come on, let's get out of here." He helped me stand, keeping his arm around my waist for balance.

Glancing down at Carson, I said, "He was going to kill me." Then it registered that there was a bullet hole, right between his eyes. "You did that? In the dark? Holy cow!"

"My gun has a light on it," he said to explain. "Plus I could see where he was sitting from outside the window before I came in."

"What about the guard?" I asked.

"That's what took us so long. We couldn't make our move until the guard came out to get the car, but you did great. You kept him occupied long enough for us to take the guard out and get the lights turned off. I was telling you to keep him occupied," he pointed to his head. "But I wasn't sure you heard me."

"I didn't." I glanced up at him. "I had no idea. I can't hear through glass or doors."

Ramos swore in his mind, and I laughed at the irony. He shook his head, thinking I was the luckiest person he'd ever known, and pushed that other thought to the back of his mind. The one that chilled his blood, whispering that I'd almost died.

Nick cleared his throat, and I stiffened, wondering how long he'd been standing there. That's when I realized they were both dressed in their black-ops clothes and had planned this attack.

"How did you know where I was?" I asked.

"Nick followed us from the club," Ramos said. "He picked me up as soon the cops let me out, and we followed you here. We even got here before Carson. We had all our gear stowed in the trunk and decided to get you out before Carson could put his plans in place."

"We'd better leave," Nick said. He glanced at Carson, his eyes widening with admiration for Ramos' shot. He was good, better than good. He offered me a small smile, amazed that I wasn't dead too. Miracles. If he didn't believe in them before, he did now.

Nick opened the door and followed us out. Ramos kept his arm around me as we walked down the drive to the gate. It was a good thing, since I was shaking so badly and kind of in a daze. "Carson was going to kill us both at the marina," I said. "He was going to tie me to the boat and blow it up when you came to untie me. I didn't know what to do. I'm glad you didn't wait."

"Me too," Ramos agreed. "What did you say to him that made him decide to kill you instead of waiting like he'd planned?" He was a little upset with me for that, thinking I should have played along a little better. Besides nearly dying, I'd almost given him a heart attack.

"Hmm... yeah, you're probably right. That was not the smartest thing I did, but he had already figured it out anyway."

"Figured what out?" Ramos asked.

"I told him for double-crossing Uncle Joey, he was already dead, he just didn't know it. It wouldn't have bothered him so much except deep down, he knew it was true. He figured that if Uncle Joey was going to kill him anyway, he'd at least get his revenge by killing me first, but before he could pull the trigger, the lights went out." The realization that I'd almost died hit me like a ton of bricks, making me shiver all over, and Ramos tightened his grip.

We came to the gate, and Ramos frowned in apology. "Sorry, but you'll have to climb over. Do you think you can make it?" He hoped I wouldn't be too embarrassed, and hoped even more he could keep from looking up my dress.

"Shut up." I said. "Besides, that won't be necessary." I pulled him to the panel and pushed the code I'd memorized from Esposito's mind. "Ta-da!" I waved my arm as the gate opened.

Show off, Ramos thought.

I nodded, giving Ramos my superior smile, and we hurried through. After a short walk, we came to the car, and Ramos disentangled me from his arms to slide like a wet noodle into the passenger seat. The shock of my ordeal was starting to go to my head, and I couldn't stop shaking. After buckling up, I crossed my arms around my waist in an effort to stop shivering. I was alive, but that was way too close. It was not an experience I ever wanted to go through again.

Ramos started the car and rubbed my hands with his for a moment, hoping to warm me up. He asked Nick to hand him his jacket from the back seat and tucked it around me. My pale face and constant shivering was making him worried. It also made him want to kill Carson all over again.

"Listen." Ramos turned up the salsa music. "Focus on the music. Listen to the beat. Nice, huh?" He was trying to take my mind off what I'd been through, and he moved his head to the rhythm. I joined in, nodding my head and feeling my muscles gradually relax.

Ramos smiled encouragingly, pushing a button to open the sunroof. As the warm night air rushed over me, we sped away. Living in the moment, the drive home passed with me in musical oblivion, and it wasn't until we pulled into the driveway that I realized we hadn't stopped at the club for the money.

"The money is safe where it is," Ramos explained when I asked. "I'll get it tomorrow."

"Sounds good," I agreed, then remembered my purse. "Do you think they'll put my purse in the safe too?"

"I'll call Max and tell him."

"Thanks," I said, then remembered my phone. "Damn! I'm supposed to call Chris tonight, and my phone's in my purse."

"You can use mine."

Nick opened the car door for me, and I got out, feeling almost back to my old self. At least the shaking had stopped. Still, I kept Ramos' jacket around me, knowing it was silly, but feeling better with it on. Ramos unlocked the door to the house and pushed in the security code. Standing just inside he said, "Wait here." He turned on the lights, and with Nick, quickly went through the house. Several minutes later, he waved me in. Normally I would have thought that was overkill, but not after today.

He handed me his phone. "Make it quick. I need to call Manetto."

"Sure," I agreed, grateful to have an excuse to give Chris as few details as possible. I couldn't go into it tonight, but once I got home, I'd tell him everything. Maybe. Or maybe that wasn't such a good idea. I didn't want to upset him, and I knew he'd be... well, probably furious, distraught, anxious, and downright grumpy. Did I really want to put him through that? Not so much.

I went up to my room and straight into the bathroom, plugging the tub, and turning on the hot water. I called it bath therapy, and I needed it bad. With the tub filling up, I was ready to place the call.

"Hello?" he asked.

"Chris. It's me."

"Oh... I didn't recognize the number. What happened to your phone?"

"It's at the club where I played the poker match. I left it there on accident, so Ramos let me use his. I'll get it tomorrow. Anyways... guess what?" I asked.

"What?" he sounded tired and a little grumpy.

"I won the poker match! Isn't that great?"

"Yeah, that's great."

"You sound tired. Are you okay?" I asked.

He sighed. "Yeah, it's just late. You're forgetting that it's after midnight and I have to go to work in the morning."

"That's right, I'm so sorry."

"No, it's fine. I'm glad you called. So you're okay? Everything's okay?" he asked.

"Yeah. I'm good. Listen, I'll let you get back to sleep, and I'll call you tomorrow."

"Sounds good," he said. "Love you."

"Love you too." I disconnected and felt my chest constrict with pain. I missed my husband with a physical ache. He sounded so far away, and right now I really needed him. Tears ran down my cheeks, and I sniffed, wishing he were here to hold me.

A knock sounded at my door, and I quickly wiped the tears away before opening it. Ramos stood there. He'd come for his phone. "Oh yeah," I said. "Here. Thanks." I handed it to him. He took in my wet cheeks and a wave of guilt rushed over him.

"I'm real sorry about what happened tonight," he said. "I never thought you'd be in so much danger."

I shook my head. "No, it's fine. It's not your fault."

"Yes it is," he said. "I was just too bullheaded to see what Carson would do. Can you forgive me?"

I looked up into his eyes and saw sincere remorse reflected in them. "Of course," I sniffed. "I don't regret it, Ramos. You're my friend. We've been through a lot together, and you've always been there for me, just like you were tonight."

"When I heard those shots and saw you lying on the floor, I thought... I was afraid you'd been hurt or worse, and it was all my fault." He raised his hands to my face and gently wiped the tears away with his thumb. He cared for me more than he thought, and thinking that I'd almost died had made him realize that. It was his fault that I was crying, and he wished he could comfort me. He gazed at me tenderly and swallowed, his need to comfort me changing into something more. I immediately sensed a wave of desire rush over him, and his sudden need to kiss me.

My heart rate spiked, and I put my hands around his wrists. "Um... wow, can you hear that? I'm filling up the tub for a bath. I hope it's not overflowing."

A goofy smile crossed Ramos' lips, and he dropped his hands. "Better go take care of it then," he said, his voice low.

"Yeah. Um... see you in the morning."

He nodded and turned away, thinking he'd wanted to kiss me, and he'd felt I'd wanted to kiss him back, but he was glad that I hadn't let that happen. There was more to me than most women. I was brave and loyal to a fault, and it gave him hope that maybe someday he could find someone he could trust like that for himself.

I shut the door and leaned against it, closing my eyes and taking a deep breath. I didn't know which had been more dangerous, nearly being killed, or nearly being kissed.

Chapter 12

I woke the next morning and realized this was my last day in Orlando. It didn't bother me in the least. I'd had a good sleep, better than I'd thought possible, and with the stress of the last few days lifted, I didn't mind putting on the same jeans I'd been wearing for the last few days. So what if they smelled a little funny. I was going home.

Since I hadn't worn my Lady Gaga t-shirt yet, I slipped that on. The song about Alejandro came to mind and I blushed, remembering the almost kiss of last night. I was glad it hadn't happened, but just as glad I had the t-shirt to remember this trip with. This t-shirt was like a token of my time spent with Ramos. It had taken on a more personal meaning for me, and because of that, I would always treasure it.

After fixing my hair and putting on a little make-up, I wandered downstairs for breakfast. I made some toast and got out a yogurt and sat at the table to eat. That's when I found the note. It was from Ramos. He'd taken Nick to the airport for an early flight out and would be back soon.

That was strange. If we were going home today, why did Nick need to leave early? What about Uncle Joey's plane?

Was it still here? Or did Nick take it back for something important? Where did that leave Ramos and me? Why didn't he wake me up so I could go too?

I was getting all worked up, and that wasn't good. There had to be a reasonable explanation, and I needed to calm down and wait for Ramos to get back so he could explain what was going on. I finished my food, washed my spoon, and had nothing to do. The pool looked inviting, but that would involve getting wet and re-doing my hair and makeup. I couldn't chance it if we were leaving right away. I didn't even have my purse to check my phone messages. So I did the only thing left and got out a diet soda, put it in a glass with crushed ice, and started guzzling.

Just then, the doorknob turned, and Ramos came inside. Finally. Now maybe I could get some answers. "I saw your note," I began. "So Nick left? Did he take Uncle Joey's plane? What are we going to do now? I still need my purse."

"Babe, chill," he said. "We have some things to take care of before we can leave, so Nick took a commercial flight. The plane's still here, but he had to get back."

"Oh, okay," I said. Ramos hadn't shaved yet, and he had on the same clothes from last night. "You look tired. Didn't you get any sleep?"

"Just a couple of hours," he said, slumping down onto the couch, and rubbing his eyes. "I had to get Carson taken care of."

"What do you mean?" I asked. "He's dead. He's not going to bother us anymore."

Ramos sighed. "Yeah, but I couldn't leave things the way they were at the house for the police to find, especially the crooked cops. They'd suspect me first thing, and I had to make sure that wouldn't happen."

"Oh. I hadn't even thought about that." I glanced at him, but he wasn't going to tell me what happened unless I asked. "So what did you do?"

"You really want to know?"

"Yeah," I said. "Or you can just let me get it from your mind."

He rolled his eyes in exasperation, knowing there wasn't much he could keep from me. "Nick and I collected Carson's body and went to the dock. We convinced Carson's men that it would be in their best interests to work with us. When they heard Carson's associates were looking for him, they decided to cut their losses and clear out. They helped us put Carson into his boat, and sent him out to sea. When his boat was far enough away, they blew it up."

"Wow," I said, my eyes widening.

"Yeah," Ramos agreed. "Last I heard, they were going back to the house to collect any valuables they wanted to keep before taking off for parts unknown."

"That's pretty ruthless," I said.

"Not really. It's just common sense. Who knows," he shrugged, "maybe one of them will try and take over his business? I told them Manetto might be interested in continuing the business relationship if they got it cleaned up. We'll just have to wait and see what happens."

"Oh, I guess so," I said. "I hadn't thought of it that way. So what now?"

"We need to get the money... and your purse," he added with a wry smile, "from Max. He should have everything ready for us."

"So, we're leaving? We're going home?" I asked.

"Well, there is one more thing." Ramos hated to ask, but it might be his last chance to find out anything about his brother.

"Oh, right," I agreed. "We need to talk to Fitch. But what are we going to tell him about Carson? He can't find out that Carson's dead, or he'll suspect you for sure."

"True, but we still need to let him know about Esposito and his buddies. I don't know if Fitch will be able to do anything about them now that Carson is gone, but maybe he can investigate them on his own."

"True," I said. "Why don't I call him and we can meet for lunch at the same place we did before?"

"Sounds good."

"Only... his number is in my purse."

Ramos shook his head. "Of course it is." He took out his phone and called Max, telling him we'd be there for the money and my purse in about an hour. "I'm going to take a quick shower and change."

With Ramos in the shower, I hurried back upstairs and packed all my things. I found Ramos' blazer and couldn't help holding it close, smelling his scent, and remembering how he'd saved me last night. I knew it was silly, but holding his jacket was like holding him, something that could never happen for real.

I carried it downstairs, and Ramos soon joined me, his hair wet and curling around his ears. His eyes held that dangerous glint of a man on a mission. Or, maybe he was just tired.

"Thanks for letting me use this," I said, handing it back to him.

"Sure," he smiled. "Glad to. Are you ready to go? We'll come back for our things after we take care of the money and talk to Fitch." He was thinking that if Javier were here in Orlando, he might want to contact him before we left, which could put leaving off until tomorrow. He glanced at me, hoping I was okay with that.

I choked back my response. I was not okay with that. Didn't he know I needed to get back to my husband and family? But how could I tell Ramos that now? I waited, hoping he'd change his mind.

He was thinking that when it came to Javier, he really didn't know what to do. He wanted to talk to him, but he also understood that it might not be the best thing for Javier.

I sighed. This was a hard decision to make, and I decided to wait and see what Fitch said before I told Ramos what I thought.

Ramos was beginning to wonder what I was thinking. He couldn't figure out why I didn't respond to his thoughts. Did that mean I didn't want to stay? He was starting to get worried. Usually I just blurted out what I thought. Was he asking too much of me? Would I do it for him?

"Let's talk to Fitch first," I said, to reassure him. "Then we can decide what to do."

Ramos let out a ragged breath and nodded. "Okay." He knew he was tired, and didn't want to overreact, but this was his brother. All these years he'd thought he was dead. He needed my help, but he wasn't going to beg.

I placed my hand on his arm. "I'll help you, Ramos. But you might have to help me too. My husband is waiting for me to come home. If it comes to that, it would help if I could tell him the real reason why I needed to stay another night. Think about it, okay?"

"Yeah, okay." He pushed thoughts of his brother away and focused on me. He was being selfish, and it came as a shock. I'd helped him so much already, the least he could do was give in on this point. "You're right. I'll talk to Chris myself, if it will help."

"Really?" I couldn't help but be surprised.

"Sure. As long as he doesn't tell anyone else." He was thinking he wouldn't tell Chris whole story. That way he wouldn't have to kill him.

"What?" I said sharply, swatting him on the arm.

"Just kidding," he chuckled, fending off my blows.

"Geeze," I said. "Talk about giving me a heart attack."

Ramos snickered, thinking he liked teasing me, but he'd never kill my husband. He might think about it for obvious reasons, but he'd never do it... for the same obvious reasons. "Let's go, or we might have to stay another night anyway."

I got in the car, feeling a little elated that Ramos really did care about me. Did that make me a bad wife? I took a deep breath and tried to put things into perspective. I knew he cared about me, but I also knew there was no way anything could come of it. He knew it too. So what had changed? Absolutely nothing.

Feeling better, I turned to him. "Can we ride with the sunroof open and listen to some more of that salsa music?"

"Sure," he smiled.

If this was our last day together, I wasn't going to spend it worrying about where we stood with each other, or something that wasn't ever going to be. Heck no, I was going to enjoy it.

The drive to the club passed in easy friendship, and Max was happy to see us alive and unharmed. "I'm glad you came out of that okay," he said, thinking he was embarrassed that we got arrested in his club. It was bad for business. "I'm sorry those cops got in here. The only thing I could think of was that Carson must have tipped them off."

"He did," Ramos said. "But we got everything straightened out."

"Good." Max pushed his curiosity aside, knowing the less he knew the better, and turned to me. "I heard you played an awesome game. I wish I could have seen it. You know, it takes a real good poker player to beat a professional like Carson. My people were impressed. Any time you want to play here, you're more than welcome. I'll even wave the setup fee."

"Thanks," I said, smiling. "I'll remember that."

Next, we stopped at the bank for Ramos to deposit the money. I opted to stay in the car and call Fitch. I found his card, and was interested to see the precinct number crossed through and another number written above it. Probably his cell. I quickly punched in the numbers and waited for him to pick up.

"Hello?" he asked.

"Detective Fitch, this is Shelby Nichols. I have some important information for you. Could you meet with me at the same place as last time in about half an hour?"

"Yes, of course. Will your friend be there?"

"Yes."

"Okay, see you then." He disconnected.

Ramos returned to the car, and we headed for the restaurant. It was early for lunch, but that made it easier to get the table in the far corner where it was more private. At least this time, we got there before Fitch.

"Since he doesn't know we know my brother's alive, how are we going to find out more about him?" Ramos asked. "I guess I could just come out and tell him I know Javier's alive, but I'd rather not do that. Fitch might warn him, and then I'd never see him."

"That's a good point," I agreed. "Somehow, you're going to have to start talking about Javier so I can pick up that information from Fitch's thoughts. If that doesn't work, I'll try and think of something that will."

"Okay," Ramos said. "But let me do the talking about Carson and the bad cops." He was worried that I might say more than I should and get us into trouble. He was probably right, so I tried not to be offended.

We ordered drinks and some chips and salsa while we waited for Fitch. He finally came in looking a little frazzled and unhappy. He was thinking that they'd found bits and pieces of a boat floating near the Titusville Marina this morning. So far they hadn't been able to identify it, but with my phone call, he figured it had something to do with Carson. He didn't want the explosion tied to Ramos, and worried about what we had to tell him.

I glanced at Ramos and whispered out of the corner of my mouth. "He's thinking about the blown up boat they found this morning and wondering if it has something to do with Carson."

Ramos nodded and stood as Fitch approached. "Fitch, have a seat."

"Shelby, Ramos," Fitch said as he sat down. "What can I do for you?"

"It's more that there's something we can do for you," Ramos began. "I have some information that would benefit you and your police department, but it's of a sensitive nature."

Fitch nodded, knowing it was something he might have to overlook as a cop. As long as it didn't involve murder, he'd be fine with that. "All right," he said. "I'll bite."

The waiter came over, interrupting us, but Ramos handled it like the pro he was. "Do you have time for some lunch?" he asked Fitch. "We can talk after we've eaten."

Fitch was thinking that with his six a.m. phone call, he'd already put in five hours, so he might as well take the time to eat. From what Ramos had said, this might be more beneficial than any fieldwork he could do anyway. "Sounds good."

The waiter took our orders, and Ramos and Fitch talked about sports until our food arrived. After we'd eaten and the table was cleared away, Ramos got down to business.

"Last night," Ramos began. "Shelby was playing a round of poker with Carson when we got interrupted by a couple of detectives and two cops."

Fitch frowned. "What did they want?"

"They arrested me and Shelby. But instead of taking us to the precinct, they let me go and took Shelby to Carson's house as a hostage."

Fitch glanced at me for confirmation and I nodded. "So these guys are working for Carson?"

"Looks that way," Ramos answered. "Maybe that's why you were never able to pin anything on him all these years."

Fitch glanced down at the table and sighed. He was thinking that it made sense, but he hoped it wasn't anyone from his precinct. If so, that meant he knew them and worked with them every day. This was bad. A cop on the take was every precinct's nightmare. But he had no reason to doubt Ramos, so it had to be true.

"Okay," Fitch said. "Besides their names, do you have anything on them?"

"No, I'm afraid not, just that they're working for Carson. Your best bet of catching them would be tying them to a money trail from Carson."

"But I can't touch Carson without probable cause," Fitch said.

"Carson might not be a problem anymore," Ramos said.

Fitch jerked his gaze to Ramos before glancing at me. "I was afraid you were going to say that. Did you..."

"Do you want a name?" Ramos interrupted.

Fitch sighed. He knew what Ramos was asking. He came to a decision. If Carson was dead, he more than deserved it.

Besides, the name of a crooked cop was more important than solving Carson's murder.

"It was self-defense," I said, not liking that Fitch thought Carson had been murdered. "There's a real difference."

Ramos widened his eyes at me, thinking I needed to keep my mouth shut. Fitch pinned his gaze on me and smiled, thinking I was a loaded gun and Ramos had his hands full keeping me quiet. With a little prodding, he might get me to tell him everything.

"You don't want to know," I said. Ramos nudged me with his elbow... hard. "Oww. So... you don't want to know?" I changed it into a question. "The name?"

Fitch frowned, confused. What was going on with me? "Yes, of course I want to know."

"No more questions about Carson," Ramos stated.

"Fine," Fitch agreed.

"The name is Esposito," Ramos said.

"And his partner is in on it," I added. "I never did get his name, but he's got receding brown hair and he's a little chubby."

"Rawlings," Fitch said. "I know them." He was grateful they weren't in his precinct, but it was still a shock. "You're sure about this?"

"Absolutely," I said. "The two cops with them left, so I don't know who they were. But hopefully you can sort it all out."

"Okay," Fitch said. "I guess I owe you my thanks, and I'll keep you out of it." He was thinking that his investigation would start with the blown-up boat belonging to Carson and go from there. "Are you both leaving town?" he asked. "Because I think that might be best."

"Yes," Ramos said.

"Good. If there isn't anything else..."

"There is one more thing," Ramos said. "I was wondering about my brother. Can you tell me any more about him?" At Fitch's surprised expression he continued. "Like where he's buried, or if he said anything about me before he died?"

Fitch's mind went blank, then he tried to think of something to tell Ramos that would make sense. "Um... your mother had him cremated, so there's no grave." He knew Ramos had missed her funeral as well, so that was pretty safe to say.

"Oh," Ramos said. He hadn't expected that. This was not going very well.

"That makes sense," I said. I rubbed Ramos' arm and smiled at him before turning back to Fitch. "You have to understand it's been hard for Ramos to come back here after all this time. He left a lot of unfinished business, and it would be nice to have some closure."

Ramos stared at me, thinking I'd gone too far. I nudged him and smiled. "When someone dies so young, you always wonder what would have become of them if they'd lived," I continued. "You know, like what kind of work they would have chosen, if they would have had a family, where they would have lived... stuff like that." I shrugged.

"Yeah," Ramos agreed, picking it up. "I figured Javier would have done something with numbers since he was so good at math, but I doubt he would have stayed around here. Not with mom and me gone. What do you think, Fitch?"

Fitch had a hard time keeping his jaw from dropping. Did we know Javier was still alive? How? It was one of his best-kept secrets. Especially with his last name changed to Moreno, he was virtually untraceable. "I didn't know that much about him," Fitch said. "But I'm sure he would have been a fine young man."

Ramos nodded and glanced at me wondering if I got what I needed. I smiled back with a slight nod.

"Well, I guess we'll never know," Ramos said.

Fitch pursed his lips to keep from blurting that Javier was still alive. It didn't matter how guilty he felt about keeping this secret from Ramos, he still couldn't justify the danger to Javier that Ramos posed. But was it his choice to make? He sighed. Maybe not, but the cycle of violence had to stop somewhere, and if that meant it was on his shoulders, so be it.

"If you're ever in Orlando again, look me up," Fitch said, standing. He was thinking that maybe at some future day he could tell Ramos the truth, and he wanted to leave the door open just in case he could.

"Sure," Ramos agreed. They shook hands, and Fitch nodded at me, then turned and walked out the door, his thoughts already centered on building a case against the crooked cops.

"So what did you find out?" Ramos asked.

"Are you going to try and contact him?" I asked. My heart ached for Ramos, but I had to agree with Fitch that if anyone knew Ramos had a brother, he could become a target.

Ramos glanced at me with surprise and confusion. Wasn't I with him on this? Did I think he would ever do anything to harm his brother again? He didn't want anything to happen to his brother, but he needed to know where he was. He wanted to see him with his own eyes. Did finding him mean he would talk with him? "I don't know," he answered honestly.

"He goes by Javier Moreno now, and he lives in Miami." I paused, giving Ramos a moment to digest this information. "He works full time for a bank and he's also going to school to get his CPA."

"That's great." Ramos smiled, pleased and proud of his brother. He was in college and was doing something with his life. It was better than he'd hoped.

"There's more," I said. "He's married and has a child."

Ramos inhaled deeply, closing his eyes as he let out his breath. He caught my gaze, then dropped his eyes to the table, not wanting me to see the moisture in them. He swallowed past the lump in his throat. "Wow, that's something isn't it?"

"Yes," I agreed. "It looks like he's doing well."

Ramos took a drink of water and composed himself. He wasn't sure what to do, but his yearning to see his brother was overwhelming all rational thought. He couldn't believe how something good had come out of all that pain. He should probably go home now, but he couldn't bring himself to do it. Not when he was so close.

"I want to see him," Ramos said. "I can't go back without seeing him. I know you probably don't approve, but after all this time, I can't just walk away. Not again."

"All right," I said, resigned to his choice. "What do you want to do?"

"Miami is about a four hour drive from here," he said, checking his watch. "But we can get there a lot quicker if we take the jet."

I chuckled. "Well then by all means, let's just jet on down there."

With that decision made, we hurried back to the house. Ramos made the phone call to Uncle Joey, which went surprisingly well. He came in from the patio with a smile on his face.

"He's really okay with it?" I asked.

"Of course," Ramos said. "Don't forget that winning a million dollars last night didn't hurt either."

"Oh yeah," I agreed. "Now it makes perfect sense. Did you tell him about your brother?"

"Didn't have to. Which is how I want to keep it. The less people that know the truth, the better. Now all I have to do is arrange everything with the pilots, but it shouldn't take long." He was thinking we'd probably get to Miami around five.

"Five?" I said. "After that we still have to find Javier." My stomach clenched with disappointment. "We're not going to make it home tonight are we?"

"Probably not," he said. He saw my shoulders slump and hurried to my side. "I know you want to get home, Shelby. But it's just one more day."

"Then you have to let me tell Chris the truth," I said. "He has to know the reason, or I can't do it."

"Okay, I know," he reassured me. "Just don't tell him everything, all right?" He was thinking about the whole sad story and how he didn't want anyone's pity or judgment.

"No, I won't. I won't tell anyone your secret, ever, I promise."

Ramos took a deep breath and nodded. "Thanks. If you think it will help, I'll talk to Chris myself and make sure he's okay with it."

"If he asks to talk to you again, that might be helpful." I really didn't know how Chris would take it. If it were me, I wouldn't like it much. But there were lots of times when he got stuck at the office, and I understood things like that happened. Maybe I could remind him that in this case, it was just like that for me? He was sure to feel better about it when I put it that way. "But I will be home tomorrow, right?" I asked Ramos.

"Yes," Ramos said. He was thinking that if for some reason we couldn't find Javier, he'd come back another time when he had more information. And maybe if he was lucky,

I'd even agree to come with him. He glanced at me, a small grin tugging at the corners of his mouth.

I grinned back, but shook my head and rolled my eyes. "I'm going to get my stuff."

Chapter 13

The drive to the airport was bittersweet, knowing it was the last time I'd be in this car with Ramos. He opened the sunroof and turned up the salsa music, and I enjoyed every minute of it.

I'd never been to the 'other' airport with the private planes before, so I just followed Ramos around like a puppy until we were walking out to the plane. The pilot and co-pilot were standing beside the stairs leading up to the small jet and greeted Ramos and me cordially.

I'd also never been in a small jet before, and my heart sped up just to step inside. Ramos explained that it was a six-passenger jet, and as I entered, I noticed the first four seats faced each other with the other two behind. The seats were extra-wide and fully adjustable. They came in a cream colored plush leather. Fold-out tables could be pulled between the seats, with cup holders spaced in the paneling along the outside by the windows. After getting comfortable in my chair, I figured I could get used to this. Ramos took the chair opposite mine, and once our luggage was secured, we were ready to go.

We taxied to the runway and got into position. I braced myself, and Ramos smiled, thinking it was a hoot to watch how excited I got. All at once the jet took off, and I held my breath. Moments later, we were airborne and I relaxed, ready to breathe again. When the pilot told us we could turn our cell phones back on, I knew it was time to call Chris.

He answered after the first ring. "Hey honey," he said. "It looks like you got your phone back."

"Yes I did. And we're pretty much done here."

"Sweet. So are you on your way home?"

"Almost," I said. "I'm actually on Uncle Joey's jet right now, but we have to make a pit stop in Miami before we head home."

"Huh," he said, his tone changing. "So what's going on now?"

"Well... I'm helping Ramos find his brother, so there's nothing you have to worry about. Ramos actually thought his brother was dead, but it turns out he's alive and living in Miami, so it's going to be pretty simple. No breaking and entering, no poker, no kidnapping, and no being arrested. It's pretty much stop by, find him, say hello, and leave. Then I'll be home. It might be tomorrow if it takes too long to find him tonight. But it will be tomorrow for sure. Is that okay?"

Chris huffed. "Does it matter? I mean... you're pretty much stuck, right?"

"Yeah, pretty much," I said. "I just don't want you to be mad at me."

"Is this something you have to do?"

"Yes," I answered.

"Then I won't be mad at you. But this is it, right? You'll be home tomorrow for sure? I can plan on that?"

"Yes, Chris. I'll be home tomorrow."

"Let me talk to Ramos," he said.

I held the phone out to Ramos. "He wants to talk to you."

Ramos grunted and took the phone. "Yes," he said. I heard Chris ask him if I was really coming home tomorrow. "Absolutely," Ramos said. "You have my word. And Chris, I don't want anyone to know about my brother. If it got out, he could be in real danger."

Chris said something like if Ramos brought me home safe, he'd forget all about him having a brother. Then he asked to speak to me. "I guess I'll see you tomorrow then," he said. "Call me when you know what time you'll get here, okay?"

"You bet," I agreed.

"Oh," he added. "And when you get home you can tell me all about the poker game, the breaking and entering, and let's see... did you say you got arrested? And what was that about kidnapping?"

"Those two kind of went together," I explained. "But it's all good now."

"I see," he sighed. "Okay then... I guess I'll hear all about it tomorrow."

"Yeah, I'll fill you in then."

We said our goodbyes and disconnected. I heaved a huge sigh myself, grateful to have that conversation over. "That went pretty well," I said to Ramos.

He shook his head, thinking that Chris was in for a shock and wondering how he handled being married to me without going insane with worry. "Are you really going to tell him everything?"

"I don't know," I said. "Even when I don't think I should, I usually end up telling him what he wants to know. You have to remember he is a lawyer and really good at cross-examination. But sometimes I can keep it vague enough that he doesn't get too upset."

"I don't think I could do it," Ramos said, thinking about all the close calls I'd been through during the course of our association.

"Yeah, but you're there," I said. "That's why he doesn't freak out. That's why he talks to you. He trusts that you'll protect me. And you always have."

"I suppose so," Ramos agreed. "I haven't thought of it that way, so I guess it works." Then he was thinking that it was a good thing nothing was going on between us, or he'd be in deep...he glanced at me, and decided to change the subject. "So it's Javier Moreno now? I guess we'll have to look him up on the Internet."

Ramos got out his smart phone and began the search. "It looks like there are a couple of listings here that could be him."

"We could always look him up on Facebook too," I suggested.

"He shouldn't be on Facebook," Ramos grumbled. "Not if he wants to keep a low profile."

We looked him up just the same, but it was a dead-end. "We'll check out the two addresses I found and go from there," Ramos said.

The flight to Miami was only an hour, but it was still a shock to find out we were ready to land. Before I knew, it we were at the car rental place. This time Ramos got a black convertible. We drove out in style, and Ramos put the top down. With the wind whipping my hair around, I got out my hair hat and put it on. Ramos laughed, thinking I looked kind of funny, or maybe like a tourist, especially with my white-rimmed sunglasses, but I didn't care.

The first address we went to was an apartment complex in a run-down neighborhood. Ramos put the top back up on the car to make us look less conspicuous, and we settled in to watch people come and go. The car was a little too nice for this neighborhood, and as several people pointed us out, I started to get nervous. It was like having a big target painted on the car for everyone to see.

Ramos tensed with each passing moment, hoping this was the wrong place and that Javier couldn't be here. It was too much like the place where he'd grown up, and he didn't like it one bit. Several cars passed, and one slowed down to get a look at us before continuing down the road. A few minutes later, a car slowly cruised down the street toward us, the radio loud and windows rolled down. There were at least four people inside, and from what I could see they were all young men with tank tops and bandanas.

Ramos swore and pulled out, quickly flipping a U-turn, thinking we were about to get carjacked if he didn't do something. It was a good thing he did, because a car coming the other way swerved around us and would have boxed us in.

The car behind accelerated to follow, and Ramos made some quick turns out of the neighborhood. He pulled onto a three-lane boulevard and maneuvered into the far lane, leaving the other car behind. "Damn!" Ramos hit the steering wheel with his palm. "That better not be where he's living."

"I can't believe Fitch would be okay with Javier living there," I said. "He must be somewhere else."

"Unless Fitch doesn't know," Ramos added, glumly.

The other place was across town and took us forty-five minutes to find. This neighborhood was not much better, but at least it didn't seem quite as bad. The address took us to a small box-like house with a yard and not much else. There was a driveway on the side of the house, but no garage. The house needed a paint job and some obvious repairs, but the porch and yard were clean and tidy.

At least in this neighborhood, our car didn't stand out so much, and no one seemed to notice us. It was the time of day when people were starting to come home from work, and we parked in the shade a few houses down, hoping we'd get lucky and catch someone coming home. After a few minutes, we were both hot and sweaty, even with the windows rolled down.

Fifteen minutes later, a car pulled into the driveway. A young woman got out and opened the back door to take a child from a car seat. She unlocked the front door and went inside.

"Do you think that's Javier's wife?" I asked, excited to finally get something.

"Maybe," Ramos said. "We're going to have to wait until Javier shows up to know for sure." He was thinking it looked good for this to be the right place, and it gave him hope that Javier would show up soon.

"Do you think you'll recognize him?" I asked.

"Yeah, I'm sure I will."

We watched for another forty-five minutes, with no Javier in sight. "Maybe he's at school?" I said. "If he works full-time at a bank, then he'd have to go to school at night."

"Maybe, or he goes to school in the morning and works late," Ramos sighed. "A lot of banks stay open until seven." He checked his watch. "It's just past six-thirty now. Let's give him a little more time to get home."

At this point we were both sweating a lot, so Ramos turned on the car and ran the air conditioning for a few minutes. I rummaged through my purse and found a granola bar, which we split. Too bad I didn't have any vitamin water left.

"Are you okay?" Ramos asked.

"Just thirsty," I admitted.

"If he's not here by seven-thirty, we'll go get something to eat and come back. Can you wait until then?"

"Sure." I settled back in my seat to wait, but every time I looked at the clock, only about two minutes had passed, and I was getting cranky.

At about seven-twenty, a car passed us and pulled into the driveway. Ramos sat up and nervous tension spilled off him. The car door opened, and a younger version of Ramos got out. He was more slender and not as tall, but he had the same angular face, deep-set eyes, and wavy dark hair.

"It's him," Ramos said, his voice a harsh whisper. He didn't take his eyes off Javier, watching with undisguised longing as he entered the house. "I wasn't sure. I mean, I guess I didn't really believe it until actually seeing him with my own eyes."

"That is so great," I said. "He looks a lot like you."

"You think so?" Ramos said. "He was always more like my mother's side."

"What do you want to do now?"

"I want to go talk to him, but... I need to think about it first." Ramos was thinking that actually seeing Javier made it all more real, and he had to be careful about his next move. He didn't want to bring trouble into Javier's life, especially not with a wife and child involved. But he wanted to do something for him. If he could do that, he could leave without any regrets.

"I want to give him some money," Ramos said. "I have more than I know what to do with, and I want to help him out."

"That's a great idea," I agreed.

"Maybe in the morning I can get a cashier's check from the bank, and we could give it to his wife. Tell her it's an inheritance from a dead relative of Javier's or something. What do you think about that?"

"That could work," I agreed. "So you want to remain anonymous?"

"I don't know. I haven't decided yet."

"What if Javier won't take it unless he knows who it's from?"

He shook his head, unsure. "We'll figure it out then. For now, let's find a place to stay that's not too far from here and work out a plan."

We left, driving slowly by the house for one more look, but couldn't see anyone inside. Now that he'd found Javier, Ramos was feeling optimistic and pleased about coming to Miami. Seeing Javier had lifted the darkness of the past and freed him from the guilt he'd carried for so long. By giving him some money, he could finally help his brother. He smiled, thinking this was the best thing he'd ever done.

Ramos turned on the GPS and asked for the nearest motels to our location. It directed us to a Hampton Inn, and we pulled up ten minutes later. Before we got out of the car Ramos glanced at me, his eyes shining with a glint of mischief. "It's our last night together," he began, lowering his voice and smiling seductively. "Want to tempt fate and share a room?"

I knew he was mostly kidding. "And if I said yes, what would you do?"

"Babe... you don't want to say that." This time he wasn't kidding.

"You are so..." I glanced up, trying to get my composure back. "Fine," I said. "The answer is no. I want my own room."

"Okay, just checking." He chuckled.

"That is so not funny," I said, pushing thoughts of Ramos' bare chest out of my mind and substituting them with thoughts of my husband. I loved my husband.

Especially when I thought about being with him tomorrow. That wasn't long. I could certainly wait until then.

"Shelby," Ramos said. "Are you coming?"

"Yeah." I got out of the car and followed him inside. He was thinking that maybe he'd pushed me a little too far that time and vowed to do better. I let out my breath, glad to hear that, and a little burst of anger came over me. He must have some idea how he affected women, right? He shouldn't do that to me.

We checked in, and Ramos gave me the key to my room. Our rooms were right next to each other on the third floor, and both had two double beds. Nothing fancy like the last time, but I was okay with that. After getting settled inside, Ramos knocked on my door. "Let's get some dinner and make plans," he said.

The restaurant across the street looked good, and we settled in at a corner booth. "So how much money are you thinking of giving Javier?" I asked, after we placed our orders.

"I was thinking fifty grand. What do you think? Is it too much? Not enough?" He was struggling with this. He'd never had relatives to worry about before.

"Sounds all right to me," I said. "He'd have a hard time saying no to that much money, plus I think he'd be pleased, especially if he thought it was an inheritance of some sort. It all depends on if you want to remain anonymous or not. You're probably the only relative he has. Do you think he'd figure it out?"

"Maybe, but I've been out of the picture for so long, I doubt he even remembers me." He shook his head. "Seriously, since I haven't shown up in his life for fifteen years, he's probably forgotten all about me."

"Okay. I have an idea. Why don't we go to the house in the morning with the check? I'll pretend that the benefactor is my client, and I'm looking for Javier as the recipient of the money. To verify his identity I could ask a personal question, like something from his childhood that not everyone would know. When he answers correctly, I'll present him with the check and my card to call if he has any questions. How does that sound?"

"That sounds really good," he said.

"That way, he'll have my number as a contact. Actually, you can use me to go through if you want to stay in touch. That would keep him safe and one step removed from you."

"Yeah. I like that. Let's do it that way," he smiled. "It will also give me a little more time to decide whether I want to actually talk to him or not." He was thinking that part of him was worried that Javier wouldn't want anything to do with him. Did Javier know Ramos thought he was dead all these years? Or did he think Ramos had abandoned him? If Javier thought that, he probably wouldn't want anything to do with him. Maybe it was better to let him think he was long gone. He just didn't know.

"We'll figure it out tomorrow," I said, patting his arm. "I can talk to Javier without you there, and I'll know what he's thinking. If he wants to see you, maybe it will make a difference in your decision."

"Yeah, okay. That could work."

We got back to the hotel, and Ramos opened the door to his room. "Babe, I know you want to come in," he teased. "But I'm beat." He was thinking that after taking care of Carson last night, he'd only had two hours of sleep. "See you in the morning?"

"Sure," I smiled. "Sleep well." His door shut, but I wasn't quite ready to call it a night. With him out of the way, I was free to head back down to the strip mall next to the hotel. I'd had enough of my jeans, and it was either get them cleaned or buy something new. I decided something new was the best way to go.

I found a nice department store and made my way to the women's section. A quick browse turned up some tan capris in my size and a cute lemon-yellow cap-sleeve t-shirt to match. Gazing in the mirror, I was pleased to find the lemon-yellow color perfect for my skin tone.

Nearby, I caught sight of some nice, tan, three-inch high, wedge sandals and had to buy those too. Now when I talked to Javier tomorrow, I'd look more professional. In the jewelry department, they had the cutest gold earrings with yellow and turquoise cut glass squares and a matching necklace, so I got those too. Not only did they finish off the outfit, but I had a tradition of getting a pair of earrings from each new city I visited, and since I was in Miami for the first time, this definitely qualified.

I got back to my room, happy with my new purchases, and finally ready to go to bed. I had to set everything down to get the key card out of my pocket and open the door. A sinister sensation of being watched sizzled between my shoulder blades, and I quickly glanced behind me.

Seeing nothing, I shook my head at how silly I was, but it kind of creeped me out, and my heart raced. I quickly opened the door and practically threw myself inside, not wasting a moment after it shut before I slid the security chain home.

Lucky for me, I'd left the lights on in my room, and I glanced around to make sure everything was all right. Nothing seemed out of place, and I tried to relax. I was getting freaked out for nothing. What was up with that? It was probably everything I'd been through lately catching up with me. Still, I wondered if I should check on Ramos. Was he okay in there, or had someone gotten to him? No, that was silly. He was fine. It was probably just that this was the first time we'd been apart since he'd come to my rescue, and I was making a big deal out of it.

I got ready for bed and tried to sleep, but I was wide-awake, so I turned the lamp back on. I tried to think rationally about my fears. Was anyone after me? Did anyone know I was here that could be after me? No and no. I was perfectly safe. It was all in my head. I was an adult. I could be alone and be okay.

I fluffed up my pillow, and turned out the light. An hour later, I turned the light back on. This was ridiculous. What was wrong with me? I kept wondering if I'd made the right decision not to check on Ramos. What if I got up the next morning and he was gone? I'd seen movies where stuff like that happened.

Exhausted, I picked up my cell and called him. It rang five times before he answered. "Ramos, it's me." I said.

"What's wrong?" he asked.

"I can't sleep," I said. "I just wanted to check and make sure you're okay."

There was a long pause before he answered. "I'm fine."

"Good. Then I'll see you in the morning." I hung up really fast, embarrassed that I'd woken him up. But seriously, what if something had happened?

My phone rang. It was Ramos, and I quickly picked it up. "Is your door locked and bolted?" he asked.

"Yeah."

"Then you're fine," he sighed. "Go to sleep Shelby, I'm right next door. You can call if you need me, and I'll be right there."

"Okay, thanks Ramos." We disconnected and I sighed, feeling like a weight had been lifted off my shoulders. After that I fell right to sleep.

The ringtone from my phone startled me awake. I cracked my eyes open to find light streaming through a gap in my curtains. What time was it? I scrambled to find my phone lying under the covers and quickly answered. "Hello?"

"Shelby," Ramos said. "Did I wake you up?"

"Um... yeah." I considered lying, but what was the point?

"I just wanted to let you know that I'm on my way to the bank for the cashier's check. I thought when I got back we could go to Javier's house. If you're ready, that is."

"Oh sure, I'll get ready while you're gone." We disconnected, and I was shocked to find it was already eight-thirty. I hurried to take a quick shower and got dressed in my new clothes just in case Ramos showed up before I had time to put on my makeup and do my hair.

It was a good thing, because he knocked before I got my hair done. I opened the door and let him in. "I'm almost done getting ready, but you can come in and wait if you want."

"Okay," he said. His brows pulled together in confusion before putting it together that I had on new clothes.

"I got them at the strip mall next door after you went to bed last night," I explained, walking back into the bathroom to dry my hair.

"Oh," he said, thinking they were nice, but he kind of liked the Lady Gaga tee I had on yesterday. It reminded him of the night I picked it up and sang, "Ale-Alejandro, Ale-Alejandro. He smiled just thinking about it.

I quickly turned on the hairdryer and got busy with my hair, a catch in my chest to think he felt the same way I did about that shirt. A few minutes later, I finished up with a little hairspray and put my earrings and necklace on, then came out into the room. Ramos was looking out the window.

"How did it go at the bank?" I asked, gathering all my things and stuffing them into my carry-on bag.

"Good," he said. "I've got the check right here." He patted the envelope in his inside jacket pocket. Now that the time had come, he was a little nervous. What if Javier was angry that Ramos had left him and didn't want anything to do with him? Maybe it was better to remain anonymous.

"You'll do the right thing," I said, sending him an encouraging smile. I sure didn't have the answer to that one. "Let's just play it by ear and see how it goes." I went through the bathroom and bedroom one more time to make sure I had everything. "Okay, I'm ready to go."

Ramos took a deep breath and nodded. He held the door open for me, and we hurried down the hall to the elevator. Checking out of the motel was a breeze, and soon we were headed back to Javier's house. Ramos left the top up on the car on account of my newly fixed hair, and I appreciated that he noticed.

We drove by the house, parking two doors down. With one car in the driveway, it was a pretty good bet that someone was home. "Is that the car his wife drove yesterday?" I asked.

"Yeah," Ramos answered.

"Then this is perfect," I said. "We can talk to her first to get her reaction. For fifty grand, I imagine she'll call Javier to come home from wherever he is, and you can give him the check yourself."

"I think you should take the check, since you'll be doing most of the talking. I mean, you are the one with the consulting agency." He handed it to me. "Just tell her you're there on behalf of your anonymous client. Then we'll see how it goes."

"Okay," I agreed, putting the check into my purse. "What personal question should I ask him? I was thinking of your mother's maiden name. Is that all right, or is there something else that's better?"

"No, that should work. Her name was Rosa Anna-Maria Mendez. She never married." He was thinking that she came to the U.S. from Cuba with his father, but they didn't marry because she could get more government assistance as a single mother. Then his father went to work one day and never came back. They never knew what happened to him, but she believed that only death would have kept him away from his family. Ramos was too young to remember much, and Javier was just a baby, but his mother was never the same after that. She used to smile and sing, but not after his father left.

"I'm sorry," I said.

Ramos shook his head. "Don't be. It was a long time ago." He took a deep breath and let it out. "Let's go."

We walked up the stairs onto the wide covered porch, and I rang the doorbell. From the way my heart was pounding, it felt like it was my long lost brother we were looking for instead of his. I figured I was picking up on some of Ramos' nervous energy. I'd never seen him so unsettled before, but it made perfect sense. I just hoped it worked out. I couldn't bear the thought of it all going wrong.

A beautiful young woman opened the door. Her hair was long and wavy, framing big brown eyes and slanting brows that drew together, questioning our presence at her doorstep.

"Hi," I said with a friendly smile. "I'm Shelby Nichols, and this is my assistant, Ramos." I waved in his direction, hoping he was okay with being relegated to assistant status. "I have a consulting agency, and I'm representing a client who I believe left some money for your husband. It's quite a lot of money, and it's been my job to find the person it belongs to. I'm hoping it's your husband. The name I have is Javier Moreno. Is he here?"

"Not at the moment," she said, opening the door and coming out onto the porch. "How much money is it?"

"It's fifty thousand dollars, but I need to verify his identity before I can give it to him. I can't just hand it over without making sure he's the right person," I said.

"Of course," she agreed. Her mind was racing, thinking how wonderful all that money would be. At the same time, she couldn't think of anyone they knew who would give them that much money. It was hard to believe Javier was the right person, but if he was... it took her breath away. "He's at school, but I'm sure he'd come home if you can wait to talk to him. Just let me call him."

"Sure," I said. "Here's my card."

She opened the door and took it. "Thanks. I'll be right back." She went inside and I heard her excited chatter through the screen door. She came back a few minutes later, opening the door wide. "He'll be here in about twenty-five minutes. Do you mind waiting?"

"Not at all," I said.

"Please come in and have a seat." She ushered us into a small living room with a worn-out couch and loveseat. There were a few toys on the rug, which she quickly picked up. "Sorry for the mess. We have a little boy, and I let him play in here." The baby chose that moment to cry from the other room. "Excuse me, he just woke up."

"That's fine. Go take care of him," I said.

Ramos stood near the door like he could hardly walk into the room. He seemed ready to bolt. "Shall we sit down?" I asked him.

He glanced in my direction, but the photos sitting on the bookcase behind me caught his attention. Drawn to them, he picked one up and studied it, his face full of shock and wonder. I turned to look, and found myself gazing at two young boys. Ramos and Javier. They must have been about six and twelve years old. Ramos had a protective arm around Javier.

Clearly shaken, Ramos put the photo down. There was another photo of his mother and Javier, and Ramos frowned, thinking he had forgotten what his mother looked like. She was so pretty and young. He didn't remember that about her. He swallowed past the lump in his throat. He didn't know if he could do this.

At that moment, Javier's wife came into the room, carrying a baby. She noticed Ramos looking at the pictures and smiled. "That's Javier's family," she explained. "That's him there, with his brother, and in that one, he's with his mom. His brother died when he was about twelve years old, and his mother soon after."

"I'm sorry," I said, surprised that they believed Ramos was dead. I glanced at Ramos, who swayed at the news.

"This is our son," she said proudly. "We named him Alejandro, after Javier's brother."

"He's adorable," I said, fawning over him. "Look at all that dark hair. How old is he?"

"Nine months," she said. "He's starting to crawl all over the place, so I have to keep an eye on him."

I spoke and listened with half an ear, while concentrating on how Ramos was taking this. He had gone so still, it was like he wasn't even breathing. After a few deep breaths, he seemed to recover, and finally looked at the baby, drinking in this miracle. He couldn't get over the fact that Javier had named his child after him. At that moment, the baby caught Ramos' gaze and smiled, moving his arms up and down.

Javier's wife glanced at Ramos. "He usually does that when he sees his father." She spoke to the baby and changed his position on her hip so we could see him better.

All at once, it was too much for Ramos. "Excuse me. I'll be outside." He hurried to the door, thinking that as much as he wanted to embrace Javier and his family, he couldn't stand the thoughts of ever bringing them harm. He wouldn't do that to them. He glanced at me, telling me in his mind that I needed to do this for him. I had to keep him anonymous, in order to keep this little family safe.

I nodded, my heart breaking for him, and he left. Javier's wife glanced at me in confusion. Why had he left in such a hurry? Was it something she said? He seemed upset.

"Don't worry about my assistant," I said. "He probably had to make a phone call or something. I'm sorry, but I don't even know your name."

"Oh... it's Anna... Annalie, but I go by Anna."

"So what's Javier studying in school?" I asked, taking a seat on the couch. I wanted to make her comfortable, and find out as much as I could about them. I was sure Ramos would want to know everything.

"He's working on his CPA."

"Oh, that's great. I'm sure this money will come in handy then."

"Yes it will, but to be honest, I don't know anyone who would give us that much money. Are you sure you have the right Javier Moreno?" She was thinking I could be wrong, and she didn't want to get her hopes up too much.

I smiled and nodded. "I'm almost one hundred percent positive, or I wouldn't have told you about it. But I do have an obligation to my client to make sure. That's why I have to ask Javier a few questions."

"I understand," she said. Excitement buzzed through her, and her eyes lit up. Fifty thousand dollars was more than she'd ever dreamed of. There was so much they could do with all that money. Javier could go to school full time and graduate this year. She might even be able to quit her job at the restaurant. But she shouldn't get ahead of herself, just in case.

"Does Javier work and go to school?" I asked.

She explained his work at the bank, and answered my other questions about him and his schooling. Then she told me how they met in Orlando when they were in high school, and their decision to get married and come to Miami to attend school. "Javier's had to work full-time while he's been going to school. That's why it's taken so long for him to get his degree."

A car pulled into the driveway, and Anna jumped up, eager to greet her husband and find out if the money really belonged to them. Javier practically ran into the house, bursting with curiosity and excitement. I introduced myself and began to explain the situation to him, wishing Ramos could have been here to see him up close.

They looked so much alike, even with some of the same mannerisms in the way they stood and spoke. I was surprised that Anna didn't notice, but if she thought Ramos was dead, it wouldn't have crossed her mind. However, there would have been no doubt if Ramos had stayed in the house.

Javier was wracking his brain, trying to think who in the world would have given them so much money.

"So," I finished my explanation. "I just need to ask you one question."

"Sure," he said.

"I need you to give me your mother's full maiden name."

His brows drew together. "Is that all?" At my nod, he quickly continued. "Her name was Rosa Anna-Maria Mendez."

I smiled broadly. "That's right," I said. "You are the one I've been looking for." I pulled the check out of my purse. "This belongs to you." He took it from my hands and opened the envelope, then staggered to see the actual amount, and his breathing turned shallow.

"This is all for me?" he asked, glancing at me, his eyes serious and questioning.

"Yes," I said firmly. "It's yours."

"I'd like to know who would do this... is there anything you can tell me?"

"I'm sorry, but it's not possible. My client wishes to remain anonymous. But there is something you could do. I gave your wife my card, and here's another one for you. I would love to hear from you every so often, at least once or twice a year. Could you do that?"

He took the card I handed him. "I've written my address on the back, but you can just send me an email. Perhaps when you graduate? And any other milestones you have in your life?"

"Of course," he stammered.

"Thank you."

"Is this so you can tell your client?" he asked. "Is he someone I knew in Orlando?" Javier was thinking it had to be someone who knew his real name if they knew his mother. He had only changed his name after his mother died because Fitch had insisted, telling him it was necessary to keep him safe from the gang and give him a new beginning. He'd moved in with Fitch, who became his legal guardian, and started at a new school. But he couldn't think of anyone from that point on, even his teachers or church leaders, who had money like this.

"I'm sorry, but I can't give you any more information," I said. Javier's shoulders fell with resignation. "However, it is my hope that at some future date it will be possible to tell you. For now, please don't worry about taking this money or let it trouble you in any way. It is a gift freely given. You don't even have to keep in touch with me if you don't want to."

"No," Javier said. "That's not it at all. It's just such a surprise."

I nodded. "Yes, I'm sure."

Javier and Anna looked at each other, excitement and happiness radiating in their faces and from their thoughts. I knew they wanted to jump up and down and share this moment together, but they were too polite to do that in front of me.

"Well," I said. "I need to be on my way. It was nice to meet you."

They both said the same to me, shaking my hand enthusiastically. Anna even gave me a quick hug, which I was happy to return. I walked out onto the porch, surprised to find Javier following me.

"Do you know him well?" he asked. "Your client?"

"Yes, I do," I answered, my eyes misting. "He's a good man."

Javier's eyes filled with tears. "Please tell him thanks for me," he said. "And that I wish to meet him someday. I'd like to thank him personally."

"I will Javier," I said, sniffing. "I promise. Now... go kiss your wife or something!"

His face split into a wide grin, and in that instant, he looked just like Ramos. I waved, then turned away to hurry to the car.

Chapter 14

I sat down beside Ramos and buckled my seat belt. "That was amazing," I said, wiping my eyes. "They're such a cute family."

Ramos nodded, unable to speak. With one last glance at the house, he pulled away from the curb and began the drive to the airport. His emotions were close to the surface, especially as he'd watched Javier talk to me on the porch. He didn't know if he'd ever see Javier again and needed some time to pull himself together.

We rode in silence for a few minutes. Then Ramos flipped on the radio and found a station playing salsa music. I smiled and started nodding my head to the beat, and pretty soon, Ramos was doing the same.

"Hey, is there another fish taco place around here?" I asked. "I kind of missed breakfast."

"Let's check," Ramos said, thinking he hadn't eaten breakfast either.

Using our GPS, we found another Hector's. Elated, I ordered three fish tacos and enjoyed each one with gusto. "I'll never think the same way about fish tacos again," I said.

"I'm even beginning to like salsa music too. How crazy is that?"

"It must be something in the tacos," Ramos said, smiling. "You know, when I left Orlando, I tried to leave all of this behind me. I was making a new life for myself and didn't think there was any place in it for what I'd left behind. I haven't listened to that kind of music for fifteen years. But now, I'm okay with it. I'm finally okay with my past."

"How does it feel?" I asked.

"Good. It feels damn good," he admitted.

As we finished up, Ramos called the pilots to let them know we were on our way. Back in the car, we turned up the music, and by the time we got to the airport, Ramos was even singing along in Spanish, surprising me with his nice baritone voice.

Smiling, I knew that from this point on in my life, I'd never hear salsa music or eat another fish taco without thinking about my time in Florida with Ramos.

It didn't take long to check in the car and walk to the tarmac with Uncle Joey's jet. The pilots were waiting like before, and soon we were settled inside, only this time, Ramos took the seat facing the front beside me. The pilot told us the flight would take about three and a half hours from here, so we should settle in and make ourselves comfortable.

Soon, we were in the air, headed for home, and this adventure was finally coming to an end. "I guess I should call Chris so he can pick me up," I said.

"Let me call Manetto first," Ramos said. "He'll probably send the limo and we can drop you off."

"Okay," I agreed.

Ramos made the call and settled the arrangements to take me home. I called Chris but it went to voicemail, so I left a message. Then I called his office and spoke to his secretary, making sure she'd let him know exactly when I'd be home. I hoped my messages got through, because I really wanted him to be home when I got there.

"I guess that's it," I said, surprised at all of the emotions going through me. I was happy to be going home, but I was also a little sad it was over. How crazy was that? I'd enjoyed learning how to play poker. Heck, I'd enjoyed beating Carson out of a million dollars even more. Plus, I'd actually stayed at the Ritz-Carlton, and I couldn't forget the great dress, shoes, and jewelry from Neiman-Marcus. But I had to admit, the best part of all, was meeting Javier, Anna, and little Alejandro.

Ramos reached over and took my hand, surprising me. "Thank you," he said. "For what you did. I couldn't have done any of it without you." He raised my hand to his lips, turning it to place a soft kiss in the center of my palm, never once taking his gaze from my face.

My heart rate doubled, and my breath hitched, but I managed a wobbly smile. "Um... you're welcome."

After a quick squeeze, he released my hand. I swallowed and got my breathing under control, picking up from Ramos that he'd noticed my difficulty and couldn't help being pleased over it. Especially since he'd managed to 'kiss' me after all.

I snorted and shook my head. "You're incorrigible!"

His lips turned up in a knowing smile. Then he got serious, and his eyes shone with curiosity. "Tell me about Javier."

I'd wondered when he'd be ready to talk about that. "He's so much like you, especially in his mannerisms, that it's kind of scary." I related everything Ramos had missed, including Javier's parting words, and my excitement that he would keep in touch with me. "I never picked up anything from his mind that he thought the money could have come from you. They both think you're dead, but if Anna mentioned that you were there with me, and maybe told him what you looked like, it might make him wonder."

"Possibly," Ramos agreed. "But she seemed pretty focused on the money."

"Yeah, she was. They were both so excited and thinking how much the money would help them out. I wanted to take a picture of them with my phone for you to have, but I figured that wasn't such a good idea."

"You're right, it wasn't," he agreed.

"But maybe someday you can get together with them, right? I know Javier would like to meet his "anonymous benefactor" and thank him personally."

"Maybe," he said. He didn't think it would ever happen. Not with his lifestyle. There would always be somebody out there who could be a threat to them. He'd made too many enemies.

"But aren't they more like Uncle Joey's enemies?" I asked.

"Babe, I'm his man. It's the same for me as it is for him."

"Well, you know Uncle Joey's getting older," I said, not willing to let it go. "He's going to retire someday. You could retire too. Maybe even change your last name again or something. Don't give up entirely."

Ramos huffed, glancing at me and thinking I wasn't going to let this go and I was a pain in the butt. "All right, if you quit bugging me about it, I'll keep that in mind."

"Good." I smiled, satisfied that I'd won this round. Plus, I had no intention of letting it go, not when I could keep him updated about Javier from the emails I was sure he'd send me. Maybe there was hope for Ramos after all.

"So, did you really tell Javier I was a good man?" he asked.

"Uh-huh, but don't let it go to your head. I know how important your bad-boy image is."

He chuckled. "Thanks Shelby."

I smiled and laid my head back on the seat. Ramos noticed and showed me how to put the seat back and my feet up, just like I was in first class. Relaxed, I closed my eyes and soon fell asleep.

"Shelby." Ramos nudged me awake. "We're almost home."

I sat up, closing my mouth and hoping I hadn't been snoring, or worse, drooling. I rubbed my face to find it dry and let out a relieved breath. I pushed my seat back into the upright position and checked my phone for any messages I'd missed. It was empty, and I was a little disappointed that Chris hadn't tried to call me back or left a text.

"When will we land?" I asked.

"In about half an hour," Ramos said.

I had time to visit the bathroom, and after freshening up, felt much better. Taking my seat, I pulled out my phone and texted Chris with the time I'd be home and telling him that I couldn't wait to see him. This time I got a text back, but it was only a smiley face. What did that mean exactly? I knew he was probably busy, but couldn't he have sent me a little more than that? I mean, I'd been gone for days. Heck, I'd nearly been killed! Of course, he didn't know that, so I cut him some slack. Still, it made me a little anxious to see him.

The plane landed smoothly, and excitement to be home swept over me. Coming down the stairs, I was surprised to find the limo parked close by. As we got closer, the door opened, and Uncle Joey stepped out, a big grin on his face.

"Welcome back," he said. The chauffeur took our bags to place them in the trunk, and Uncle Joey took my hands. "I'm glad you came through that all right. Ramos said it was close."

"Yeah," I stammered. "Thanks for sending him after me."

He lifted his brow. "It was the least I could do since you were only there because of the letter I asked you to deliver." He ushered me inside the limo, and I sat down in the section behind the driver. It was nice that Uncle Joey was being so reasonable. Then I picked up the other reason he was so pleased, and that was the million dollars I'd won.

Uncle Joey and Ramos both sat opposite me, and we were soon on our way. "I wish I could have been there to see you play poker," Uncle Joey said. "Now that would have been fun. Would you consider playing with some of my friends sometime?"

"Sure, as long as they don't try to kill me when I beat them," I answered.

Uncle Joey chuckled. "Don't worry about that."

"And you could play too," I added.

"Oh no, not me. I know better, but it would be fun to get the boys together. What do you think Ramos?"

"You'd definitely be entertained. And I think Shelby would really enjoy beating everyone."

He knew me well. "That's true," I agreed.

"We'll have to set it up sometime," Uncle Joey said. He asked mundane questions about our trip before the conversation turned to business matters between Ramos and Uncle Joey. I tuned them out, watching the road and hoping the driver knew where he was going. I didn't want to end up at the office. I listened to his thoughts, hearing enough to know that he did, and I could quit worrying. But that wasn't all I heard, and my stomach tightened with alarm.

We pulled up to my house, and the chauffeur got out to get my bag from the trunk. With him gone, I could finally talk. "Uncle Joey, did you know your chauffeur is a spy?"

"What?" he sputtered.

"It's true," I said. "He's been listening to all of your conversations and thinking about reporting them all back to his boss."

"Do you know who his boss is?"

"Not by name," I said. "He just calls him the judge." At that moment the chauffeur opened my door.

"Thank you, Shelby," Uncle Joey said, his brows drawing together. "I've certainly missed having you here." He was thinking this was a fine mess, but now that he knew, he could do something about it. Plus, he'd have my help. "I'll call you tomorrow."

"But it's the weekend," I protested.

Uncle Joey pursed his lips, clearly not caring about ruining my weekend, or the fact that I'd just come home after nearly three weeks of being gone.

"Monday," Ramos said, pulling Uncle Joey's attention away from me. "It can wait until then."

Uncle Joey glanced at Ramos and then sighed, sitting back into his seat. "All right," he conceded. "I'll call then." He frowned, unhappy, but knowing this wasn't a battle worth fighting for, especially since I had Ramos on my side. When had that happened? This trip had changed us. He'd felt it when we first got in the car. What was going on?

"Thanks," I said quickly, wanting to interrupt his thoughts. "And thanks for the ride. We can definitely talk on Monday." I started to get out, but Uncle Joey stopped me.

"Your purse," he said, pointing.

"Oh, yeah." I grabbed it.

He was thinking that he'd certainly rattled me. Interesting. "Have a nice weekend," he said.

"Um... you too. Bye." I couldn't get out of the car fast enough. I grabbed my bag from the chauffeur and narrowed my eyes at him. This was all his fault. He blinked and backed away from me, surprised I wasn't thanking him like a normal person. What was wrong with me?

I inhaled sharply, and marched quickly up my driveway. Uncle Joey was way too perceptive for his own good. Of course, what the heck was I worried about anyway? There was nothing going on between Ramos and me. Nothing. Though I had to admit, I'd enjoyed my time with him, and I might miss that a little, but it wasn't like I'd never see him again. Even so, I doubted that I'd ever spend so much time alone with him again. Which for me and my marriage, was definitely for the best.

I took a cleansing breath and let it out before opening the door. My heart quickened to find it unlocked. That had to mean someone was home. I entered the house, relief pouring over me to be home and safe. I dropped my bags and listened for my kids, but the house seemed strangely empty.

"Hello!" I shouted. "I'm home."

Hearing nothing in response, I wandered through the living room and into the kitchen. From here, I could see into the backyard and caught sight of the patio table. A long tablecloth covered it, and in the center stood a vase with flowers. The small flames from two candles swayed in the breeze, and the table was set for two with my fine china and crystal goblets.

Wow! My heart melted a little, and I opened the patio doors to find Chris standing at the grill, cooking up something that smelled divine. He glanced up and our gazes met. His smile made me dizzy, and I ran to him in delight, catching him in a tight squeeze. "Oh Chris, I've missed you so much!"

He hugged me back. "I've missed you too, babe." He held me tight, then slowly released me. "I'm glad you're home." His lips met mine, and nothing ever felt so good. Before I was ready, he pulled away. "Dinner's ready."

"What? Can't we eat later?"

"No," he said, forcefully. "I haven't gone to all this trouble to eat a cold meal. Now take a seat." He turned me around and swatted my bottom to get me moving.

"Okay," I said, taking a seat at the table. "What are we having?"

"Rib-eye steak, just like you like it," he responded. "But we'll start with a green salad."

We ate the salad, and he told me that Josh and Savannah were at sleepovers for the night. While eating the steak and baked potato, we chatted about everything that had been going on at home without me.

"That was amazing," I said. "Thank you so much for doing this."

Chris nodded and twined his fingers with mine. "I'm just glad you're back safely. Now it's your turn to tell me what's happened to you in the last few days. Start at the beginning, when you left the hotel to deliver the letter."

"Sure," I said. "But you already know that part."

"Um... sort of, but sometimes when you tell me things over the phone, it doesn't always make a lot of sense. So I'm okay with hearing it again." He raised his brow expectantly, and I knew I wasn't going to get off the hook that easy.

I just shrugged and told him the whole story. I left out Ramos' past, but I did tell him about Fitch's secret that his brother was alive, and how I didn't know if I should tell Ramos. Chris only interrupted a few times to clarify things, and I left out a few of the details that weren't relevant, like Ramos' wound, and that sort of thing.

He loved hearing about the poker match and how angry Carson got. "Carson couldn't figure out what he was doing wrong or how I was reading him so well. It drove him crazy."

"I wish I could have seen that," he said. "So what happened after the game?"

Chris tightened his grip on my hand when I told him about the crooked cops, and how they took me to Carson's house without Ramos. I kind of left out the part where Carson shot at me before Ramos came, making it sound like Ramos killed him before he shot up the couch. It wasn't the whole truth, but it was close enough. Chris was still pretty upset about it, and a little mad at Ramos that he'd let me get into such a dangerous situation. Not that it was his fault, but he was supposed to keep me safe.

It was nice to end on the high note of giving Javier the cashier's check, and how cool that was. "I guess you're supposed to forget about that," I added. "But I'm sure glad you know why I had to stay another day."

"Yeah," Chris nodded. He glanced at our hands, rubbing his thumb across my knuckles. "But I have to be honest. I wasn't real comfortable with you spending so much time with Ramos. I mean, you're alive and safe, so I guess we should just leave it at that."

I brought his hand to my face, rubbing his fingers against my cheek. I kissed his knuckles, then turned his hand over to his palm and kissed him there, especially since I knew that was a pretty sensitive spot.

"Chris," I said, holding his gaze. "I'm all yours. You alone hold my heart... all of my heart."

He let out a deep sigh, and I felt his relief pour over me. He suddenly smiled and a mischievous glint came into his eyes. "How about playing some strip poker?"

I burst out laughing. "Sure," I agreed. "But you know I'll win."

"You know what? I don't really care."

"You're on," I said, standing. Chris pulled me onto his lap, and kissed me until I was breathless. "Hmmm... maybe we should skip the poker."

"Honey," he replied. "We've got all night."

I chuckled and jumped up, grabbing his hand to pull him to his feet. "Let's get started then."

"Oh baby, oh baby."

Thank you for reading **Secrets that Kill: A Shelby Nichols Adventure.** Ready for the next book in the series? **Trapped by Revenge: A Shelby Nichols Adventure** is now available in print, ebook and audible formats. Get your copy today!

If you enjoyed this book, please consider leaving a review on Amazon. It's a great way to thank an author and keep her writing!

NEWSLETTER SIGNUP For news, updates, and special offers, please sign up for my newsletter on my website at www.colleenhelme.com. To thank you for subscribing you will receive a FREE ebook.

ABOUT THE AUTHOR

USA TODAY AND WALL STREET JOURNAL BESTSELLING AUTHOR

As the author of the Shelby Nichols Adventure Series, Colleen is often asked if Shelby Nichols is her alter-ego. "Definitely," she says. "Shelby is the epitome of everything I wish I dared to be." Known for her laugh since she was a kid, Colleen has always tried to find the humor in every situation and continues to enjoy writing about Shelby's adventures. "I love getting Shelby into trouble...I just don't always know how to get her out of it!" Besides writing, she loves a good book, biking, hiking, and playing board and card games with family and friends. She loves to connect with readers and admits that fans of the series keep her writing.

Connect with Colleen at www.colleenhelme.com

Made in the USA
Monee, IL
22 November 2023